After Thought

a novel

P. A. CRENSHAW

Published by P. A. Crenshaw Books
www.pacrenshaw.com

ISBN (paperback): 978-1-7367752-0-2
ISBN (ebook): 978-1-7367752-1-9

Library of Congress Control Number: 2021904202

Cover design and formatting by Streetlight Graphics, LLC
Edited by Suzanne Johnson

Dedicated to my family and friends who
have encouraged and supported me.

Chapter 1

WHO KNEW A TRIP TO the mailbox could irrevocably change a person's life? Certainly not the unsuspecting Adam Lancaster, who paused on his way to the mailbox to look out the window at the iconic spire of One World Trade Center in the distance. After living in his high-rise studio apartment for several months, and making the same trip to the bank of mailboxes almost every day, he still marveled at the magnificence of the Manhattan skyline every time he saw it. He couldn't believe he had finally realized his dream of having his own place in New York.

When Adam reached his mailbox, he mechanically retrieved his mail and sorted the stack as he walked.

Junk mail. Ads. Junk mail. Electric bill for Mr. Adam Lancaster, Apartment 810. Oh the joys of reaching adulthood. Letter from Mom—not so much adult-like. Package for Madeline Smith, Apartment 811.

Adam paused.

He always seemed to get other residents' junk mail, which he usually threw away. He figured they wouldn't miss it. However, in this case, he guessed the package was probably not junk. He made an about-face to return the package, but paused again when he realized there was no way to fit it in the tiny mail slot of the correct mailbox. He didn't want to just leave it sitting in the hall. Someone would surely call the bomb squad about a suspicious package. Instead, he decided to knock on the door of apartment 811 to see if anyone answered. After all, he should make an attempt to meet more of his neighbors.

If he was lucky, Madeline Smith might be really hot. With his luck, she would be a nice, old lady. Either way, it would be good to put a face with the name.

Adam knocked on the door and waited and listened. No response. He knocked again and waited a few moments longer. Still no response. He turned to walk away but stopped when he thought he heard footsteps on the other side of the door.

"Who is it?" he heard a muffled, feminine voice say.

"Um, I didn't think anyone was home," he said. "It's your neighbor."

He heard the *ker-chunk ker-chunk* of at least two deadbolts being unlocked. The door opened a crack and caught on a couple of swing-type door guard bars like the ones in hotel rooms.

Paranoid much?

Adam could barely make out two squinting eyes peering at him. The eyes looked a little unfriendly…or suspicious…or annoyed… or maybe all of the above.

"What do you want?"

The abruptness didn't surprise him. Many New Yorkers were that way—they didn't trust strangers until they got to know them.

"Um, I'm looking for Madeline Smith," he said.

She paused for a moment and finally said, "Who are you and how do you know that name?"

"I'm Adam Lancaster. I live next door. A package for Madeline Smith at this address was delivered to my mailbox mistakenly."

More silence. Then the door closed and Adam heard the creak of metal from the remaining locks being unlocked.

When the door finally opened, there before him stood the most beautiful woman he had ever seen. She appeared to be in her early-to-mid-twenties with sleek, baby-doll blond hair that fell just below her shoulders. Her pale-blue eyes looked like ice crystals fringed with long, thick lashes. A natural beauty, she wore no makeup, except for the subtlest hint of a glossy shine on her full lips. Her white V-neck Beatles t-shirt conformed to her full breasts and accentuated her slim waist. His eyes drifted down to her skinny jeans that displayed her curvy hips in a sexy, yet tasteful way.

Adam caught himself gawking at her and regained his composure.

"M-Madeline?"

Please let her be Madeline. Please let her be Madeline.

She must have noticed his…admiration. With one eyebrow slightly raised and her lips curled into an amused half-smile, her eyes scanned him up and down.

"That would be me. It's very nice to meet you, Adam."

She extended her hand, palm down. Adam stared at it for a split second. He didn't know whether to shake it or kiss it like the queen. It seemed rather odd. He ventured on the cautious side and went with the handshake. Her hand felt warm and soft in his. He didn't want to release it.

She brought him back to focus when she said, "But please call me Maddie. All my friends call me Maddie."

"Oh, gotcha…Maddie," he said. "But Madeline is a beautiful name."

She smiled a dazzling white smile that revealed perfectly straight teeth.

A movie star smile.

"Thank you. But I think Madeline is a bit old-fashioned. Don't you?"

"Not at all, but if you prefer Maddie, then Maddie it is."

She smiled again, nodded slightly, and then looked down at the package in his hands. He followed her gaze.

"Oh, right. I guess I should give you this," he said as he handed the package over.

"Thanks."

"You're welcome."

Adam didn't want the conversation to end. He usually had no trouble talking to the ladies, but with her he felt nervous.

After an awkward silence he said, "Have you lived here long?"

"Oh, only a few months or so," she replied offhandedly. "What about you?"

"I just moved in a few months ago as well, and I don't know many people yet. I thought I'd take this opportunity to meet one of my neighbors."

She nodded and said, "Well, welcome to the neighborhood."

"Welcome to the neighborhood to you too," he said. "I love it here."

"It certainly is a great city," she mused. "One of the best skylines in the world."

Maddie held his gaze for a few moments and then looked down at the package in her hands. She looked up, held the package up slightly, and said, "Well, thanks again for delivering my package."

She took a step back. He needed to think of something to say... anything.

"By the way," he said. "Nice shirt."

Maddie raised a curious eyebrow.

"I mean...the Beatles," he said. "I think they're amazing. It's cool that you're wearing a Beatles shirt."

"Big fan?"

"Definitely. I'm a music fanatic. I like all kinds of music genres from all ages. In fact, I'm the lead singer of a band and we jam in my apartment sometimes. I hope the music hasn't bothered you."

She shook her head. "No, it hasn't bothered me at all. I guess the walls have good insulation. Now that you mention it, though, I have heard music coming through every now and then, but it wasn't terribly loud. From what I could hear, it sounded good."

"Really? You liked it?"

"Seriously. I thought it was coming from iTunes or something. Does your band have a name?"

"It's an alternative rock band called Night Fury. Ever heard of it?"

She pursed her lips, wrinkled her eyebrows, and looked up as if trying to recall. After a few moments she said, "Sorry, I don't believe I have."

"No need to apologize. We're not exactly famous yet. But we have recently landed some steady gigs at some of the biggest and hottest nightclubs in town. Our goal is to get a recording contract and hit the big time."

"That's really cool. I love alternative rock. I'm also a music fanatic of all genres and ages."

"That's pretty sick," said Adam.

She seemed genuine when she said, "I think it's admirable to have such big dreams."

She smiled that dazzling smile again. Adam thought he would melt. He decided to take a chance.

"We practice in the residents' lounge every Thursday night," he said. "You should come watch us sometime. It's an open invitation. Several of the residents, our friends, fans, and significant others come to our practices. We hang out, drink beer or whatever, and there is always plenty of good food to munch on. It's just as much social time as it is a rehearsal."

"It sounds like a good time. I just might do that. Well, thanks again for delivering my package. It was a pleasure to meet you."

She took a step back, indicating the end of the conversation. He wondered if he had come on too strong. She didn't give him a definite 'yes,' but it wasn't a flat-out 'no,' either. Adam glanced down at Maddie's left hand and smiled inwardly when he saw no ring.

"It was very nice to meet you, too, Maddie. Hope to talk to you again soon and maybe see you at rehearsal."

As he turned and walked away, he gave himself an imaginary high-five. His friends would not believe this. He couldn't wait to tell them.

Chapter 2

MADDIE PACED BACK AND FORTH in her kitchen, waiting for her friend to answer the phone.

Why was she not answering?

Maddie tapped her foot impatiently and called again. She really needed to talk to her.

Then, finally, she heard a voice—her best friend, Sancha. After a short greeting, she asked, "What took you so long to answer?"

Sancha replied with mock exasperation, "I was out in the garden. I didn't hear it ringing. I'm fine, by the way. Thanks for asking."

"I'm sorry. I just need to talk to you about something."

"It's fine. I'm just teasing you. What's on your mind, *dulce amiga*?"

"Well, I met one of my neighbors today," Maddie said as she continued pacing.

"Is everything okay?" Sancha interjected before Maddie could say anything else.

"I'm fine. It's fine. Everything's okay. It's just…"

"Really? Are you sure?" said Sancha, sounding worried.

"Yes. Yes. I'm sure. It's just…" Maddie paused.

"Well, spill it then. What's his name?"

Maddie started to speak, realized what Sancha had just implied, and paused again before saying, "Who said it was a he?"

"Well, if nothing is wrong, then what else would it be? Am I right?" Sancha said smugly.

Maddie sighed and said, "You know me too well. Do I really only call you when something is wrong?"

Sancha laughed and said, "No, don't be silly. Well…so, maybe you do, but it's okay. That's what best friends are for. Go on. Is he *muy guapo?*" Very handsome.

Maddie thought about it a moment and said, "Actually, he's… beautiful."

Sancha paused and then said slowly, "Really? I don't often hear someone describe a man as 'beautiful.' "

"True," Maddie agreed, "but that is the best word I could think of to describe him."

"Wow, he sure must be something then. Tell me all about him."

Maddie twirled her hair as she said, "He lives in the apartment next door. His name is Adam Lancaster. My mail was accidentally delivered to his mailbox and he stopped by to deliver it and introduce himself. He's in an alternative rock band, and he wants to be a rock star, which is really cool. He's tall with dark hair. It's kind of like a modern pompadour, you know the style, with short, faded sides, longer on the top, and combed into a high mound in front. It looks like he works out a lot because his arms and shoulders looked cut. He's got indigo-blue eyes that draw you in. And he actually seems really nice."

"All of that sounds great," said Sancha. "So what's the problem? Why the urgent call? Do you want me to get my connections to run a check on him?"

"I think he's harmless, but you probably should, just in case."

"Did he ask you out?"

"Not exactly. He did mention that his band rehearses in the residents' lounge every Thursday night and he invited me to stop by. He said there are always lots of people hanging out and having a good time."

"So if he checks out okay, you're going, right?"

"I don't know."

"Why don't you know? Do you think he's secretly freaky or something?"

"Geez. No, I don't think he's secretly freaky. Do you really think I should go?"

"Sure. Why not?"

Maddie hesitated and said, "You know why I'm hesitant. That's why I'm calling you for advice."

"The answer seems obvious to me. He likes you enough to ask you to come hang out, and you seem to like him too, so you go."

Maddie paused for a moment then said, "Do you think it would be safe?"

Sancha sighed and said, "Try not to worry so much."

"I have a good reason to worry, and you know it," protested Maddie.

She sat down on her barstool and poured herself a glass of wine.

"You know I understand more than anyone," said Sancha. "But you are due to have some fun in your life. You need to get out and meet people, make friends, date, and have a good time. You can't just waste away your life in that apartment, being a recluse."

Maddie silently contemplated her friend's words. She knew Sancha had a point, but her intuition told her to be cautious.

"I don't know. There's a part of me that wants to go, and a part of me that thinks I shouldn't even start anything."

"Well, you called me for advice and my advice is for you to go. Go—have a good time, socialize, meet some new people, and quit worrying. Just because you go doesn't mean you are starting something. If nothing else, maybe you'll make some new friends."

Maddie didn't respond.

Sancha apparently sensed her hesitation and continued more forcefully, "Maddie, I want you to promise me you will go."

"I don't know if I can do that. I still haven't made up my mind."

Sancha cut her off, "Then I'm making your mind up for you because I love you. And I think it's about time you let go of everything from your past and get a life."

Maddie knew her friend truly cared about her and meant well. She sighed. "I know deep down that you're right. I just don't know if I can do this."

"Of course you can do this, *cariño*. Promise me you will go to the rehearsal. And I want a full report."

Maddie silently debated.

"Okay, I don't normally do this, but you've forced me. If you won't do it for you, then do it for *me*," said Sancha.

Maddie whined, "That's not fair, Sancha."

Sancha ignored her and went on, "It's not very often that I ask you to do something for me. So now I'm asking you, sincerely, please do this for me."

Maddie sighed again and said, "Okay, okay, already. I'll do it. I'll go. Against my better judgment, I'll go."

"Great! You'll be so happy you decided to go. Trust me. You'll be fine, and you'll have a great time. And even if all that comes out of this is you make new friends, it will be a step forward. Now, aren't you glad you called? You can thank me later."

"Yes, so glad," said Maddie sarcastically, not quite convinced.

"Deep down I think you know I'm right. I'm not telling you anything you don't already know. You just needed confirmation."

Maddie mumbled, "We'll see."

"Cheer up, girl. Everything is going to be fine. I'd better go now. I've got to get back to the garden. Remember, I want a full report on Friday. *Adios, amiga.*"

"Yes ma'am, and good-bye."

Chapter 3

TIME SEEMED TO SLOW TO a snail's pace as Adam waited for Thursday night to come. When it finally did, he had a bounce in his step and a gleam in his eyes when he entered Blondies Sports Bar to meet the guys for their customary pre-rehearsal gathering. "The guys" also affectionately included Lacey, the keyboardist, her girlfriend, Sam, and Claire, Zach's girlfriend. One of the largest sports bars in the Manhattan area, Blondies served up TVs at every angle and free-flowing pub grub and suds. Adam spotted his friends at the usual table and headed to join them. His best friend and lead guitarist, Zach, waved him over.

Adam pulled up a chair. Zach gave him a fist bump and handed him a beer. Lacey seemed to notice his excitement first.

"Why the extra-big, creepy grin?" said Lacey, true to her blunt, no-nonsense self. "You look like The Joker."

"I can always count on you for a compliment, Lacey," said Adam. "I'm just excited for tonight's rehearsal, that's all."

"Um-hmm. Right," said Lacey, looking unconvinced. "Am I right, Sam?"

Sam laughed and rolled her eyes as she nodded.

Claire's eyebrows rose as she studied Adam's face. Ever since she had started dating Zach, she and Adam had also developed a close friendship, although it hadn't always been that way. Admittedly, Adam had been jealous when Zach and Claire's relationship had grown so serious. He missed the shenanigans he and Zach always seemed to get into. When Claire had come along, Zach often invited him to hang out, but Adam often felt like the third wheel since he had not yet found a serious relationship of his own.

"Seriously, Lancaster. For being The Joker, you have no poker face. What's going on with you?" said Claire as she dipped a pretzel bite into the cheese and popped it into her mouth.

"I'm just happy to see all of your bright, shining faces," said Adam.

Claire rolled her eyes. Lacey shook her head.

Zach chimed in. "You're so full of bullshit, Adam. Just tell us already."

Adam feigned being hurt. "What? Am I that transparent?"

"You're so transparent you're like a fuckin' ghost," said Luke as he took a swig of his beer and then began to chant, "Tell us. Tell us. Tell us. Tell us. Fuckin' tell us."

"What are you, a child?" asked Adam as he taunted back.

Jason interrupted, "Damn, please put us out of our misery and shut him the hell up."

Adam laughed. "Okay. Okay," he said. "I met someone—a girl who lives in my apartment complex."

He tried to sound nonchalant about it but wasn't sure he pulled it off.

"Big fuckin' deal," said Luke. "You meet girls at our shows all the time. You never seem to have a shortage of them after you."

Adam tuned out the resulting chatter on his supposed prowess with the ladies. Although Luke spoke the exaggerated truth, Adam still sometimes wondered what women saw in him. Although he portrayed himself as self-confident on the outside, sometimes he felt like that insecure, skinny, gawky, nerdy-looking, messy-haired high school kid he used to be. The kid that doubted a beautiful woman like Maddie would be interested in him romantically. He didn't normally get nervous around women anymore, but with Maddie, he felt like a high school boy again, waiting to see if the girl he liked would like him too.

Chapter 4

THE RESIDENTS' LOUNGE IN ADAM'S apartment building looked like a hotel bar. A bartender manned the small area just inside the entryway on the left. High-top tables were strategically placed throughout the center of the room. The band crammed all of their equipment, speakers, microphone stands, and instruments on a small stage at the back of the room, just behind the dance floor.

The apartment manager had agreed to let them practice in the residents' lounge every Thursday night for free, as long as they opened the rehearsals to the residents. He figured they could provide free entertainment and attract residents to the bar, and in exchange the band got to practice performing in front of a live audience, regardless of the size of the crowd. They posted a disclaimer that the events were live rehearsals, not paid performances, and most residents were cool with that. They were there to drink, relax, socialize, and listen to some good music.

In addition to the residents, some of the band members' friends, family members, significant others, and fans often stopped by to hang out. Night Fury drew in some of the same people each week—the regulars. The crowd seemed to steadily grow with new faces as word about the band spread. It went from a handful of people in the audience on the first rehearsal, to a crowd that filled almost every seat on most nights, and left standing room only on the best nights. On this night, the regulars arrived early to get good seats.

Of course the band members always arrived early to set up. Adam went through the usual motions of setting up his equipment, running cables, and doing sound check, but as soon as he finished, he found himself too nervous to stand still.

He wondered if Maddie would show up.

Several of their friends had already arrived and staked out their tables close to the front of the stage. Adam mingled and greeted everyone as they entered; all the while, he scanned the crowd for any sign of Maddie.

Rehearsal started promptly at 8:00 p.m. and had no set end time. Some nights everyone left by 11:00 p.m., but other nights the party went on into the wee hours on Friday mornings. It all depended on the mood of the crowd.

At 8:00, Maddie hadn't arrived yet, but the show had to go on, so Night Fury began their first set. People routinely came and went throughout the rehearsals, so Adam hadn't given up hope. But as they finished the last song in the first set and she still hadn't shown, Adam slouched on his stool to start the second set. He normally liked to keep the energy high during performances, and he rarely sat while he sang. He tried to shake off his disappointment. He had really hoped to see her again. He wanted the chance to get to know her better and, to be truly honest, to show off for her—to impress her. Singing in front of a live audience always put Adam in his zone.

During the second song of the second set, just as he began to get really bummed out, Adam glanced at the door in time to see Maddie enter. He inhaled sharply as a jolt of excitement spread through his body. He barely knew her—barely knew anything about her. He wondered how she had this effect on him.

She stood at the back of the room, leaned against the wall, and fixed her eyes on him. Adam's jaw clenched when he saw several men near her check her out. She looked just as beautiful as he had remembered, and the other men took notice of it too.

As he performed the set, the showman—and the show-off—in him emerged. He smiled and gave her a nod and a wink, his signature flirty stage move. She waved at him and smiled a breathtaking smile. He felt his heart melt a little. He wished the set would hurry up and end so he could talk to her, but at the same time he had no idea what he would say.

As the second set wrapped up, his heart rate accelerated. He switched the microphone to his other hand and wiped his sweaty palm on his jeans. Normally confident during performances, Adam had not been nervous at a rehearsal in as long as he could remember. But the thought of talking to her during intermission only made him more nervous. He didn't know what to say.

When the set ended, Adam announced over the microphone— "Everyone give a shout-out to my neighbor, Maddie"—as he held out his hand in her direction.

When everyone turned their attention on her and clapped, hooted, and hollered, she shrank back against the wall, lowered her head slightly, and let her hair fall forward to partially cover her face. Adam hoped he hadn't made a mistake by singling her out. Had he embarrassed her? She sheepishly grinned and lifted her hand in a half wave. Adam put his mic in the stand, took a deep breath, and strode to greet her.

As he approached, he noticed she held a large, brown paper bag.

"Hey, Maddie," he said. "I'm so glad you made it. Are you enjoying the show so far?"

He rubbed both sweaty palms on his pants and hoped his nervousness wasn't apparent.

She smiled and said, "Your band is really good. I'm so impressed with your vocals, Adam. You're very talented."

He had been told that before, but for some reason the compliment meant a lot coming from her—and she had even remembered his name.

"Thank you. Come with me and I'll introduce you to everyone. Can I give you a hand?"

He motioned toward the bag she held.

"Thanks, but I've got it."

She followed him to the table where the band always gathered for breaks between sets. The regulars often brought finger foods to share while everyone had a drink or two. He introduced her to Zach and Claire, the rest of the band, and all of the regulars. She seemed to fit right in with their crowd.

Luke, the most uncouth guy in the band, blurted out, "What's in the paper bag, Maddie?"

She didn't miss a beat when she said, "I wanted to bring something to contribute."

Everyone's curiosity was piqued as they gathered in to see the mystery contents.

"Adam, what is your favorite beer?" she said.

"I never met a beer I didn't like. Hmm. Let's see." He thought for a moment and said, "Lately, we've been trying different imported beers at Blondies. There's this one called Shark Fin I really like, but it is rare, and most people have never heard of it. It has a big shark fin on the label and the bottle is really cool-looking. I can't find it anywhere except at Blondies. It's…"

Before he could finish his sentence, Maddie reached into the bag, pulled out a twelve-pack of Shark Fin and smiled triumphantly. Adam's eyes widened as he stared at the beer, then back at Maddie. Everyone seemed frozen in place—stunned.

Luke shattered the silence when he bellowed, "That's fuckin' awesome!"

He grabbed a beer.

Everyone else clapped and shouted their approval as they moved in for their share. Still a little stunned, Adam grabbed two beers and pulled Maddie aside so he could talk to her over the noise of the crowd. He handed her a beer and took a sip of his.

"Okay, what's your secret?" he said. "How did you know which beer I was going to choose? Are you a magician or something?"

She laughed and said, "No. It was just a lucky guess."

Adam shook his head and said, "There is no way you could have guessed that. Did you hear me talking about it through the walls of my apartment?"

Suddenly paranoid, he wondered what else she could hear through the walls.

In mock horror, he said, "What else did you hear?"

She laughed again and said, "Don't worry. I didn't hear anything."

Still not convinced, he said, "Do you like Shark Fin too? I mean, where in the world did you find it?"

She hesitated a moment and said, "I don't know if I like Shark Fin. This is the first time I've tried it. I just dropped into a package store on a whim and thought the design on the bottle looked interesting, so I bought it."

"Seriously? What a crazy coincidence. Where'd you buy it from? I'd like to know. I haven't been able to find it in any of the stores around here."

She thought for a moment and said offhandedly, "I don't know if I can remember the name of the store. Like I said, I just stopped in on a whim and didn't think to take note of the name of the place."

She took a sip of her beer. Adam looked at her skeptically, but he didn't want to press her too much.

He said, "Well, what do you think? Do you like it?"

She nodded and said, "It's pretty good. I'm not really into beer. I prefer wine. But this beer has a good, medium flavor. Not too light, not too dark."

"I agree. Well, if you happen to remember the name of the store, or even just the location, let me know. Thanks for the beer."

He lifted his beer to hers for a toast and said, "To Shark Fin."

She laughed as she clinked her bottle against his and said, "Cheers. I'm glad it was a hit."

She beamed that smile of hers again and he thought his heart might beat out of his chest.

What was it about her?

Adam and Maddie talked and sipped their beers for the rest of the break. He began to relax a little. He felt strangely comfortable with Maddie, as if he had known her for a long time. The beer probably helped a little as well.

Toward the end of the break, one of the regulars, Cristy, introduced herself and several of her friends to Maddie. She invited Maddie to join them at their table during the next set. While Maddie found a seat among the regulars, Adam nodded his thanks to Cristy for taking Maddie in. Adam thought she looked good there.

As he prepared for the next set, he found himself glancing their way frequently. From what he could tell, it appeared Maddie had seamlessly joined right in on their conversations. However, to his delight, Maddie turned her full attention on him when he started to sing. She smiled, clapped, and sang along to the cover songs. Every now and then she would chat with the ladies, but mostly she watched the performance. She watched him. It seemed as if she knew exactly how to make him feel special. With her attention focused on him, he performed to the best of his ability. He really wanted to show her what he could do. He performed for her and her alone.

The rehearsal ended around 11:00 p.m. With such a good vibe in the air, he didn't want the night to end. Many people left early because they had to work on Friday. He did an inward fist pump when Maddie stuck around as the party moved to the rooftop terrace. He couldn't wait to see what else the night had in store.

Chapter 5

PERCHED ATOP THE APARTMENT BUILDING, the lively rooftop terrace provided sweeping views of the city. Elegant-but-cozy seating surrounded several gas-burning fireplaces that took the chill out of the evening air and lent to the ambience, along with strategically hung solar light strings and lanterns. The party continued for another hour or so. The group slowly dispersed as people left one and two at a time, until he and Maddie were the only two left.

Maddie sat in a lounge chair across the table from Adam as they talked. Relaxed by the alcohol and more at ease in her presence, he marveled at her beauty in the glow of the city lights at night. He couldn't imagine ever growing tired of looking at her.

"Maddie, you said you work from home. What do you do?"

"I'm a freelance writer. I write for magazines, newspapers, and I've even published a few books."

Adam leaned in, intrigued, and said, "Cool. Which books? Maybe I've read them. Or if I haven't, I'd like to."

"I use a different pen name every time I write something. It helps me to remain anonymous. I'm not looking for fame or recognition. I just love to write. I'll give you a list of my work and some sample writing the next time I see you."

He grinned. She was already talking about seeing him again.

"It's great that you can work from home doing what you love and make a living out of it. That's my philosophy exactly. It's why I started day trading from home," he said.

She nodded in agreement and said, "You'll have to teach me about stock market trading sometime."

Again, she had hinted about future encounters.

Maddie continued, "Another great benefit of writing is that I can do my job wherever I go. I get to travel, meet people, and experience new cultures when I want to. And if I don't feel like traveling, I can stay in one place for a while. I like that kind of freedom."

"I guess the same is true for day trading," he said. "Although day trading doesn't sound as glamorous or exciting as writing."

She laughed. "I don't know if writing is all that glamorous or exciting. But speaking of glamorous and exciting, your band is really good. Exceptional, really. *You* are exceptional. I don't think you guys will have any trouble getting a recording contract."

Adam smiled and said, "Thanks. That means a lot to me. I guess I'm different from you in that I crave the spotlight. It's been a long-standing dream of mine to live the rock star life. You know: have a recording contract, go on tour, have legions of adoring fans and fortune and fame, the whole nine yards."

"I think it's admirable that you're living out your dreams. It's important."

Their eyes met as Adam pondered this for a moment. She seemed so sincere, almost imploring him to understand a deeper meaning as she looked into his eyes.

Adam felt at ease talking with Maddie, but he found his thoughts drifting occasionally. He watched her lips as she talked. He wanted to kiss those lips. His mind wandered to other things he could think of doing with her as well. He kept having to mentally nudge his thoughts back into the conversation. He wondered if she had similar thoughts.

For some inexplicable reason, Adam got the impression she wasn't the type of girl who would jump into bed with a guy on the very first meeting. She seemed reserved. So, he figured he had better take this one slowly, a little cautiously. He didn't want to make the wrong move. He would leave it up to her. If she just wanted conversation, then he would talk with her for as long as she wanted.

He fidgeted under the scrutiny of her gaze, and finally said, "So, Maddie, what do you like to do for fun whenever you're not writing?"

"Well, I guess you could say I'm an outdoorsy-type person," she said. "I like to go hiking, camping, or just being in nature and enjoying the scenery. I also like running and exercising outdoors. I even like fishing."

"Well, Madeline," he said in mock formality, "I would've never pegged you for an outdoorsy-type lady."

He winked at her.

Her eyebrows creased as she said, "Why do you say that? You don't think I can do all those things?"

He sensed he had offended her and quickly tried to recover by saying, "No...I mean...yes. I do think you can do all of those things. It's just...you are so...I mean..."

He looked away as he felt his cheeks burn red. He rarely got embarrassed. What the hell was wrong with him?

In an attempt to recover from his blunder, he cleared his throat and said, "Madeline Smith, I believe you can do anything you set your mind to."

Her eyes widened as she grinned and said, "You're starting to get me, Adam. You don't even know how right you are."

He exhaled slowly, relieved that she didn't appear to be offended.

He said, "I grew up in upstate New York. My family likes

outdoor activities as well. I haven't been fishing in ages, but when I was a young boy, my family used to go camping and fishing quite often. We'll have to go fishing sometime."

She nodded and seemed pleased with the idea.

"Yeah, that would be fun," she said. "Now it's my turn to ask a question. Tell me something about yourself that might surprise me."

He thought for a moment and said, "I love to cook."

"Really? A budding rock star who loves to cook? Intriguing. Tell me more."

He pretended to be offended and said, "What? *You* don't think I can?"

"Touché, Adam. I get you."

He winked and said, "I dabble in gourmet cooking. I'm self-taught. I watch the Food Network a lot throughout the day while I'm working. You know, I have it on in the background most of the day. Wolfgang Puck is my hero. I like to entertain and I love good food, so I am continually trying out new recipes on my friends. I'll have to cook for you sometime."

"I'd like that."

"Now it's my turn. Maddie, tell me something about yourself that not many people know."

She thought for a moment and said, "Well...like I said before, I really love music. You might be surprised to hear that I play an instrument too. I play the violin. I've played it for a number of years and I am fairly accomplished at it—if I do say so myself."

"That's awesome! You'll have to play for me sometime. You should bring your violin to our rehearsal one night and play it for everyone."

"I could do that," she said and nodded in agreement. "Or maybe I'll just play it for *you* sometime—a private audience."

Her lips turned up in a mischievous smile as he became aroused. He fought back the urge to move around the table and take her in his arms. But for some reason his instincts told him to hold back and play it cool. He did enjoy just talking with her, after all. But as much as he wanted to kiss her—and do so much more than kiss her—he didn't want to spoil a great evening by making the wrong move. Instead, he took her hand in his and said sincerely, "I'd really love that."

Again, their eyes locked as she softly said, "So would I."

But she made no further move, so Adam let it be and just focused on enjoying the time with her. They talked a while longer about their interests, hobbies, and music. They opened up to each other more than Adam expected, and he didn't want the evening to end.

He snapped out of this thoughts of an endless night with Maddie when she stood up abruptly and said, "Adam, I've really enjoyed tonight and getting to know you and some of your friends. I haven't enjoyed myself this much in a really long time. Thank you so much for inviting me."

Adam jumped and stuttered awkwardly, "Oh…yeah…of course. I've really enjoyed it too. I'm so glad that you came."

He also stood. Maddie smiled at him, but it seemed different. Did he detect a hint of sadness? Why was she leaving so suddenly? Maybe he was overanalyzing again.

She said, "Unfortunately it's getting late and I guess I better get going. I have a lot to do tomorrow, and I need to get at least a few hours of sleep."

He tried not to show his disappointment. Instead, he fake-smiled and said, "Sure. I completely get it. I'll walk you to your door."

They continued their conversation on the way to her apartment, which was so convenient next to his. As they walked, Adam tried to think of a way to set up the next encounter with her. He didn't want to let her go before he asked her out, or at least got her phone number.

When they arrived at her door he said, "We're playing at the Venus De Milo tomorrow night. Have you ever been there?"

"No, I haven't ventured out much since I moved to the city," she said. "What exactly is it?"

"It's a huge, three-level nightclub on MacDougal Street, with live music on the main floor every night, a DJ dance hall, and a game room. Many famous alternative rock bands got their start there. You never know which famous musician will drop in to play with the house bands. Only the best bands are offered standing weekend gigs, and Night Fury recently landed Friday nights. You should come by and check out the show. I'll even make sure you get a VIP pass for backstage."

He winked.

She grinned and said, "I just might have to do that."

"I guarantee our real performances are a lot different than our rehearsals in the residents' lounge. It would really be worth your while."

She nodded. "This I might have to see. What time do you go on?"

"The show starts at nine o'clock tomorrow. We get there at least an hour ahead of time to set up and do sound check and stuff. You're welcome to come at any time. You can even ride over with me if you want to."

She thought for a moment as if mentally checking her calendar and said, "I'll have to see how things go tomorrow. I'll try to make it, but I can't make any promises. Don't wait for me. If I decide to come, I'll meet you there. Again, I really enjoyed tonight."

He leaned on her doorframe and said, "Thank you again for the Shark Fin beer. I still can't believe you just happened to randomly pick it out for us. That's crazy."

"I'm glad you liked it. Goodnight, Adam."

She leaned over and kissed him gently on the cheek. Her lips felt soft and warm. It sent pleasurable pulses of heat throughout his body.

"Goodnight, Madeline."

He inhaled deeply as he watched her unlock her door and go inside. This girl was special. This girl was hot. He really enjoyed her company and he couldn't wait to see her again.

Chapter 6

T HE NEXT DAY MADDIE CALLED Sancha to give her the full report. Sancha must have been waiting for the call; she answered on the first ring. "Well, how did it go? I'm dying to find out!"

Maddie laughed at Sancha's excitement.

"It went great. I had a really nice time and met some of his friends. The band is extremely talented, and it was fun watching them rehearse."

"Go on. Go on."

"Well...Adam and I hit it off. He's so sweet and gorgeous, and easy to talk to. We had a great time."

"Really? That's wonderful!"

"Yeah, we sat outside on the rooftop terrace after everyone else left and talked for hours. I felt oddly comfortable talking to him. He seems like a really good guy, and did I mention that he is really sweet and so good-looking?"

Sancha laughed. "I believe you did mention that once or twice. Does he seem interested in you as more than a friend?"

"I definitely think so. We flirted a little bit. I haven't had that much fun in a long time. And yes, you were right, Sancha. I'm really glad you made me go."

"Well, that's wonderful news. So, did he ask you out on a date or anything like that?"

"He did ask me to go to a nightclub tonight to watch the band perform. They're playing at a club called the Venus de Milo. He even offered to let me ride with him."

"And you said yes, right?"

"I told him I would probably go."

Maddie could hear the frustration in Sancha's voice. "You would probably go? Wrong answer. I believe the correct answer is 'yes.' Are you trying to play it cool with him or what?"

"Not intentionally—you know I'm not like that. I'm not trying to play games with him. It's just that I'm still hesitant about this whole thing. It's been so long and there's still the possibility that..."

Sancha cut her off. "Don't think so negatively. You know better than that. You've got to keep your thoughts positive, and you can't let the events of your past stop you from living a full life. You've been on your own long enough, Maddie. Now go out and have some fun."

"I know, I know."

"Then why do I have to keep telling you?"

"I don't know why. I can't explain it. I just have this feeling that something bad will happen. I'm not trying to be negative. I'm just trying to be realistic."

"You of all people know the consequences of negative thinking. Tell me what harm could be done by going to the nightclub to watch him perform."

"I don't know. I guess I'm just being silly and paranoid."

"So, are you going tonight?"

Defeated again by her friend's reasoning, Maddie sighed and said, "Yes, I'll probably go. I'd like to see their stage performance. Adam said it's even better than their rehearsals, so I'd like to see if for myself. And, to be totally honest, I really want to see Adam again. But I will drive myself, just in case."

Chapter 7

FRIDAY NIGHTS AT THE VENUS De Milo were always wild. With different styles of music on each of the three levels, it drew an eclectic and dynamic crowd. The band never knew what kind of audience they would get.

The band members were doing their usual setup, sound check, and warmup when Luke said, "Hey, Adam, that chick...Maddie was it? You were right about her. She is smokin' hot!"

Jason chimed in, "Yeah man. Dude, did you ask her out?"

"Yeah, give us the scoop. How did it go last night? Did you get lucky?" Zach joined in.

Lacey, always the mediator, interrupted, "You jerks leave Adam alone. He'll tell us if he wants to."

"Well, if you didn't ask her out, I'm going to," Luke blurted. "She is so freakin' hot!"

Even though Adam knew not to take Luke seriously most of the time, it wasn't above Luke to move in on someone else's girl, not even a friend's girl. Adam could usually take Luke's ribbing with no problem, but for some reason it rubbed him the wrong way when Luke talked that way about Maddie.

Annoyed, Adam said, "You already said that once, Luke. You're sick, man, and I don't mean that in a good way. Like she'd want to go out with you anyway. Besides, I saw her first, so back the hell off."

"Oh, so it's like that?" Luke taunted. "Well, what are you going to do about it? Try and stop me, bitch."

Lacey intervened, "Chill out, boys!"

Zach said, "Adam, you're keeping us in suspense. We're waiting to get the juicy details. Come clean with it already. Did you ask her out or not?"

Adam knew they were relentless and would never give up. He sighed and said, "I asked her to watch our performance tonight. That's all the details you're getting."

Claire leaned forward and said, "And did she agree to come to the show tonight?"

Adam felt his face fall just a tad, but he tried to remain upbeat.

"She didn't commit to anything, but she said she'd try to make it. I took that as a good sign because that's the same thing she said when I asked her to come to rehearsal. I'm hoping she will come tonight as well."

Jason said, "Speaking of that, how long did she stick around after everybody left? She was still there when I left around midnight."

Adam shook his head knowingly.

"I know what you're angling for, Jason, and I'm not biting. But if you must know, I'm not even sure what time it was. To tell you the truth, I was enjoying talking with her so much that I lost track of time. We talked for hours and got to know each other a little better."

Luke bellowed, "Just how well did you get to know each other? Tell us. Did you get lucky last night? That's all we really want to know."

"Pigs!" Lacey feigned disgust as she leaned in closer to hear better.

Adam shot Luke the "go to hell" look.

Undaunted, Luke continued, "That means no. You bombed.

Blue balls. I can tell by your reaction. You would've been bragging about it if you had."

"I'm not a kiss-and-tell bastard like you, Luke. I don't divulge that kind of information," said Adam as he grew more irritated. He clenched his fists.

Luke retorted, "Oh yeah, Mr. Holier-than-thou. That's bullshit! You've *divulged* plenty of information to us in the past."

Adam clenched his teeth and said, "Well it's different with Maddie."

This piqued Zach's interest. "Oh really? How so?"

Adam's anger melted away as he thought of Maddie and their night together.

"I don't know exactly. She just seems like a... how should I describe her? A very nice, intelligent, classy lady. The type of woman that you take things slow with."

Luke snorted and said, "Nice, intelligent, classy lady, my ass. You just wussed out. I bet she was waiting for you to make a move and you didn't. You probably disappointed her. So now she'll come running to me."

Adam couldn't imagine Maddie ever having an interest in someone like Luke. That did a lot to dampen any lingering irritation he felt toward his bandmate.

"In your dreams, asshole. Everything went well. Just let me play it my way, Luke. You worry about your own love life. Or should I say lack of it?"

Adam added the last with a sneer. Nope, the irritation wasn't completely gone.

Luke flipped him off.

"Bite me! You're just grumpy because you didn't get laid last night. That's all."

Everyone laughed at Luke's comment. Adam rolled his eyes and went about his business of plugging in his amp and setting up the equipment.

A little self-conscious after that exchange, Adam tried to be inconspicuous when he repeatedly scanned the crowd for any sign of Maddie. He wanted to play it cool in front of his friends, but inside he started to feel nervous again. The realization of the effect that Maddie had on him made him feel uncomfortable. As showtime approached, he scanned the crowd again and spotted the regulars setting up camp at their usual table in the front row, but still no sign of Maddie. His shoulders slumped as he sighed and started their first number.

Halfway through Night Fury's first set, Adam looked toward the entrance and saw Maddie as she scanned the crowd for familiar faces. His heart jumped in his chest.

Amazing. He couldn't believe that just looking at her made him feel this way.

Energy surged through him as he strutted around the stage.

He set his sights on her as he sang. She made her way down to the table where Cristy and the others sat. They waved to her to come join them. She sat down, made eye contact with Adam, and gave him a little wave. He winked at her as he pulled the mic out of the stand and strutted toward her. He flirted with her and all of the ladies at the table. He was in his element.

The club owners had invested in a pyrotechnics display that they regularly used to enhance the stage show for many of the house bands. On that night, they had special lighting, a smoke machine, and the pyrotechnics display to help blow the audience away.

The fans—fueled by copious amounts of alcohol and drugs—grew into a frenzied, undulating mob. They were packed like sardines as they screamed, danced, and banged their heads. To Adam's delight, Maddie joined them. Adam's chest filled with pride at the effect their performance evoked.

As is the tradition in most concerts, the band left the stage when they finished their last number and went backstage to wait for the crowd to chant and cheer them back for the encore. Not to disappoint, the audience chanted and stomped and clapped and illuminated their cell phone flashlights. When the band didn't come back immediately, the audience chanted louder, hooted, hollered, and screamed until Night Fury came back onstage.

They were midway through the first encore song, with the strobe light flashing, smoke filling the air, and pyrotechnics blasting, when the screaming of the crowd began to escalate and change tones. The screams became shrill cries. People pointed at the stage, their eyes wide, as they scurried in various directions. At first Adam thought the crowd had worked itself into an even wilder frenzy due to the band's awesome performance, but then he realized that something seemed different. Something wasn't quite right. He couldn't place the strange looks on their faces.

Was that surprise or fear?

He scratched his head absentmindedly. The crowd continued pointing, climbing over one another, and backing away from the stage. Had the band done something to turn them off? It didn't make sense—until he saw a sudden flash of orange behind him. Adam spun around and realized some of the curtains at the back of the stage had caught on fire from the pyrotechnics and were rapidly being enveloped in flames.

Eyes wide, he spun back around and looked for Maddie. She wasn't where he had last seen her. His pulse quickened as adrenaline surged through his veins. He scanned the crowd and couldn't see her anywhere. He hoped she had fled to the nearest exit and escaped. He prayed she would be alright.

In a flash of memory, Adam recalled the fire that had occurred at The Station nightclub in Rhode Island several years before. The story had been covered heavily by the press. Pyrotechnics had caught the nightclub on fire and many people were killed because they had panicked and couldn't escape.

Adam alerted his bandmates to the fire and motioned for them, and anyone nearby, to follow him. The nearest escape route was through the backstage door, but the fire had spread quickly and blocked the exit. Adam tried to remain calm and clearheaded as he looked out over the crowd to find the next nearest exit. The crowd appeared to be in full panic mode. They were piled up at the exits, climbing over each other, and pushing each other down. He imagined, to his horror, that the outcome would be just like the Rhode Island nightclub fire scene.

The lights were dim, and smoke filled the room quickly, making it increasingly hard to see. Adam focused on trying to locate an exit. Since they were up on the stage, the band members were closest to the fire. Mobs formed at every available exit. Adam's heart beat rapidly as he raked his fingers down his face. He felt panic rising from deep within as he stood frozen in terror.

Suddenly, he felt someone grab his hand in the darkness. He strained to see who it was, and realized it was Maddie, looking surprisingly calm. Relief flooded through him as she pulled him toward her and yelled, "Come with me, Adam. Call for everyone in the band and follow me."

Adam shouted into the mic for Zach and the other band members to follow them. Maddie led them through the crowd toward an area of the club that, to his knowledge, did not have an exit. He wondered if she had gone mad. Had the smoke affected her thinking? As far as he could see, there was no exit in sight, only a wall with a large, heavy stage curtain covering it. He assumed it served no purpose except for decoration, and he knew there weren't any exits near there.

Adam had been in and out of the club many nights and he had never seen anyone enter or exit there. Several people blindly followed them like a flock of sheep, assuming that they knew an escape route. As the smoke filled the room, visibility decreased. People coughed and wheezed violently, and some passed out due to smoke inhalation. It appeared they were trapped. He had to do something fast, or people were going to die.

Adam, convinced that Maddie had suffered from confusion or delirium from panic or from the smoke, made up his mind to take control. He grabbed Maddie by the arm to pull her and the others away from the wall to safety. She jerked away from him, grabbed the large curtain, and pulled as hard as she could. His mouth fell open as the curtain fell and revealed a large garage-like, rollup door. He rubbed his eyes.

How could she have known a door was there?

He realized it wasn't the time to ponder the situation and quickly helped Maddie grab the large chain pulley to raise the door. It moved a little, but seemed to be stuck from lack of use. Several of the guys also grabbed the chain and pulled as hard as they could. To everyone's great relief, the door finally gave way and began to open.

People poured out of the door even before it rolled all the way up. The next thing Adam knew they were standing outside coughing and sputtering, but they were alive. No one near them appeared burned or hurt. When he finally regained his composure and realized they were safe, he turned to Maddie and said, "Are you okay?"

She coughed and replied, "Yes. Are you?"

He looked himself over and said, "I think so."

She visibly gave a sigh of relief and said, "I'm so sorry about that, Adam. I was so worried about you. You don't know how glad I am that you're alright…that we're all alright."

Adam furrowed his brow. "Sorry? It's not your fault. I was worried, too. I have to admit that was the scariest thing I've ever been through."

She didn't reply. He scanned the faces of the people that were in the vicinity while he did a mental inventory. To his relief he saw all of the band members and all of their friends who had been seated closest to the stage.

"Is everyone okay?" he shouted.

He heard several positive responses and saw nods. He also heard the sound of the approaching sirens.

He turned back to Maddie and said, "How in the world did you know that door was there? As long as we've played here, I've never seen anyone entering or exiting through that door. Have you been in this club before?"

She hesitated briefly, as if choosing her words carefully, and said, "I've never been in this club before. I didn't know for sure it was a door. It was a lucky guess."

A lucky guess?!

He looked at her incredulously. He couldn't quite put his finger on it, but something about the way she said it made him doubt her story. He could believe that she had never been to the club before, but he found it odd that she, or anyone for that matter, would have guessed a door loomed behind that curtain just by looking at it, especially in a moment of panic. Maybe he had put her on the spot. Maybe she knew more than she wanted him to know. Anyway, it wasn't the time to overanalyze things. Thankfully, she had been right about the door, no matter how she knew of its existence. Adam shivered as the realization sank in that if there hadn't been a door there, they might not have made it out alive. Maddie had saved their lives.

As if reading his mind, Claire rushed up to Maddie and hugged her as she said, "Maddie, you saved our lives! Thank you so much."

Claire's voice caught as she barely held it together. "I was so scared. I couldn't see anything and I was getting to the point where I couldn't breathe. I thought we were all going to…"

She broke off as Zach took her in his arms, patted her back, and comforted her with calming words. "It's okay. You're okay. We're all okay, thanks to Maddie."

He gave Maddie a grateful nod as Claire buried her face in his neck and sobbed.

Luke patted Maddie on the back and, in a serious manner hardly ever witnessed by anyone, he said, "We owe you one, Maddie. Good going."

He too gave her a respectful nod of gratitude. Several others verbalized their thanks and gratefulness. Maddie said nothing, but just stoically nodded back as if to tell them all *"you're welcome."*

Adam attempted to lighten the mood and said, "Maddie, you're my hero."

Maddie didn't smile. She still looked shaken. "Well, I just did the best I could. I'm so sorry. I was so afraid for you, Adam. You could've been killed in there."

Sorry? Why was she apologizing?

"It's not your fault, Maddie. I'm fine."

She looked at the ground and said, "I don't think anybody was hurt badly. A few people have been taken off by ambulance."

Adam thought it was a miracle that nobody had perished. As he pondered the implications of this, he saw Maddie shiver. The temperature had dropped, and in the rush to get out, she had left her jacket in the club. He usually wore some type of rocker-style leather jacket during performances, and tonight was no exception. He took off his jacket and placed it around Maddie's shoulders.

She tried to protest. "Adam, don't do that. There's no sense in both of us freezing out here."

"I insist," he said. "Besides, what kind of jerk would I look like now if I took it back?"

She finally laughed a little. "Good point. Well, if you insist, then how about this?"

As the jacket rested on her shoulders, she held it open with both hands and wrapped her arms around his waist. It enveloped them both like a small blanket. She pressed her body against his, and rested her head on his chest.

Sudden warmth came over him, and only partly from her body heat. Through the smell of smoke that permeated their clothes and hair, he could smell her subtle perfume and the scent of her. He became aroused by the closeness of her body to his and marveled at her effect on him.

He wrapped his arms around her waist and pulled her closer as he answered her question. "This will do just fine. I could stay like this all night and not get cold at all. And it just might take all night for them to let us back in to get our equipment out. But as much as I would selfishly like for you to stay with me like this, you should probably get out of the cold and back to your warm apartment."

"I really don't mind staying for a while," she said. "I'm warm now myself. Do you think your instruments and equipment will hold up to the fire and smoke?"

"Some of it will, and some of it may not. We won't know the extent of the damage until we recover everything and clean it. I imagine the metal mic stands and instruments will fare okay, but the wooden, string instruments might be damaged beyond repair. We've all put a lot of money into our equipment, but Zach has the most to lose. His guitar is a vintage classic 1965 Gibson Firebird III with a reverse body in cardinal red. He put a lot of cash and T.L.C. into his 'baby' and will be crushed if it is lost."

As Adam spoke, he watched Zach pace back and forth a few yards away, and he knew that he must be thinking the same thing.

As everyone else in the crowd dispersed, their little group waited in a small huddle for the fire department to give them the word that they could reenter. About an hour and a half later, they were finally cleared to go in and retrieve what they could. It wasn't as bad as they had anticipated. It looked like mostly smoke damage. It would take some major scrubbing and elbow grease, but most of the equipment was salvageable—even Zach's beloved Gibson. Zach nearly cried when he saw that 'his baby' had suffered no permanent damage. No one would have ribbed him about it, either. They all had the ultimate respect for the vintage classics.

They finally wrapped it up at about two o'clock in the morning, and Adam offered to follow Maddie home to make sure she made it safely. Like him, she still seemed pretty shaken up. He had to admit the fire was probably one of the scariest things he had ever experienced.

He and Maddie walked hand in hand in silence from the parking garage to their neighboring apartments. They were both still in shock and exhausted from the horrific events of the evening. He felt glad that she had stayed behind to help. He also wondered what, if anything, the rest of the night might have in store for him and Maddie. He considered himself a typical guy when it came to sexual expectations, fire or no fire, exhaustion or no exhaustion, and he could only hope.

When they got to her door, she stopped and said, "I'm so thankful that everyone made it out tonight. I could see there was no escape for the band and I was so afraid for all of you."

She paused for a moment and continued, "So despite the fact that there was a fire, the nightclub almost burned down, and people almost died, I had a great time."

Adam grinned at her attempt at humor.

"It's good that we can joke about it now. But seriously, though, I'm touched that you were worried for me. I was worried about you too. I'm glad everything turned out okay."

"You guys are really awesome performers, and I really enjoyed the show. Thanks for inviting me," she said as she stepped forward, put her arms around his neck, and kissed him gently on the mouth.

He felt heat spread throughout his body. As she stepped back, he stepped closer to her, pulled her back to him and said, "I'm so glad you came to the show. It meant a lot to me." And he kissed her back, gently at first, and then, with the passion building, a little more firmly.

Her lips parted and a slight moan escaped as the kisses grew deeper and their bodies pressed closer together. They stood like that for several minutes enjoying and exploring one another. Adam was just beginning to think that she might invite him in for the night when she stepped back and said, "I hate to be a mood kill, but I really need to get some sleep. I've got a lot of writing to do tomorrow and I'm up way past my bedtime. I need my beauty sleep."

She winked and added, "But I really had a great time...up until...well, you know."

Adam forced a smile to hide his disappointment. After all, they hadn't even been on an official date. He actually found it somewhat alluring that she didn't jump into bed with him right away. But he didn't want her to get away before he could get a chance to officially ask her out.

"Trust me. You don't need any beauty sleep," he said. "I can't imagine you getting any more beautiful. Listen, I want to keep my word and cook you that gourmet meal I promised."

"I'd like that, Adam."

"Are you free on Tuesday night?"

She grinned and said, "I believe my calendar is open that night. When should I come? And what should I bring?"

"How about six o'clock? And don't feel like you need to bring anything. Leave everything to me. I love showing off my cooking prowess."

She raised an eyebrow and said, "I can't wait to experience your *prowess*, and your culinary skills."

She looked at him seductively and winked.

Damn, she was killing him. It was going to be a long wait until Tuesday.

They exchanged cell phone numbers and shared one last, lingering kiss. Then she gave him a big, heartfelt hug and said, "Good night, Adam," as she turned and walked into her apartment.

"Good night, Maddie," he said dreamily.

That night definitely felt like a dream—a nightmare turned happy ending.

Chapter 8

MADDIE CALLED SANCHA THE NEXT morning to tell her the news about the fire. After she replayed the horrifying events, Maddie said, "Sancha, I can't explain why, but something felt wrong to me."

Sancha said, "Well, excuse me for stating the obvious, *mi hermosa amiga*, but fires in nightclubs usually feel wrong."

Maddie rolled her eyes and said, "You know that's not what I mean. I don't think the fire was an accident."

"You mean, you don't think the pyrotechnics caused it?"

"Oh, I'm sure the pyrotechnics ignited the fire, but I don't think they caused it."

"Do you think that an arsonist was in the nightclub? Like a terrorist?"

"I suspect someone evil caused it, but they weren't necessarily in the nightclub."

Sancha sighed and said, "I'm not following you."

Frustrated, Maddie sighed too and said, "Sancha, do you think that Paul could have anything to do with this?"

After some consideration Sancha said, "I really doubt it, Maddie. We've been monitoring the situation and we haven't seen any activity in your area. You've been well hidden lately and nothing has happened in the past few months, so why would you suspect Paul?"

Maddie picked at her lip nervously and said, "I don't mean to sound paranoid, and it is very likely that it was just a random fire, but I just can't help but wonder if Paul was involved in some way. What if I'm in danger? Or worse, what if I'm putting others in danger?"

"We'll get someone to check it out. Did you see anyone familiar in the crowd? Anyone that looked suspicious? Do they know what caused the fire?"

"I didn't see anyone or anything that looked suspicious. And right now they're saying the cause was the pyrotechnics display."

Sancha paused a moment and said, "Based on what you've told me, let's just go with the thought that it was a random event that had nothing to do with you. But I'll make some calls and do some checking around just in case."

Maddie put her hand on her forehead as she paced back and forth.

"But what if we're wrong? What if Paul was involved? I could be putting Adam and everybody else in danger."

"*Mi amada amiga*, how many times do I have to remind you that you can't live your life in fear? Everything turned out okay and you just need to move forward and think positively. Now, let's change the subject. How did it go with Adam?"

Maddie grinned. "Up until the fire, everything was going great. Well, actually it went great even after the fire, despite everything that happened."

"Tell me more."

Maddie felt like a giddy schoolgirl. "He invited me over for dinner on Tuesday."

"And you're going?"

"Yes, I'm going. How could I refuse when a man offers to cook for me?"

"That's wonderful! A man that can cook. You need to snatch him up, Maddie."

Maddie laughed and said, "He's also a good kisser."

"Hmm," said Sancha. "A good cook and a good kisser…sounds like a keeper."

"That remains to be seen. I'm going on the date, but I just want you to know that I am still leery about this whole situation."

Maddie could practically hear Sancha rolling her eyes. "I understand. I'm happy as long as you're moving forward. Well, call me and let me know how your dinner date goes. I'll call you if anything turns up."

Chapter 9

ADAM FLITTED AROUND HIS APARTMENT and made preparations for the dinner he planned to cook for Maddie. He often entertained his friends and had gotten quite adept at it, but he wanted to make their first official date extra special. He decided to call on his personal dating consultant—Claire.

Since Zach and Claire had been together, Claire had often offered Adam dating advice—whether he asked for it or not. And most of the time he found her advice to be extremely helpful—whether he liked it or not.

He liked to think he had mastered the art of entertaining, especially when it came to the ladies, but for reasons he couldn't even explain to himself, he felt the need to make everything perfect for Maddie. And he knew Claire could offer a woman's perspective on how to make it just so.

Claire helped him decide on a menu of his specialty dishes. For the appetizer, they chose mozzarella and tomato bruschetta with fresh basil and garlic. The salad would be a classic Italian with his special version of homemade vinaigrette. He decided to go with lemon chicken piccata in a tasty lemon, butter, and capers sauce for the main dish. And finally, for the dessert he chose to make his own version of Emeril Lagasse's tiramisu recipe. Claire suggested that he serve a chilled white zinfandel wine with dinner and offer coffee or cappuccino with dessert as an added special touch.

Claire also advised him to have some nice, relaxing mood music playing quietly in the background throughout the evening, and some candles placed strategically throughout his apartment for just the right ambience. She assured him that if he followed all of her advice he couldn't go wrong. She even offered to come show him how to set the table "the proper way" right before Maddie arrived.

Adam had decided to time the meal preparation so that it would be about halfway done when Maddie arrived. That way she could watch him prepare the meal and he could show off his culinary skills. He figured she could also help with the dinner preparation if she wanted to. Getting guests involved with the cooking always seemed to be an icebreaker. He called her earlier in the day and reminded her to bring her violin so she could play for him.

Adam stared at the clock and tapped his fingers on the counter—6:00...6:01...6:02. He checked on the food and glanced at the clock again—6:03...6:04. He ran his fingers through his hair.

Maybe she changed her mind and wasn't coming. Maybe she was purposely being fashionably late.

He jumped when he heard a knock on the door. His eyes darted to the clock—6:05. He breathed a sigh of relief. When he opened the door, he inhaled sharply at the sight of her. She looked absolutely stunning.

He tried not to appear like a total Neanderthal as he forced his eyes to look at her face first. It lit up with that dazzling smile again, and he could tell she had spent a little extra time on her hair and makeup. Her normally straight, blond hair curled subtly and fell whimsically around her face and shoulders. She had applied more of an evening look with her makeup, a smoky gray around her eyes that brought out their brilliant blue color and gave her a sensual look. Her full lips were tinted with a shimmery gloss that made him want to kiss her deeply.

Later. Take it slow.

He then let his eyes drift to the tastefully sexy little black dress that showcased the curves of her voluptuous body perfectly and showed just the right amount of cleavage. He had to fight the urge to take her in his arms and take it off her. But he refrained. He wanted to savor the evening. He noticed that she held a bottle of wine in one hand and her violin case in the other.

"Good evening, Ms. Madeline. You look absolutely stunning, as always. Welcome to Casa de Lancaster. Your table awaits you. Please allow me," he said in mock formality.

He reached for the wine and violin case.

She smiled that beautiful smile that he loved so much and said, "Thank you. It smells wonderful in here. And by the way, you're looking pretty gorgeous yourself."

She winked at him as she walked past.

This is going to be an amazing night.

She followed him to the kitchen. Along the way she said, "The place looks great. I love all the candles."

Thank you, Claire.

"I know you told me not to bring anything, but I wanted to contribute something to the meal, so I brought my favorite wine for you to try."

"That sounds great! We can have some while I finish cooking dinner."

As Adam examined the wine label, it occurred to him that he didn't have a corkscrew.

Damn!

After all of the planning and preparation to make the evening perfect, he couldn't believe he had missed that important detail. The last time he had looked for a corkscrew in his utensil drawer, where he would normally keep it, he couldn't find it.

He was almost positive it had disappeared during one of the wilder parties he had hosted, but he decided to look one last time. He opened the drawer and dug around just in case he had missed it before. Finding nothing that even resembled a corkscrew, he leaned down for a better view, looked in the back of the drawer, shuffled things around, and looked again. No corkscrew.

Damn!

"You know what, Maddie, I'm sorry but I don't think I have a corkscrew. It disappeared during one of our particularly rowdy parties and I've never replaced it. I hate to ask, but do you have one?"

She stepped toward the drawer and said, "Well, let me see if I can find it," as she began rummaging.

Convinced that she wouldn't find a corkscrew in the drawer, Adam started to protest, "I'm pretty sure you're not going to find…"

But before he could finish his sentence, she said, "Oh here we go," as her hand emerged from the drawer holding a corkscrew.

Adam's eyebrows shot up as he stammered, "What the..? How did you..? Wow, am I going blind or what? I can't believe you found that. I've searched that drawer a few times and I've never seen it. You look for a microsecond and immediately find it. How did you do that? I swear you're a magician or something. Was that a sleight-of-hand trick? Come on, spill it. First the Shark Fin beer, then the corkscrew. What's your secret?"

She laughed the same way she did when she had amazed the band members with the Shark Fin beer at rehearsal and said, "I don't know. I guess I have good searching skills."

Adam glanced at her sideways. He thought too many strange coincidences occurred in Maddie's presence. But what else could explain it? He got the slightest feeling she wasn't being truthful with him. Not in a malicious way, but in a way he couldn't quite explain. He could have sworn there had not been a corkscrew in that drawer. Why would she lie, though? That would be a weird thing to lie about. He decided to let it go.

He shrugged and said, "Allow me."

She handed him the corkscrew. As he opened the wine, he noticed that the corkscrew didn't look like his. Maybe somebody had left one in the drawer the last time he had guests over. But he had just looked in the drawer and he didn't see it. He scratched his head.

Oh well. That was just strange.

He went on about the business of opening up the wine. He poured them each a glass and she gave him a lesson in the etiquette of wine tasting. Although he didn't normally drink wine, he was open to trying anything once, especially since she had brought it.

She said, "This is Beringer, Cabernet Sauvignon—Private Reserve, Napa Valley 2001. I usually only buy it for special occasions."

Adam was definitely not a wine connoisseur, but even he could tell it was what he considered an expensive bottle of wine. Warmth spread through him, partly from the wine, but mostly because she had considered their first date to be a special occasion.

Their eyes locked for a moment as they sipped the wine.

She is so sexy, he thought as he tried to imagine what she would look like with her dress off.

He would have gladly skipped dinner altogether and gone straight to bed with her. Patience, Grasshopper. Wait for it. He had definitely watched too many "Kung Fu" reruns.

He snapped back to reality and said, "Well, I need to chop some basil to add to the pasta dish when it's almost done. You don't want to add the fresh herbs too soon or they'll cook too much and wilt and you won't get the full flavor."

She raised her eyebrows and nodded—the 'A student' at a cooking lesson.

Adam retrieved his chef's knife from the cutting board and

started chopping rapidly, emulating the famous chefs he had seen on the Food Network.

Maddie said, "How do you do that so quickly? I would have already chopped off a finger. If I had to chop all of that it would take me an hour."

He stopped and looked at her. Sometimes he took his culinary skills for granted. Chopping quickly was second nature to him now, but it often amazed other people.

He held out the knife to her and said, "Here—you try."

She shook her head and said, "Not unless you want to wait an hour to eat."

"Come here," he said. "It's not as hard as you think. There's a certain technique. I'll show you."

She put down her glass and hesitantly took the knife from him. She gave him a pleading look for help. Adam stepped behind her and put his arms around her so that he could hold each of her hands in his. Something stirred deep within as his body drew closer to hers.

She glanced over her shoulder at him and said in a sexy voice, "I like this method of chopping already."

He inhaled sharply as he became aroused. Her hair touched his cheek. He inhaled the crisp cleanness and a subtle hint of perfume. He closed his eyes and breathed in again, savoring the smell of her. He had the urge to kiss her neck. He refrained. Instead, he carefully guided her hands and spoke softly to her as she chopped.

"Stack the basil leaves into a pile of about five leaves. Roll the stack, starting at the stem side and moving toward the tip of the leaves. Put the tip of your knife down and keep it steady so it always maintains contact with the cutting board. Now raise and lower the knife in a quick, rocking motion. A good chef's knife will easily chop through the leaves."

He guided her hands for a few more chops until he thought she had the hang of it, and then he let her try it on her own. She bit her lower lip as she chopped away at the basil, awkwardly at first, but then more quickly and proficiently as she gained confidence in the technique.

After a few minutes, she looked up at him through her lashes, handed him the knife, and said, "I think I'd better leave it up to the chef to finish this off. I'll drink my wine and learn by observing."

He continued with the final dinner preparations while they talked and sipped on the wine.

"I noticed you brought your violin," he said. "Why don't you play while I finish dinner?"

"Don't mind if I do."

She gingerly opened the case and removed a beautiful violin. By the looks of it, he guessed it must have been worth enough for a down payment on a Manhattan Brownstone.

"Yeah, this is my baby," she said. "My very special investment."

She took out the bow and tuned the violin for a moment.

"This is Bach's *Chaconne*," she said as she gently pulled the bow across the strings.

Adam stopped what he was doing and fixed his gaze on Maddie. Although he had no experience in playing the violin, he could tell that she was quite accomplished.

"That's amazing! You're so talented."

She smiled and nodded a silent thank you while she continued to play. She was a classy lady, and it made her even more appealing to him.

"We should feature you in one of our songs sometime," he said.

"When you get your recording contract and you need a violinist, I'll be there."

A slight, close-lipped smile spread across Adam's face. He liked her reference to the future. He could really get used to having her around. She played a few more songs while Adam put the finishing touches on the meal.

When he was ready, Adam motioned for Maddie to join him

at the dinner table. She carefully returned her violin to the case, and took her seat across from him. They lingered over their plates, eating and sipping wine in the dim candlelight as they made small talk. Chatting with Maddie was easy. Again, he felt as if he had known her for a long time, just like he had that night on the rooftop terrace.

At the end of the meal, Maddie dabbed up the last bit of sauce on her plate with a piece of bread. She popped it in her mouth, leaned back, and put her hands on her stomach.

"Can you tell I thought it was terrible?" she said, winking. "Would you be offended if I licked my plate?"

Adam laughed. "I won't judge. But you better save a little room for dessert."

"I am soooo full, but there's always room for dessert."

He served the tiramisu with chocolate-covered strawberries and cappuccino.

"That was absolutely delicious," said Maddie as she helped him clear the table. "Who needs restaurants?"

Adam had planned to clean up later, but she insisted on helping him. They stood side by side, laughing, joking, and flirting while they washed the dishes. She washed and he dried and put the dishes away.

Afterward, he said, "I hope you don't mind, but I took the liberty and picked out a movie. Claire recommended it. She said it's a chick flick for the most part, but Zach liked it too. I thought we could watch it."

"Sure, that sounds good. I love watching movies."

So despite the fact that he was completely stuffed, he popped a bag of popcorn in the microwave—because that seemed like the thing to do when watching movies. He also poured them both another glass of wine.

They moved into the living room. Adam was as nervous as a high school boy out on his first date. He found the movie on Amazon, dimmed the lights, and—while he sat on the couch with his wine in one hand and the remote in the other—wondered exactly how he was going to position himself next to Maddie. Should he motion for her to sit close to him? Give her some space? He relaxed when she solved the dilemma by sitting right next to him, the sides of their legs touching. He reached for the popcorn bowl and put it in his lap to hide his arousal.

He started the movie and leaned back on the couch to get comfortable. He stretched his arm out across the back of the couch. Maddie leaned back as well, snuggled right up next to him, and laid her head on his shoulder. His fingers seemed to have a mind of their own as they gently stroked her soft, fine hair.

Adam kissed the top of Maddie's head and closed his eyes as he breathed in the scent of her hair and perfume again. He thought he would never grow tired of being close to her. He glanced at her, observed the shape of her nose, the fullness of her lips, and the light from the TV as it danced off her hair and eyes. With heightened senses, he was aware of her breathing and felt her body touch his.

Suddenly, Maddie laughed. Adam jumped. She tilted her head and looked at him with furrowed brows, wondering why he hadn't laughed too. When their eyes met, her smile, still lingering from the laughter, faded as he stared at her intensely.

Adam leaned over and gently kissed her lips. A bolt of electricity ran through his entire body. He had never experienced this with any woman. He kissed her gently for a few moments. She leaned into him. As the passion ignited in him, he kissed her a little more firmly. Her lips parted and their tongues met. Deep, sensual kisses followed. Adam moaned softly. This woman made him feel like no other woman ever before, and he wanted more.

He lost track of time as he kissed her and stroked her hair, face, and neck. Her fingers ran through his hair and her nails scraped down his neck and back. His lips moved to her neck and he heard the slightest moan of pleasure escape her lips. Encouraged by this, he laid her down on the couch as he ran his hand down her neck and side, and cupped her breast through her dress.

She responded and pulled his body a little closer so he was almost on top of her as he kissed her passionately. Her breasts were full and soft in his hand. He wanted to taste them. He wanted her badly. They were caught up in the passion—their hands and arms moved over each other's bodies more frantically as fingers touched, grabbed, stroked, and caressed. He felt her fingernails dig into his back and chest, scratching and massaging as their bodies pressed together.

His hand moved slowly down her body to her upper thigh, where he felt the hem of her dress. He grabbed it and started to pull it up. He was ready to remove the dress, ready to reveal her body to him. But as he pulled her dress up past her hips, her hand stopped his. She sat up abruptly and pulled her dress back down. She breathed heavily as tears shimmered in her eyes.

She whispered, "I'm sorry, Adam. I'm not ready for this."

His eyes widened as he sat up and absentmindedly straightened his shirt. One moment everything was going well—they were both into it, there was no denying that. The next moment, things had come to a screeching halt. His brow creased as he ran a hand through his hair.

He said, "I'm sorry if I did something wrong."

She shook her head and said, "No. No. You didn't do anything wrong. I'm sorry. It's me. I just…I don't know if I'm ready for this."

She jumped up off the couch and made a beeline for the front door. Adam froze. He didn't know what to do. Should he follow her? Should he let her go? Dumbfounded, he just sat there. He had never experienced anything like this before.

When she reached the door, she turned to face him. Her bottom lip quivered as she said, "Adam, I am truly sorry. I had a wonderful night tonight. The meal was amazing, and I really enjoy spending time with you. I'm just not ready for this. I hope this doesn't ruin things between us."

He tilted his head and narrowed his eyes as he tried to understand. It made no sense to him. Still unsure of what to do or say, he stood, walked to her, took her by the hands and said, "It's okay, Maddie."

She buried her face in his chest. As his arms moved to envelop her, she pulled back and looked down at the floor.

"I really am sorry."

She wiped a tear off her cheek with the back of her hand, then turned and walked out. Just like that the date was over.

Adam stood dumbfounded. He rubbed his face with his hands. What the hell?

He paced as he went over it again and again in his mind, trying to figure out exactly where and why things had gone wrong. Was it something he had said? Something he had done?

He was pretty sure she had enjoyed herself. When they were making out, she had seemed to be into it. He felt as if she had wanted him as much as he had wanted her. There must be something more to it. But what?

What should he do now? Should he call her? Knock on her door? Leave her alone for a few days? Let her contact him?

He recalled the last thing she had said before she walked out...
I really enjoy spending time with you. I'm just not ready for this. I hope that this doesn't ruin things between us.

What did that mean? Maybe he should just quit overanalyzing everything. She probably got scared that they were going too far, too fast, and freaked.

He flopped down on the chair and covered his eyes with his hands. As he sat there sulking and pondering, he glanced through his fingers and noticed her violin case across the room. Had she left it on purpose? He doubted it, but it gave him a glimmer of hope. They would definitely be in contact again. She'd have to come back to get it, or he'd have to take it to her. Either way, it gave him a reason to contact her. He decided not to do anything for the night. Just let it go for now and seek counsel from Claire in the morning.

He finished cleaning the kitchen and tried to go to sleep, but sleep evaded him as he replayed the events of the night in his mind. It had been a wonderful date. They'd had a great time. He recalled what it felt like to kiss her, the way she made him feel. He had loved every moment of it. He hated the complete disappointment that he felt from her abrupt departure. Was he falling in love with Maddie? Was he already in love with her? The night's events continued to replay over and over in his mind as he tried to make sense of it all. Eventually, he fell into a fitful sleep.

Chapter 10

T HE NEXT DAY ADAM VISITED Zach and Claire. He needed some advice from his relationship counselor. He relayed the entire story to them and emphasized that everything seemed fine until the very end.

"Claire, what should I do next? Should I wait? Should I call her?"

"I think you should give her some space. I mean, based on the fact that she told you that she had a great time and that she didn't want to ruin things between you, makes me think she wants to see you again. She was just scared for some reason. Maybe she's old-fashioned and believes in a long courting period. Maybe she likes you more than she wants to admit to herself."

"If only," he sighed.

"Seriously," she said. "I wouldn't call her. I would play it cool. Give her time to come around on her own. She knows there's an open invitation to rehearsals on Thursday nights, and she knows what gigs you have at the clubs on Fridays and Saturdays. Not to mention that she happens to be your next-door neighbor. So, if she wants to see you, she'll find a way. She'll come around."

Adam knew that Claire was probably right, but waiting would be excruciating for him. He wanted to call Maddie badly. He wanted to apologize if he had done something wrong. But at the same time, he wanted to play it cool. He didn't want to upset her any further and scare her off even more. In the end, he took Claire's advice and didn't call her. It would be a long wait until Thursday's rehearsal, wondering if Maddie would come.

Chapter 11

WEDNESDAY CAME AND WENT WITH no word from Maddie. By the time Thursday night rehearsal came around, Adam worried that she wouldn't show up. The longer he went without contact with Maddie, the more insecure he became. He had taken Claire's advice and had not called her. He had given her space. He hoped Claire was right.

When the rehearsal started, there was still no sign of Maddie. He had even stalled the rehearsal start time for a few moments, just in case she was running late, but to no avail. So, with shoulders slumped and a heavy heart, he performed the opening number. He went through the motions robotically and scanned the crowd frequently for any sign of her.

About midway through the first set, Adam glanced at the door—like he had done a thousand times that night—and spotted her as she walked in. His heart began to beat rapidly, partly because he was excited to see her and partly because he didn't know what was going to happen next. He didn't think he could handle being rejected by her. He would be crushed. It had to work out between them. He could hardly wait to get through the last song of the set.

She stood at the back of the room and watched him with a face blank. He looked away and rubbed his sweaty palms on his shirt. As soon as he belted out the last lyric, while the instrumentals finished up, he left his mic in the stand and headed toward the back of the room to meet her.

As he approached, her eyes met and held his gaze. Adam had no idea what he was going to say to her. Where would he begin? He would just wing it. When he finally reached her, without saying a word, she threw her arms around him, pressed her body against his, and buried her face in his neck. Caught off guard, he stiffened momentarily before he put his arms around her and hugged her tightly.

She pulled back just enough to see his face and said, "Adam, I'm so sorry for freaking out on you the other night. I hope you can forgive me. I'm really into you and I want you to know it wasn't anything you did."

His eyes searched hers. His heart pounded so loudly that he wondered if she could hear it. Relief flooded his body as he closed his eyes and hugged her tightly.

She continued, "I'd rather not go into the details right now, but just know that I've had some bad experiences in the past and I'm just a little cautious. So, if you don't totally hate me, and you don't mind taking it slow, I'd like to continue seeing you."

He exhaled slowly. That was all he needed to hear. Yes, she confused the hell out of him, but he couldn't imagine not having her in his life. He kissed her gently, touched his forehead against hers, and whispered against her lips, "I'd really like that, Maddie."

She closed her eyes and inhaled and exhaled deeply. He was instantly back on top of the world again. He kissed her for a few more moments then took her by the hand and led her back to the table where Cristy and the regulars were seated.

Zach and Claire exchanged knowing glances, and Claire gave Adam a wink as if to say, "See, I told you so."

He nodded and winked back, a secret understanding between them, and hoped his gratitude was apparent.

That night, Maddie joined him on the rooftop terrace, just like she had done the night of the first rehearsal. This time they snuggled on the couch. He sipped beer. She sipped wine. They talked and made out for hours. He was very careful not to make any moves that might scare her away. He tried to be respectful of whatever it was from her past that made her fearful.

Even though they had not yet been intimate, he knew he was falling in love with her. Those few days in which he didn't know what would happen or what she was thinking were unbearable. The joy he felt when she came back to him was indescribable.

If this was all he could get from Maddie right now, if this was all she could give, he would gladly take it. Adam knew he would wait as long as it took, as long as she needed. This realization surprised him a little. He knew deep down that he really didn't have a choice, after all. She had captured his heart.

Chapter 12

DURING THE NEXT FEW WEEKS, Maddie and Adam were inseparable, and it was wonderful. Their relationship grew stronger by the day. Sometimes Adam couldn't believe things were going so well.

Maddie became a regular part of their crowd. They accepted her. She came to all of their rehearsals and performances. She was always there watching him, supporting him.

They spent many nights making out for long periods of time and doing some heavy petting, but he never pressured her for more, fearful of making any moves that would scare her away again. He figured she would tell him when she was ready, but he made it no secret that he wanted her badly.

Zach, Claire, and some of their friends had planned a skiing trip to upstate Vermont the upcoming weekend, and they invited Maddie and Adam to come along. Everyone booked cabins for the entire weekend. Maddie and Adam booked a cabin together. He secretly hoped this might be the weekend they would consummate the relationship.

When they got to the ski resort, everyone hit the slopes immediately. Maddie and Adam spent a good part of the day on the green and blue intermediate trails. When they got tired, they would take breaks in the lodge, snuggle by the fire, warm up for a while, have some refreshments, and then head back out.

The weather was perfect. It was a nice, sunny day. The weekend forecast called for clear skies and temperatures in the high forties all weekend. As they thoroughly enjoyed their time together, Maddie and Adam didn't realize how late it was getting. The last lift to the top of the mountain closed at five o'clock. They jumped on the chairlift to take one last downhill run.

Maddie looked between her dangling skis to the ground far below and said, "What a beautiful view."

Adam gazed at her and thought the same, exact thought. He smiled and nodded his head in agreement, but it wasn't just the view of the landscape that he thought was beautiful. He leaned over and kissed her cheek. She turned to face him. He cupped her chin in his gloved hand and gently pulled her face closer to his so that he could kiss her more deeply.

After a moment, she pulled away from him and said, "I think I'm ready."

Adam furrowed his brow and said, "Ready to try a black diamond trail? Let's do it."

She giggled and said, "No, I don't mean that."

He narrowed his eyes and turned to face her.

She looked up at him through her thick lashes and slowly repeated herself. "I think I'm…ready."

And then it hit him. She wasn't talking about skiing. His eyes widened as he inhaled slowly and absorbed the implication.

"Are you sure? I don't want to pressure you into anything."

She leaned over and kissed him gently as she whispered against his lips, "Absolutely."

He involuntarily sucked in a breath. His heart beat fast in his chest as he became aroused. He pulled her closer and deepened the kiss. He knew he had already given himself to her the first moment he saw her, and now she was ready to give herself to him—completely.

Suddenly, the wind whipped around them and dark clouds gathered rapidly overhead as they approached the exit for the intermediate slopes. Below them a man flagged everybody to get off the lift and a blinking billboard sign flashed weather alerts, storm warnings, and trail closings. They continued kissing. The man shouted at them to get off. Maddie stopped kissing Adam and tilted her head slightly.

"What's that sound? I thought I heard a voice."

Adam twisted in all directions and looked for the source. They simultaneously looked behind them and spotted the man frantically waving his arms as the distance between them continued to grow. It was too late. They were so far past the lift exit at that point that jumping off would be quite a drop. Adam wasn't sure they could make it without getting hurt.

They stared at each other, wide-eyed.

Maddie said, "What's going on?"

Adam shrugged and said, "I think he wanted us to get off back there. It looks like we might be trying a black diamond trail today, like it or not."

Maddie ignored his lame attempt at humor as she looked at the sky and the surroundings and said, "Look at the black clouds overhead. Where did those come from? I thought it was supposed to be clear and sunny all weekend."

"The weather forecast didn't call for any storms," he said. "I've heard of freak blizzards appearing from out of nowhere in the mountains, but shouldn't there have been some warning signs?"

The wind bursts increased in intensity, so much so that the chairlift swayed and rocked. They gripped the safety bar. Adam didn't mention his growing concern to Maddie. He didn't want to scare her. He watched as small ice particles landed on his goggles and melted. He felt them spray on his face with each gust of wind, as more dark and menacing clouds gathered over the mountaintop. Maddie shivered and moved closer to him. With the wind and the sudden cloud blockage of the sun, it grew darker and colder by the minute. Adam wrapped his arms around her as she quietly stared ahead and bit her lip.

Bewildered, she said, "The forecast certainly didn't call for snow today. What if we get to the top of the mountain and I don't have the skills to maneuver the more advanced trail?"

"Well, if it gets that bad, worst-case scenario is that we take our skis off and walk down, or even slide down on our asses if we have to. I've seen people do that before. Don't worry about it. You'll do fine. Besides, with this storm getting worse, they'll probably have the trails closed and the Ski Patrol will be up there to tell us what we need to do."

She furrowed her brow and quietly said, "I hope so."

The wind continued to grow in intensity, swinging the chairlift even harder. Maddie wrapped her arms around Adam's waist and gripped him more tightly. He couldn't help but think of the nursery rhyme lullaby that his mother used to sing to him as a child:

Rock-a-bye baby in the treetop
When the wind blows the cradle will rock
When the bough breaks, the cradle will fall
And down will come baby, cradle and all

He hoped this bough wouldn't break anytime soon. It was even more unsettling when they noticed that there was nobody else on the lift. They were the only ones who hadn't disembarked at the intermediate run drop-off because they were too busy making out. Stupid as it was, Adam thought it was worth it—that is, worth it if they made it out of this mess unscathed.

As they approached the drop-off point for the top of the mountain, Maddie shouted over the sound of the wind. "Do you think we should ride the lift back down?"

Adam had been pondering the same question. "I'm not sure. Are you up for the challenge of a black diamond trail today?"

"I'm not sure either," she said. "I don't know if I can handle it with the wind and visibility getting worse."

"We'll probably get down the mountain quicker if we ski down rather than ride the lift back down. It feels like the wind is getting stronger and I don't relish the thought of getting whipped around in this thing all the way back down. But on the other hand, like you said, maneuvering down the mountain in these conditions might make it more difficult. I don't even know for sure if anyone realizes we're still on the lift. It's possible we could get halfway and they shut it down, leaving us stuck."

Maddie looked straight ahead, her face a blank mask as she said, "We left our cell phones in the cabin. What if no one knows we're up here? Surely the man that was signaling us to get off earlier reported it to someone."

The snow flurries increased in size and intensity. Visibility grew worse as the wind gusted around them and the dark clouds overhead grew more ominous. The temperature dropped rapidly.

As they debated whether or not they should ride the lift all the way back down or get off at the next drop-off point, the decision was made for them. When they were almost to the exit, the lift slowed and stopped completely a few feet away from the actual drop-off point.

"Great," they said simultaneously.

Adam leaned over as far as he could without rocking the chairlift to see how far they would have to jump. He estimated it to be a ten-foot drop. There was no way they would make that with their skis on.

He glanced sideways at Maddie. She looked at him, wide-eyed, failing to disguise her fear any longer.

"We're going to have to jump for it," he said. "I'll go first and then maybe I can help you. It's probably best if we throw our skis and poles aside so that they don't get in the way of our landing."

He took Maddie's ski poles and tossed both sets as far as he could from the landing point, but close enough so that they could retrieve them once they were safely on the ground. Then, they carefully removed their skis and threw them in the same vicinity as the poles. They would certainly need them if they tried to make it down a black diamond trail.

Adam scooted to the edge of his seat and waited for the swaying chairlift to swing in the right direction. When he felt the timing was right, he launched himself off the chairlift with as much force as possible so that he could clear the ten-foot drop without falling backward down the mountain. He managed to land upright on his feet, fell forward, and caught himself with his hands just in time to stop a face-plant.

He looked up at Maddie and said, "Your turn. I'll stand to the side so I won't get in the way, but I'll be able to catch you if you start to fall backward."

She took a deep breath and launched herself. She landed on her feet, but they slipped out from under her as she fell backward. Adam caught her by the arm and helped her up. They retrieved their skis and poles and stayed put for a moment to assess the situation. They spotted a small, shed-like building close to the ski lift with a sign that read "Ski Patrol."

Adam said, "I don't have a good feeling about this. There aren't any lights on. It doesn't look like anyone's in there."

Maddie followed him into the Ski Patrol shack. Just as he had suspected, it was abandoned. He flipped the light switch—nothing. Maybe the storm had knocked out the power.

Damn!

Maddie rummaged through a desk drawer and found a flashlight. Adam put the handset of the landline phone against his ear—no dial tone.

Damn!

Maddie said excitedly, "Look, a CB radio. Do you know how to work one?"

Adam scratched his head.

"I've never used one."

They took turns trying various knobs and tuning to different frequencies. Occasionally, they would hear other people talking in choppy, interrupted sentences as the signal faded in and out, but it seemed that no matter what they did, no one could hear them. Adam's hands clenched into fists as he paced the room.

Maddie shone the flashlight on a map of the ski trails that was posted on a bulletin board.

Adam studied the map and said, "We could wait out the storm here in the ski shack. But with the power out and the temperature dropping so fast, it's going to get really cold up here."

Maddie frowned and said, "We don't know when the storm is going to end. And what if we get snowed in here for several days? We don't have any food or water. And if we're snowed in, no one can get to us to help."

Adam raked both hands down his face and said, "Then our only other option is to try to make it down the mountain. If we find the shortest trail, we should be able to get down in an hour or less. If we keep moving, we should stay warm enough to avoid frostbite or hypothermia."

In an attempt to lighten the mood, Maddie glanced over her shoulder with a cheeky grin and said, "Then we'll be back in our warm, cozy cabin with a hot tub and a nice fire going, and some good wine, and…"

Adam pulled her close and kissed her. "That sounds fabulous to me. Are we in agreement to give the mountain a go?"

"I think it's our only option," she said as her eyes searched his for encouragement.

He nodded somberly. It was unfortunate that neither of them could foresee the consequences of their decision.

Chapter 13

ADAM WONDERED HOW IT HAD come to be that they were stranded at the top of the mountain in a snowstorm with no other souls in sight. He and Maddie carefully examined the ski trail map and tried to find the shortest trail they thought they could navigate, skill-wise. All of the trails at this location were black diamond and double black diamond trails—the highest level of difficulty. But even among black diamond trails, some were harder than others to navigate. Some double and triple black diamond trails could contain ice crevasses, moguls, soaring cliffs, and avalanche risks. They had to choose carefully. They settled on a single black diamond trail that appeared to be the shortest.

Maddie shivered as they emerged from the ski shack. She covered her mouth with her gloved hands as she scanned the area. Visibility had decreased to less than twenty feet. She squinted to make out the signs as the wind and snow stung the exposed areas of her face.

Adam said, "We need to stick together, no matter what."

Maddie nodded. They retrieved their skis and poles and made their way to the trail entrance. Even though they were anxious to get down to warmth and safety, Adam made a conscious effort to keep the pace slow for Maddie. When they first started out,

Maddie's teeth chattered, but as long as they kept moving, the cold was bearable.

Through the dark clouds, they could barely make out the orange hues in the sky as the sun began its descent behind the mountain. At first the trail didn't seem too difficult as it meandered across the mountain somewhat horizontally. But when they got to the ridge and looked down, there was a steep slope with big moguls everywhere. Adam gripped his poles tighter and swallowed hard.

This was not going to be good.

Maddie glanced at him, wide-eyed.

"You can do it," he shouted over the wind.

He tried to keep his face blank to disguise his growing apprehension. She nodded as they began the slow process of navigating their way down, barely able to see what was coming ahead of them. Adam feared that it might become a complete whiteout before long, but he kept that thought to himself. Maddie was quiet, her eyes on the trail, her face contorted as she concentrated intently on her every move.

Based on his memory of the trail map, Adam estimated that they were approximately halfway down the mountain when he heard a loud, rumbling roar in the distance.

Was that thunder? A train?

He stopped and strained to hear. He couldn't quite make it out, and then his eyes grew wide when it occurred to him where he had heard a sound like that before. His pulse quickened as he recalled a television show that he had seen about a month ago in which the extreme skiers compared the sound of an approaching avalanche to the sound of a freight train.

The rumbling steadily grew louder as the realization hit him. He quickly looked at Maddie, and judging by the panicked look on her face, she knew it too.

He shouted, "Pick up the pace," as he squinted and searched for anything they could use as shelter—a rock or a fallen tree that they could get behind—but suddenly the avalanche was upon them.

In the next instant, Adam felt himself tumbling down the mountain, caught up in a slide of snow, ice, and debris, tumbling over and over, out of control, tangled in his skis and poles. He couldn't see or hear Maddie. He began to scream her name over and over, but he couldn't even hear his own voice. All he could hear was the rumbling roar of the avalanche.

He tumbled for what seemed like several minutes, although he didn't know how long it actually was. His hand flailed as he desperately grabbed for stationary objects but couldn't get a grip. He arched his back and dug in his ski poles and his heels, but he couldn't overcome the force of the avalanche. He was helpless.

His body jerked as he crashed against something hard, possibly a large bolder. He bounced off whatever it was like a rag doll and crashed back down onto another hard surface. He felt excruciating pain as something in his leg snapped.

"Ahhh!" he screamed out in pain, but he hadn't stopped tumbling. Then everything went black.

Chapter 14

WHEN ADAM FINALLY CAME TO, his eyes shot open. Maddie's face hovered above his. Tears streamed down her cheeks as she frantically dug in the snow.

"Adam, wake up! Are you okay? Can you hear me?"

He tried to ask how long he had been out but couldn't speak. His eyes widened as he realized that his mouth was packed with snow. He tried to move his arm to get the snow out of his mouth but an unknown force held it down. As he became more alert, he realized his entire body was buried in snow. He breathed rapidly as he tried to flail around to free himself. He was drowning in the snow.

Maddie saw him struggling and quickly scooped the snow out of his mouth with her finger. He sputtered and coughed and gasped for air.

Maddie blurted out, "Adam, you're alive! Oh my god! I was so scared that you were dead. Are you okay?"

All the while tears continued to stream down her face as she continued to dig his head and upper body out of the snow.

He barely managed to get the words out. "I…don't…know. I'm in a lot of pain. It's my right leg."

She began digging his legs out of the snow. When she had

moved enough snow to see his leg, her face contorted. She covered her face with her hands and tried to hide her reaction, but it was too late. Adam saw her look of horror, which confirmed his fears.

Maddie sucked in a deep breath, steeled herself, and said, "Your leg is badly broken. Try not to move."

She began to pack the snow back on top of his leg.

Once his entire leg was re-covered with snow, she said, "The snow will keep the swelling down and help with the pain—hopefully."

Adam's teeth chattered audibly and his body began to shake—probably as much from shock as from the cold—as the temperature grew more frigid and the sky grew darker. He felt dull-headed and couldn't organize his thoughts. It finally occurred to him to check to see if Maddie had been hurt. As his eyes scanned her over, he noticed that she had a big gash on her left forearm that spanned the length of her arm from the inner elbow to the wrist. Blood streamed out of the wound and stained the snow crimson.

The sight of Maddie being hurt snapped him out of his stupor. His concern for her made him temporarily forget about the pain in his leg—maybe the freezing snow helped with that too.

"Your...arm...is...bleeding," he managed to say through chattering teeth.

She glanced down at her arm and back at him and said, "Don't worry about that right now. I'll be fine."

Adam sat up, despite the excruciating pain that he felt in his leg. His head spun and for a moment he thought he was going to pass out. He shook his head and forced himself to sit up and focus. He started to unzip his ski coat.

"Adam! What are you doing?" she screamed. "Stop it! You're going to freeze to death."

He ignored her and continued to unzip his coat. He reached in under his sweater and ripped off part of the t-shirt that he wore underneath. He tore the shirt into strips and wrapped them around Maddie's arm to stop the bleeding. When he was satisfied that the bleeding had stopped and that she would be okay, he collapsed back into the snow without even bothering to re-zip his coat.

He winced in pain. It was becoming unbearable. He closed his eyes as Maddie re-zipped his coat. He felt himself fading and wasn't sure how long he was going to be able to remain conscious. When he opened his eyes again, the look of panic was back on Maddie's face. She was saying something about needing to get him down the mountain and to a hospital as soon as possible. He was losing the ability to focus on what she was saying.

Adam thought he heard her say, "Do you think you could walk if I helped to support you?"

"I don't know," he mumbled. "I...can...try."

His own voice sounded distant to him. She tried to lift him. He screamed and tasted bile. The usually simple act of sitting up and trying to stand almost made him puke and pass out.

"Please stop," he pleaded weakly.

Maddie seemed to be talking to herself as she said, "Stay calm, Maddie. Stay calm. I wonder if I can drag you down."

She gripped his jacket and tugged hard. She managed to move him a couple of inches. Adam gritted his teeth and growled in an attempt to stifle a scream of agony.

"Stop!"

It was then that they both realized the full extent of the dire situation. It was unlikely that anyone would be able to find them on the mountain in the midst of the storm. Besides, who knew where the avalanche had taken them? And even if any rescuers knew where they were, they would not be able to get to them. There was no way Adam could make it down the mountain unassisted, and Maddie wasn't strong enough to carry him.

Maddie looked up at the western peak and glimpsed the last sliver of the setting sun through the dark clouds and flurries. Adam thought it seemed like the snow was intent on completely covering them and erasing their very existence.

His body shivered uncontrollably. Through the fog of the pain and shock, Adam came to the terrifying realization that they would almost certainly die on the mountain. It was going to be their last night on the earth. How did they go from a having great day to this?

Maddie still had a chance, though. She could probably make it to safety. He couldn't allow both of them to die. His heart warmed at the thought of her surviving. It gave him a sliver of hope. He had to convince her to try. From that point on, all he could think of was saving Maddie's life.

Focus on saving Maddie. Ignore the pain. Ignore the urge to slip into unconsciousness right now. Don't let her see your fear.

Adam stared at Maddie and wondered what she was thinking. Her contorted face told him that she had come to the same conclusions.

He said, "Maddie, you're going to have to go for help."

Her eyes widened in disbelief as she said, "No! I'm not leaving you."

"You have to try," he pleaded. "If you don't go, we're both going to die on this mountain."

"There's no way I could make it down in time," she sobbed. "Besides, even if I did make it down, how would anyone be able to get back up here in this storm?"

"I can probably last through the night knowing that you're safe. You can bring help in the morning," he said weakly.

She stared at him, horrified. Tears continued to stream down her face. Some seemed frozen in place. She tried to wipe them back with her gloves.

They both fell silent for a few moments and let the gravity of their situation sink in. Then something passed over her face. Was it a look of peace?

She must be about to lose it too.

Or was it a look of resolve? Maddie straightened suddenly, as if

74

set in determination. She lowered her face inches away from Adam's and looked directly into his eyes, as if her next words were of the utmost importance. She cupped his face in her gloved hands.

"Adam, listen carefully to me. I'm not leaving you on this mountain. And we are not going to die tonight," she said with conviction.

She said it with such certainty that Adam wanted to believe her. But he knew that she was just putting on a brave face for his sake. His head started spinning again. He tried one more attempt. Maybe begging would help.

"Please listen to me, Maddie!" he pleaded. "Now is not the time to be strong-willed. I don't want you to die. I could never forgive myself for that. I'll be fine. You go get help. It's the only way we might have a chance. Please!"

"No! I am not letting you die up here alone! We are going to make it!" she screamed.

She spoke the words so forcefully and with such resolve and determination that he knew she meant them. He couldn't talk her out of it. He felt his body slump further into the ground. Sadly, he realized that she would not leave him. His last sliver of hope for her survival was snuffed out. As much as she tried to hide the truth with her words, he knew without a doubt that they would freeze to death on the mountain. Adam loathed this complete and utter helplessness. He felt despair crush his chest as he struggled to breathe. But he wanted to, had to, stay composed for her.

She lay down in the snow and faced him as she pressed her body close to his. In happier times, this would've been a welcome gesture. But seeing her give up and prepare to die with him was more than he could bear. He closed his eyes and, with a childlike hope, thought that if he couldn't see what was happening, then it must not really be happening. He tried to erect a mental block from all the pain and despair and hopelessness.

He felt her wrap her arms around him and the warmth of her

breath on his cheek. He knew this was going to be their last moment together, their last embrace, but he had no words to say.

What do you say when you and the person you love the most in this world are about to die?

There was only one thing to say. He wrapped his arms around her as best he could and said, "I love you, Maddie."

A fresh batch of tears welled up in her eyes as a smile spread across her face. She hugged him even more tightly and said softly, "I love you, too, Adam. Don't worry. I promise you, we are not going to die on this mountain."

He had to smile at her earnest attempt to comfort him, even though he knew that the promise she had just made could not be kept. She loved him, and that was all he needed to hear. He clung to that thought as they lay there in the snow together, arms wrapped around each other in their last embrace.

Adam started to feel himself losing consciousness, and he didn't think he could fight it any longer. He heard his own voice as if it were coming from somewhere far away, say, "Maddie, kiss me."

She moved in closer and pressed her lips to his. This would be their last kiss. All of the love that he felt for her spread throughout his body. He hoped that she could feel it too. If he had to die, this was the way to go. Knowing that she loved him was enough. He closed his eyes again and gave in to the powerful urge to go to sleep and never wake up.

As he drifted into unconsciousness, he heard her ghostlike voice comforting him, like a mother comforting a child.

"That's right, Adam," she said. "Just rest now. Think warm thoughts."

She quietly repeated, "Think warm thoughts. Think warm thoughts."

In his last conscious moments, Adam felt a sudden warmth spread over his entire body. He thought he must be close to death. It wasn't the kind of warmth that comes from another person's body heat—there was no way that Maddie's body could have generated that amount of heat in the snow and freezing temperatures. He felt the kind of warmth that one feels from the sun on the beach in ninety-degree weather. What a wonderful, welcome sensation. He was enveloped in a warmth that comforted and relaxed him. His body quit shivering. His teeth quit chattering. He couldn't hold on any longer. He drifted off into oblivion.

Chapter 15

ADAM AWOKE TO A BLINDING light and a faint beeping noise. He squinted as his eyes grew accustomed to the light.

Where am I?

He glanced to his right, where the intense light streamed in from a large window. He quickly looked down to avert his eyes. His brow furrowed when he saw that he was in a bed with metal railing and tubes attached to his arms. His eyes darted to the foot of the bed.

Was that a cast on his leg?

The beeping sound came from some sort of instrument on a pole next to the bed. A woman he assumed to be a nurse adjusted the settings. He looked to his left. Maddie sat beside the bed reading a book. When she heard him stir, her head snapped up and she stared at him with wide eyes. She jumped to her feet and threw her arms around his neck.

"Adam, you're awake!" she cried. "Oh my god! I'm so glad you're okay!"

Tears streamed down her face.

Why was she crying?

He heard another familiar voice say, "Easy now, don't squeeze him so hard that you hurt him."

There were other people in the room. He slowly turned his head in the direction of the voice and saw Zach, Claire, and his parents. They moved closer to the bed and gathered around him. They all looked relieved and happy.

Adam heard his dad say, "Son, you had us so worried."

Maddie moved back to let his mother and father hug him.

His mom was crying too. She kept repeating, "I thought we had lost you. Baby, I thought we had lost you."

Adam pursed his lips and knitted his brow.

What the heck was going on?

He rubbed his eyes and tried to remember. Zach and Claire hugged him too. It was good to see them, but he couldn't make sense of it all. Then, memories began to flash in his mind: skiing, a storm, an avalanche, a broken leg. Adam glanced down at his leg again, which was hoisted up at the foot of the bed and covered with a very large plaster cast from his foot to mid-thigh.

He remembered lying in the snow with Maddie. He remembered thinking they were going to die. But they hadn't.

He strained to remember anything beyond that.

His eyes met Maddie's and he said in a hoarse voice, "Are you okay?"

"I'm fine," she said as she smiled her beautiful smile, wiping tears away.

Adam noticed that she had a large bandage wrapped around her arm where the gash had been. She saw him look at the bandage and rubbed it absentmindedly as she said, "It's okay. It just needed a few stitches."

"A few?" said Zach. "More like forty."

Maddie shot him a look as if to say '*shut up.*' Claire hit Zach on the arm and gave him a disapproving look as well.

Zach continued, "Dude, you've been out for like twenty-four hours. Now that's some serious Zs."

Zach had a way of lightening up a conversation.

Twenty-four hours?

It felt like only moments ago that Adam had prepared to die on the mountain.

His mom said, "They did surgery on your leg. The doctor says it was a success and everything's going to be fine. You'll be up and walking in no time."

"They told us it was a miracle that you two survived on the mountain," his dad chimed in, his voice breaking a little when he said the word "survived."

How did they survive? How long were they on the mountain? How were they rescued?

Adam honestly didn't know. He had so many questions.

Mom said, "Do you need anything, sweetie? Let us know if you need pain medicine or something to eat. The doctor is on his way to examine you."

As his parents and Zach and Claire continued to talk to him, Adam noticed that Maddie had retreated to the back of the room. She looked sad as she stared straight ahead out the window.

He had to ask, "Exactly how long were we up on the mountain?"

Zach glanced at Claire and Maddie, then leaned in and said, "Man, you guys were up there all night! The rescue party didn't find you until the next day. Both of you were covered in snow. They almost didn't see you. The doctors said it's a miracle that you survived the well-below-freezing temperatures. And neither one of you had any frostbite. It's a damn miracle, bro!"

Claire chimed in. "We're all so thankful you made it. The rest of the guys said to tell you 'hey' when you woke up, and that they're pulling for you. They'll be by to see you later."

It certainly must have been a miracle. How else could they have survived?

And then Adam remembered the warmth enveloping him right before he lost consciousness. Had he been hallucinating?

"God must've been looking out for you," said Mom. "I was praying for you both all night long, from the moment I got the call that you hadn't returned to the lodge. The meteorologist said it was a freak storm. They didn't see it coming until it was too late. It just came out of nowhere. They said a storm like that happens very rarely. And the two of you surviving it was an even rarer occurrence."

Her voice broke as she fought back tears. Adam glanced at Maddie. Maybe the recollection of the horrible events was too much for her.

As Mom, Dad, Zach, and Claire continued on with the conversation, Maddie remained mostly quiet. If someone asked her a question, she would answer, but otherwise she didn't speak. Maybe it was a self-defense mechanism for post-traumatic stress. Adam didn't know. He wasn't a damn shrink, but he could tell something wasn't quite right.

After a few hours, everybody left to go get a bite to eat, except for Maddie. Adam was glad she had stayed behind so they could have a private conversation. He wanted to ask her if she could recall anything about the rescue.

She sat in the chair next to the bed and held his hand. She still had that strained look on her face. It was almost the same look of anguish or sadness that she had on the mountain when she had thought they were going to die.

Maddie leaned forward and stroked Adam's hair with her other hand. He wondered why she looked so sad. They had made it to safety. This was a time for happiness and celebration, yet there was that look.

"That feels good," he said.

Her smile didn't quite reach her eyes. As she held his hand and stroked his hair, she looked into his eyes and lowered her voice just above a whisper. "I am so thankful you made it. I thought you were going to die. I had to see for myself that you are okay."

"Well *we* made it, Maddie," he said, trying to sound cheerful. "Everything's going to be okay."

Why did he feel like he was trying to convince himself of this more than he was trying to convince her? He felt a nervous feeling in the pit of his stomach. He didn't like the way she was looking at him.

And then she confirmed his apprehension when she said, "Everything is not okay, Adam."

Tears ran down her cheeks again.

What the hell was going on? What was she talking about? His eyes narrowed and his brow creased. She looked so damn sad.

"You're not going to understand this, and there's no way I can ever explain it, but it was my fault that we almost died on the mountain."

Adam's eyes grew wide, incredulous. Had she lost her freakin' mind?

"What are you talking about?" he said quietly. "It couldn't have been your fault. Don't blame yourself. We made the decisions together. The storm and the avalanche were just occurrences of nature. How could any of that be your fault?"

She sighed and looked at her hand in his, then back to his eyes.

"Like I said, I can't explain it to you. I just know it was because of me that you almost died. And I couldn't have lived with myself if that had happened. I can't continue putting you in danger."

Was she serious? Adam felt like he was waiting for the punch line. Surely, she must be joking. But this was no joking matter. Maybe she was having a mental breakdown from the traumatic events. Maybe the cold had messed with her head. Or maybe she had hit her head.

"Maddie, you're not making any sense," he said. "You're not putting me in danger. You bring joy and happiness into my life, but not danger."

She stared straight ahead and said, "I know that what I'm telling you doesn't make sense now—and it probably never will—but it's for your own good. I want you to always remember that it's not your fault. I always want you to remember that I meant what I said on the mountain. I do love you with all my heart. And for that very reason, I have to leave you. After today, you won't see me again."

Adam's eyes widened as his heart froze. Was she breaking up with him? What the hell was she talking about?!

He couldn't comprehend what she was saying. He heard the words, but they weren't making any sense. His eyes searched hers questioningly.

She leaned over and kissed him so tenderly that he ached for more. He reached to pull her closer to him, but she pulled back suddenly and backed across the room. Tears poured down her face.

She strained to get the words out as she began to sob. "I hope that someday you can forgive me, Adam. I am so sorry!"

She turned and ran out of the room. Adam wanted to run after her. Damned cast and all these tubes. He was trapped in the hospital bed.

He called out at the top of his voice, "Wait, Maddie! Come back! What are you doing? It wasn't your fault! Damn it, Maddie!"

But she didn't come back. He frantically scanned the room and tried to figure out how to get unhooked from all of the tubes. He spotted his cell phone on the side table next to the bed. Someone must have left it for him. In a desperate attempt, he grabbed it and called her. She didn't answer. He slammed the phone down and raked both hands through his hair. He felt an indescribable pain in his chest and wanted to scream, but he couldn't breathe. He thrashed around and tried to get out of the bed and pull the tubes out of his arm. The nurses ran into the room and restrained him. They put something in his IV that they said would 'calm you down.' Very soon afterward, he drifted off to sleep.

Chapter 16

WHEN ADAM AWOKE AGAIN, HE tried to convince himself that it had all been a terrible nightmare and that Maddie had just gone to get something to eat. She will be back soon, he told himself.

Visitors came and went. Nurses checked his vital signs every two hours. Doctors did rounds. Meals were delivered and left uneaten. No sign of Maddie. He didn't tell anyone about his final encounter with Maddie because he still held out hope she would change her mind the way she had after freaking out on their first date.

That night he tried to stay up all night, hoping she would change her mind and call, text, or come back. She never did. The remainder of his time in the hospital was more of the same—still no word from Maddie. His life had turned into a living nightmare.

Adam was crushed. When Maddie left him, it was as if his heart had been ripped out of his chest. How could she have done this to him? Why would she leave him when he needed her most?

Try as he might, he couldn't make sense of her final words to him as he mulled them over again and again...*I do love you with all my heart. And for that very reason, I have to leave you. After today, you won't see me again.*

He held on to hope for three or four days after she left, but it soon became apparent that his hope was in vain. He sank into a deep depression.

On the day of Adam's discharge, Zach and Claire offered to drive him home and help him get settled. Claire stuffed pillows behind his back while Zach situated his casted leg on the ottoman. Once everything was situated, Zach sat down on the edge of the ottoman, careful not to disturb Adam's leg, and blurted out, "Okay man, spill it. Don't think we haven't noticed that Maddie is MIA. And you've been moping around like someone knocked you sideways. What's going on?"

Claire shot Zach a disapproving look but said nothing.

Adam sighed, slouched down farther into the couch, and raked his hand across his face.

"Zach, I don't want to talk about it."

"You don't have to tell us," said Claire.

"Oh, hell, he doesn't," retorted Zach. "I'm his best friend. We tell each other things. I've given him enough space. Now he needs to talk about the elephant in the room."

Claire glared at Zach and then looked at Adam apologetically. Adam sighed loudly again and rolled his eyes as he raked his fingers through his unkempt hair.

"Fine," he said. "I'll tell you. But first, get me a beer."

"Aren't you on painkillers?" asked Claire.

Adam shook his head and said, "Only prescription-strength ibuprofen, as needed. I'll be fine."

Zach shrugged and headed to the kitchen. Claire followed closely behind. Adam could hear their whispered arguing. He couldn't hear what they were saying, but he honestly didn't care. He didn't care about anything.

They eventually returned with three beers, each kept one and Zach handed Adam the third.

Adam grabbed the beer without a word of thanks, popped the top, and proceeded to chug it down in less than thirty seconds.

He then proceeded to release a rather large belch as he pointed at Zach's beer and said, "Are you going to drink that?"

Stunned, Zach and Claire looked at each other quizzically as Adam yanked the beer from Zach's hand and chugged that one down as well.

"Damn, man," said Zach. "That's enough beer for you for now. Now get on with the story."

Adam belched even louder and said dejectedly, "What's there to tell? You've already figured out that we broke up. What more do you want me to say?"

He couldn't bring himself to even say her name. He wished Claire would quit with the look of pity.

"What happened?" asked Claire softly.

"She had to leave," said Adam as he stared blankly ahead. "We were having a great day skiing before the accident and the next thing I know she tells me she's sorry but she has to leave."

"What a flake," said Zach angrily.

"Zach!" reprimanded Claire. "Please stop."

Zach stared at her, aggravated.

"Why did she have to leave?" said Claire.

"She had to leave on a work assignment," Adam lied. "She didn't know how long she would be gone so she thought it would be better if we broke up."

He didn't want tell the real reasons she gave for leaving because he didn't want them to think she was crazy, although he was beginning to wonder if she was.

"She couldn't even fuckin' wait until you got out of the hospital?" spat Zach. "Her job is more important than you? How selfish is that?!"

Adam cringed. Zach was his best friend, after all, so of course he would side with Adam. He didn't respond. Instead, he stared straight ahead. He realized that maybe he should've thought of a better lie. He could have said her father was ill and she had to leave to be his caretaker. That would have been more palatable. As upset as he was about Maddie leaving, he still loved her and felt the need to protect her reputation. Even so, a small part of him sided with Zach and felt she deserved whatever was coming to her.

"If she ever shows her face here again, I'm going to give her a piece of my mind," said Zach.

Adam stared straight ahead.

"Babe, maybe we should let Adam rest for a while," said Claire as she rested her hand on his shoulder.

Zach looked as if he wanted to say more, but he took Claire's hint and nodded.

Claire said, "Adam, we'll be back to check on you tomorrow. Call us if you need anything."

Adam nodded but didn't look at them.

Zach patted him on the back and said, "Try to get some rest, man. We're here for you if you need us. I'm just glad you're home and on the mend. You had us all really worried for a while there."

Adam looked at them both and said, "I appreciate it. I really do."

They both hugged him before they walked out and left him to wallow in his sadness alone.

Chapter 17

ADAM FOUND IT DIFFICULT TO resume his life—life before Maddie. He couldn't muster up the will to do anything. All he wanted to do was lie in his bed and feel sorry for himself. The pain in his chest never let up, and he knew that he would never learn to live with it. Zach assured Adam that the pain would subside over time, but Adam doubted it. How could Zach know? He had never lost someone so dear to him.

Zach and Claire dragged Adam to his physical therapy appointments so he could slowly learn to walk on his badly injured leg again. Adam figured that he didn't really need to learn to walk again since he never planned to get out of bed again. He didn't try very hard, which he knew frustrated everyone.

With Zach's prodding, Adam started going back to rehearsals and performances with the cast on his leg, but he wasn't into it anymore. He couldn't find the joy in it. He didn't want to go out, or hang out, or see people. A part of him was gone, and he was permanently changed.

The nights were the worst. Almost every night Adam awoke from the same nightmare. He was tumbling down a mountain in the snow. It was almost as if he could actually feel the bitter cold and the centrifugal force spinning him over and over as he screamed

Maddie's name. When he awoke, he found himself breathing heavily, as if he had just run a marathon, and sweating profusely. His heart would be pounding in his chest, and then the recollection would begin. The feelings of despair, loneliness, and loss would return, along with the realization that she was really gone. His wounds were reopened every night when he mentally relived his final conversation with Maddie. He would analyze every sentence and dissect each one into pieces that he hoped would make sense someday. It was unbearable.

Maddie had said he would never understand, and she was right. Adam wished he had been bold enough to ask her more about her past when he'd had the chance. He wondered what had happened in her life before he knew her.

What had gone on with this girl?

Adam was fairly certain she must have suffered some traumatic event, or events. But he had tried to remain respectful of her privacy and believed that when she was ready, she would confide in him. Whatever dark secrets she held, she never shared them with him.

Over the next four weeks, the pain and hurt gradually developed into anger and frustration. His only remaining link to Maddie, her cell phone, was disconnected. When she said Adam would never see her again, she apparently meant it. She disappeared without a trace. He never saw her move anything out of her apartment, so he assumed her belongings were still in there. He also never saw her— or anyone else, for that matter—go in or out of her apartment. He wondered where she was living. Did she have another home that he had never known about?

It appeared her mailbox had grown full because he could see pieces of mail protruding from the slot. He thought about taking the mail and saving it for her, but he couldn't bring himself to touch it. If she did have another home, she certainly didn't bother to have the mail forwarded to it. Maybe she thought Adam would somehow be able to track her down if she had left a forwarding address.

Adam tried to go on with his life. He tried to get over the pain. He tried to forgive her. But he couldn't. She had hurt him deeply, and he resented her for that. He was angry that she had left him just when they were about to make a breakthrough in their relationship. She left at the point when he thought they were closer than they had ever been. If she had truly loved him, how could she have turned her back on him? He would have never done that to her. If she had loved him, how could she put him through this pain?

As the level of his anger and resentment escalated, his will to live declined. He wondered if he would ever be able to forget her and pull himself out of his paralyzing depression.

Chapter 18

ABOUT EIGHT WEEKS AFTER ADAM got out of the hospital, his leg was healing nicely and he had graduated to a walking cast so he could walk without crutches. This made it much easier for him to resume rehearsals and performances with the band.

On this particular Friday night, Night Fury's normal gig had been canceled because some VIP had reserved the club for a private party, and they were bringing in their own band. The rest of the band members had decided to hang out at a different club that night. It wasn't often that they got to go out and be the ones in the crowd these days since they were always working nights and weekends. They had asked Adam to join them, but he wasn't feeling up to it. All he felt like doing was staying home alone and being miserable.

Around 9:30 that night, when the band would have normally been well into their first set at the club, Adam sat in his apartment and surfed the web. Suddenly overcome by boredom, he began to look for a distraction. Since he hadn't checked the mail in days, he decided it would be good for him to get out and walk around for a few minutes.

He hobbled out of his apartment and down the hall to retrieve the mail. Walking was a little tricky with the walking cast, but he had gotten used to it fairly quickly and could get around relatively well. The doctor was hopeful that he would only have to wear the annoying thing for another couple of weeks. He couldn't wait to get it off. He was ready to put it all behind him: cast, Maddie, and all.

Since the accident, every time Adam approached his apartment after being out, he couldn't resist the urge to look at Maddie's door. He didn't know what he thought he would see. Maybe subconsciously he hoped for some sign that she had returned, but he knew that was wishful thinking. He told himself that he would quit the habit, but it hadn't worked so far.

As he turned the corner on his trek back from the mailbox, he vowed to not look at her door this time, but he couldn't help it; he looked in spite of himself. What he saw caused him to freeze in place.

Maddie stood at her door with her keys in her hand, ready to unlock it. At first Adam thought he was hallucinating. He blinked. Maybe his subconscious had materialized her image. He shook his head to clear it. She was still there. His eyes narrowed as he caught his breath.

In that instant, her eyes met his and he saw her look of panic, like that of a child who had been caught doing something they weren't supposed to be doing. She froze momentarily, eyes wide.

Adam's automatic reflexes must have kicked because he didn't remember willfully moving, but he felt himself approach her.

"Maddie, is that you?"

He felt like he was in a dream. He rubbed his eyes. She didn't respond. There was no look of happy recognition or gladness to see him. Instead, she looked as if she might bolt at any moment. Not exactly the reunion of his dreams.

Her gaze darted from Adam to the keys in her hand as she fumbled with them and tried frantically to get the key in the keyhole. But her hands shook and made the task more difficult.

Adam picked up his pace, as best as he could in the walking cast. Instinctively, he knew that if she got into her apartment and got the door shut and locked before he got there, he might never see her again. She continued to fumble with her keys as he approached.

Adam said, "Maddie, wait."

She didn't look up. She finally got the key in the lock and started to turn it quickly with trembling fingers. Adrenaline kicked in, and he walked as fast as he could toward her. He wasn't going to let her get in that door and shut him out. He could feel all the pent-up frustration and anger well up inside of him. She didn't even have the courtesy to say hello to him. Instead, she gave him no more acknowledgement than a complete stranger.

Finally, she managed to get the door open and attempted to hurry inside as he lunged toward her. He made it to the door right as she was about to slam it shut. Without thinking, he thrust his walking cast between the door and the doorjamb right as the door slammed on his foot. A dull, jarring pain shot up his leg. It wasn't excruciating, and he didn't even care because he had managed to stop the door from shutting.

From the other side of the door, he heard Maddie yell, "Adam! What are you doing?"

"Let me in! I need to talk to you," he yelled back.

Adam could hear the anger in his voice and he knew that she could too. He was not going to let her get away without an explanation—and without giving her a piece of his mind. He pushed on the door. She tried to hold it shut on the other side.

Her angry tone matched his as she said, "Move your foot so I can close my door!"

Oh, now it was on. Through gritted teeth Adam said, "I can't move my foot with you pushing on the door."

She was pretty strong and she managed to hold him out for a moment. But she couldn't match his strength and he eventually pushed the door open.

She stepped back with a look of dismay on her face and screamed, "What the hell do you think you are doing? Get out!"

His voice was low and shook with anger.

"I'm not leaving until we talk."

"You were supposed to be at your gig. I didn't expect to see you."

"Really, Captain Obvious?" he snarled sarcastically. "Tell me why you came back tonight."

She glared at him, ignored the question, and said, "Adam, you don't know what you're doing. Leave now."

His heart pounded as he stepped toward her. She took a step back. She was every bit as beautiful as he had remembered. Seeing her face-to-face again brought back all the feelings of love and passion he had tried to suppress. At the same time, he felt the hurt and anger burning in his chest. He took a few more steps toward her. She continued to back away. A storm of emotions raged inside his body and mind.

Faintly, he heard her say, "I told you we can't be together."

"I am not leaving until I get an explanation," he said.

He had lowered his voice, but his anger and the seriousness of his intention was unmistakable.

She pleaded, "Don't do this, Adam. I know you don't understand, but you just need to go."

"I'm not going anywhere," he hissed.

He continued to walk toward her as she continued to back up until her back pressed against the wall. She had nowhere to go. He didn't realize that he had pressed his body against hers. He held his hands up and took a small step back to give her space, but his eyes remained trained on hers. She didn't move.

Still pleading, she said, "Please, don't do this. Please."

It looked as if the fight was leaving her. Being this close to her, Adam thought that his heart would explode within his chest. He knew that he had to speak his peace and get some answers from her, or he might never get the chance again.

He tried to appear calm as he swallowed hard, took a chance, and said, "Look me in the eyes and tell me you don't have any feelings for me. If you can do that—if you can honestly say you don't care for me at all—then I'll turn around and walk out the door and leave you alone forever."

He stared directly into her eyes. His heart pounded so loudly that he was sure she could hear it. She held his gaze for what seemed like an eternity, and then she looked away as a tear rolled down her cheek. He sucked in an involuntary breath as he gently wiped the tear from her cheek.

She couldn't do it. She couldn't tell him that she didn't love him.

It gave him hope.

"Don't cry," he said softly.

Adam felt Maddie's determination dissolve as she returned her gaze back to him. She didn't look angry anymore. On impulse, he leaned closer and gently kissed her cheek where the tear had been. She quietly sighed and closed her eyes, but didn't try to resist. He brushed his lips against hers. The slightest moan escaped her lips as they parted. He pressed his lips to hers as he took a step closer to her and kissed her softly at first and then more passionately as she gave in to his kisses. He felt her give in to passion as her body arched closer into his and she started to kiss him back. Her tongue met his as the kiss deepened, causing his stomach to flip as he became aroused. He was so hurt and angry with her, but he still loved her. Kissing her again stirred up the feelings that he had tried to stuff away. He had to have an explanation. He deserved one.

Moments passed as they melded together in the familiar embrace. Lips moving, hands stroking, bodies pressed close together. And then he tasted the saltiness of her tears.

Chapter 19

ADAM PULLED BACK, LOOKED AT Maddie's face, and saw that tears streamed down her cheeks. She looked defeated and angry at the same time.

Her voice cracked as she said, "You don't even know what you're doing, Adam."

His determination was renewed. "I want an explanation. I've had a lot of time to think since you left me in the hospital, and I'm not leaving here until I get one."

He crossed his arms. She shook her head.

Then his words frantically spilled out. "We should've died that night on the mountain. We should've frozen to death up there, but something unexplainable happened, something miraculous. At first, I thought you were just being brave and trying to comfort me when you told me that we weren't going to die. But then you told me to think warm thoughts and everything changed. I thought I was really dying because suddenly it felt like I was on a hot beach in ninety-degree weather. I thought I was in heaven. And then there was the fact that neither one of us got frostbite, not even the slightest bit. That's impossible, Maddie. I've thought about it a lot."

She hung her head as she continued to cry.

"And then there were all the little things. Look, the scar on your arm and the marks from the stitches are completely gone. How do you explain that?"

She absentmindedly rubbed her arm where the wound had once been.

"And what about the fire in the nightclub? You claimed to have never been to that club, but you just happened to find a door that nobody else knew about. Coincidence? I don't think so. And what about on our first date when I cooked dinner for you? I know that I didn't have a corkscrew in the drawer, but you found one. How convenient. And you just happened to show up at rehearsal the first night with Shark Fin beer, and you didn't even know us at all. There is no way you could've just randomly picked that out. You told me the avalanche was your fault. You told me that being with you puts me in danger. How can that be? And most of all, how could you tell me that you love me and then just leave?"

She wiped the tears with the back of her hand, sighed, and said in a low, defeated voice, "I told you that you wouldn't understand. I was trying to save your life, Adam. Being around me is dangerous. Don't you see?"

He stood there with his arms crossed and stared at her. There was no holding back now.

"No, I don't see. Don't I get a choice in this, Maddie? Did it ever occur to you that maybe I would rather have died on that mountain than live without you?"

Her eyes met his and she winced almost imperceptibly.

"What is going on with you? What is it from your past that you are not telling me? Why were you afraid to be intimate? In some ways I feel so close to you, like I've known you forever, and in other ways I feel like I don't know you at all. Who the hell are you, Madeline Smith?"

Her face was unreadable. Maybe she finally believed he was not leaving. Maybe she was just tired of fighting. She stood there silently with a look of ambivalence. She had stopped crying.

Adam suddenly realized the room was cold and shivered involuntarily. Maddie noticed him shudder.

"Are you cold, Adam? How about a fire?" she said stoically.

Before he could respond, she pointed to the fireplace while never taking her eyes off him. Instantly, he heard a whoosh like the sound of a fire being lit with an accelerant, and a fire sprang to life. Adam was stunned. How had she done that?

He tried to recall if she had gas logs with a remote starter. No, it was a wood-burning fireplace. He remembered stacking the logs and lighting the fire on the cold nights they had spent together at her place. The hairs rose on the back of his neck. Wide-eyed, he looked at her expectantly and waited for an explanation.

She stared at him without any emotion as she said, "You might want to sit down and get comfortable. How about a beer?"

She pointed to the couch. As he robotically turned to move toward the couch, he noticed a Shark Fin beer on the coffee table, as if she had just placed it there for him. But she hadn't moved. He was pretty certain the beer had not been there before. Goose bumps rose on his arms, and not from the cold. He sat down slowly, looked at the beer in amazement, and then looked back at her. There was a glass of wine in her hand where there hadn't been one before. He grabbed the beer and noticed that it was ice cold. He took a huge gulp.

Her face was still unreadable when she said, "What do you want from life? Fortune? Fame?"

Her empty hand closed into a fist and opened again as she pretended to toss something to him. To his astonishment, several one-hundred-dollar bills appeared out of nowhere, flew toward him, and floated down all around the room like confetti. Astonished, Adam picked one up and examined it. It looked and smelled like the real deal. His eyes widened even as his blood ran cold.

"Do you want a mansion? How about eternal youth?"

She paused for a moment and waited, he assumed, for a response. He took a few more gulps of beer.

He whispered hoarsely, "How the hell did you do that? What are you? A witch?"

She smiled in spite of herself and said, "Well, I've been called a witch before, but no, Adam, there's no such thing as far as I know."

"Are you a magician or a sorcerer?"

She shook her head.

"Are you a superhero? I give up. What the hell is going on?"

Even though all of the things that he had just witnessed—and the other strange events that had revolved around Maddie in the past—went against what he knew of reality, he also knew he hadn't imagined these things. She had just proved it. She could do things that were not humanly possible. Still, he couldn't quite believe what he had just witnessed.

Adam repeated the question, "What are you?"

Her eyes looked to the ceiling as if deep in thought, and then slowly back to him as she said, "Well, if you have to give it a label, I guess you could call me a manifestor."

"Manifestor?" Adam repeated, not sure if he had heard her correctly.

"I know you've heard of term 'manifest.'"

"You mean like to make things appear out of thin air?" he said.

She nodded. "Right. That's what I do. Whatever I think of, I can manifest. If I think it, I can make it real in this world. It sort of gives new meaning to the word 'afterthought.' Get it? After... thought."

She laughed halfheartedly.

Adam didn't know what to say. He was speechless. He just sat there and stared at her in amazement. He wouldn't have believed it if he hadn't witnessed it for himself. He tried to process everything that had just happened. It all seemed impossible. But at the same time, he knew deep down that this was the only explanation that would piece everything together. Now they were getting somewhere. Maybe she *had* saved his life that night on the mountain. Maybe she *had* saved his life at the nightclub. But there were still things that she hadn't explained to him—so many unanswered questions.

As if reading his mind she said, "It's a very long story, Adam."

He shook his head in disbelief and said, "I've got as long as it takes."

Chapter 20

MADDIE PICKED UP A TISSUE, wiped the remaining tears off her face and eyes, and sat down beside him. She appeared calmer as she slumped back into the cushions of the couch with her glass of wine. She sighed heavily and said, "Adam, I want you to understand that if I tell you the truth, I'm exposing you to the very thing I was trying to protect you from by leaving. There will be no turning back."

Again, he felt chills run down his spine as he said, "I understand. I need to know, regardless of the outcome."

She looked down at her hands as she quietly said, "I thought that I was making the right choice, or I would never have left and hurt you. I'm sorry. I truly am. I thought it was for your own good. I knew that you wouldn't be able to make the right decision because you didn't have all the facts."

"Then give me the facts," he said. "I assure you that—even after everything I just witnessed—there is nothing you can say that will change the way I feel about you."

He took her hand in his, intertwining his fingers with hers.

Her eyes welled with tears again as she said, "I do love you, Adam. I couldn't bear the thought of something happening to you because of me."

"I love you, too," he whispered.

He kissed her gently for reassurance and put his arm around her shoulders. Even though he was still a little angry with her, he couldn't stand to see her in pain.

Maddie looked down at her hands again for such a long time that Adam thought she might have clammed up again, when she finally said, "Where do I even begin?"

Thinking the question was rhetorical, he waited.

After another awkward silence, he said, "Tell me about the fire and the avalanche. You claimed responsibility for those events. You said that being with you had exposed me to danger. How could those things be your fault? Why would you cause something like that to happen?"

She furrowed her brow and shook her head vehemently. "Not me. I never said that *I* caused those things to happen. I believe it was someone else."

He still had no clue what she was talking about, but he was relieved to see that she was finally willing to open up to him.

"Who would do such a thing?" he said slowly.

"My ex-husband," she said so quietly that it was almost a whisper.

Adam felt as if he had been dealt a physical blow to the gut, but he tried not to let it show. It was yet another shocker. He had no idea she had been married before. She had never mentioned it, and he had never seen any evidence of another man in her life. No old wedding pictures. No mention of him in conversation. No nothing. It made him bristle at the thought of her being married to another man, but at least she had said *ex-husband*.

She was studying his face as she slowly said, "I'm not the only one who has the ability to manifest. There are many people out there, like my ex-husband, who are manifestors."

"How many others?"

"No one knows for sure. Hundreds. Maybe thousands."

"Are these people born with special powers or something?"

"No. It doesn't take special powers. In fact, anyone can master it, given enough training."

"When you say 'master *it*,' what exactly do you mean?"

"Ancient practitioners called it The Power Within. In pop culture, it's been referred to as the Law of Attraction, The Power of Positive Thinking, New Thought, The Power, auto-suggestion, positive mental attitude, quantum mysticism, or magical thinking. The people who taught me and I call it Refined Transcendent Power, or RTP for short. Some people believe it's a form of faith and there are references to the use of RTP in many religious texts. In a religious context, it has been described as the cosmic force of infinite intelligence, the universe, God, God within, Allah, Buddha, and others. The basic concept is that whatever you focus your thoughts on, you can attract into your life. Think it, believe it, and manifest it. Regardless of your personal, spiritual, or religious beliefs, the point is, it doesn't matter how you label it, we *all* have the ability to do it."

Adam couldn't fathom what he was hearing. He said, "If anyone can do this, then how come I've never seen or heard of anything like this before? I mean, I have heard of people having faith and thinking positively. But I have never seen anyone materialize things right out of thin air like you do."

"Believe it or not, most people use RTP in their daily lives, to a lesser degree, without even knowing that's what they are doing. And many high profile people have mastered using RTP over the centuries, such as Rameses the Great, Moses, Beethoven, Einstein, Thomas Edison, and Andrew Carnegie, to name a few. I've heard that some modern-day celebrities and political figures have used it to achieve their successes. I don't have first-hand knowledge of that but I do know that some people, like my ex-husband, Paul, use it for evil and illegal purposes and personal gain. They disregard the law and believe that knowledge of RTP should be kept a secret.

They'll do *anything* to keep the awareness of it from the general public."

Adam rubbed his face with both hands. "What do you mean 'they will do anything to keep it a secret?' "

"Many years ago, Paul formed a group called the 'Keepers of Transcendent Power,' known to us outsiders as 'KTP.' The KTP use Refined Transcendent Power for evil, such as revenge killing, illegal gambling, racketeering, and oppression. They have tried, and succeeded in many cases, in forcing peaceful practitioners of RTP to join their ranks. Anyone who refuses to join is put to death."

Adam's eyes widened in horror. This was the most bizarre thing he had ever heard.

"Those of us who are peaceful, and who do not want to join the KTP, have entered into a sort of self-imposed witness protection program. We have gone underground and changed our identities so that we cannot be located."

Adam felt a sinking feeling in his stomach. It was becoming painfully obvious that he knew way less about this woman than he thought. In fact, he knew absolutely nothing about her true identity.

Did he even want to hear more? Maybe she was right—there was no turning back now. He took another gulp of beer, swallowed hard and said, "So your name's not even Madeline Smith?"

She looked at him sheepishly—like a kid who had been caught in a lie—and shook her head as she said, "My first name really is Madeline, but my true last name is Locke."

"Why didn't you change your entire name?" he said.

"Well, my name changes depending on where I am living at the time. Like now that I'm living in New York City, it is pretty safe to keep my original first name. Do you know how many Madeline Smiths there are here? Probably hundreds. It would take a long time for someone to figure out which one was me. Plus, I'm guessing they probably wouldn't expect me to use my real first name, so that would throw them off. I've moved around so many times over the years that I've learned how to blend in well. I never stay in one place for very long. Because if I stay put for too long, eventually they will catch up with me."

Adam let her words sink in for a few moments before saying, "Are you saying Paul knows where you are now?"

"I don't think he knows where I am now because if he did, I think he would've already shown himself. I haven't seen any physical signs of him or his followers. But my sources tell me that in recent times his ability has grown stronger. He has found a way to use RTP...remotely, if you will, to control the forces of nature. They are speculating that even though he doesn't know my location, he can use negative thoughts about me to cause bad things to happen to me, such as the fire and the avalanche."

"So, you think Paul was the one who caused those things to happen?" Adam said incredulously.

"I'm not sure," she said. "It could be possible. But if he has learned to channel RTP in that way, then that is not good at all. He could use internet searches and news reports about the events to narrow down his targets' locations. We should all be very afraid."

"But what does he want?"

She sighed and said, "That's the long part of the story. We'll get there."

Chapter 21

ADAM AND MADDIE SAT QUIETLY for a few moments. His mind was racing, trying to process all of the incredible information. He had so many questions. She had indicated that it would take a long time to tell the entire story. But out of all the questions he had, one troublesome thought kept occurring to him.

He broke the silence and said, "Earlier, when you were demonstrating your powers to me, you mentioned something about eternal youth. What exactly did you mean by that?"

She studied his face as she spoke, as if gauging his reaction. "People only age because they *think* they are supposed to. We have been conditioned all of our lives that it is an indisputable fact that we all must grow old and eventually die. Some people summon it upon themselves by thinking and believing they must age. I don't believe in aging, so I don't."

Still not comprehending, Adam said, "What do you mean by that? You... don't age? Exactly how old *are* you?"

She smiled slyly and said, "If you're asking me how old I feel, or how old I want to be, then I'm twenty-eight. That's a good age, isn't it?"

Adam was puzzled. Had she said twenty-eight because that was his age too? He said, "Let me rephrase the question. How many years have you been alive?"

She stared past him, her eyes fixed on some point across the room as if recalling a distant time and place and said, "I was born in 1833 in Manchester, England."

Adam couldn't help it. He felt his eyes widen and his mouth drop open, but no words came. This was too much. How was he supposed to believe the woman he loved was over 150 years old?

Impossible.

She didn't look a day older than him. But everything else he had learned about her defied all logic as well. This was just par for the course. He managed to close his mouth and regain his composure—somewhat.

Observing his reaction, Maddie stood and went to the bookshelf. She removed what appeared to be a very old photo album and returned to her place beside him. Without saying a word, she opened the album to the first page.

The pictures reminded him of his grandmother's old photos from when she was a little girl, and also the pictures of his great grandparents that were proudly displayed in his parents' house. They were black and white with the photo paper slightly yellowing with age. They looked like photos of the Old West that Adam had seen in museums and on TV. A group of people surrounded what looked like an old horse-drawn, covered wagon. The men wore wide-brimmed hats, boots, handlebar mustaches, and holsters with pistols proudly displayed. There was also a woman and a young girl. They wore long dresses with lacy cuffs on the sleeves, hair pulled back, wide-brimmed hats, and they too sported guns. There were even a few people dressed in what appeared to be Native American attire. Everyone wore serious expressions. No smiles.

Adam's eyes kept going back to the woman and young girl. The woman looked a lot like Maddie, but he could tell that it wasn't her.

He figured it had to be a relative of hers. He looked closer at the girl, at her eyes, the lips, and the nose.

Was it? No, it couldn't be.

Maddie pointed at the girl in the picture and said, "When I was a young girl, my parents—like many others during that time—immigrated to the United States with hopes of finding land, settling, and striking it rich during the great California Gold Rush. They believed in the American Dream, freedom, and the promise of prosperity.

"When I was fifteen years old, we were traveling the Santa Fe Trail through New Mexico. The Mexican-American war had just ended in 1848, and New Mexico had officially been declared a part of the United States. There was still a lot of upheaval and unrest, and traveling in the area was dangerous.

"One night we stopped near Fort Union to find shelter for the night. While we slept, a nearby tribe of Apache Indians raided the fort. The inn we were staying in caught on fire. I awoke coughing and barely able to breathe. Smoke was everywhere. I couldn't see my hand in front of my face. I was screaming for my parents, but I never heard a response over the loud crackling of the flames and the roaring fire. I crawled blindly across the floor, next to the wall, until I managed to find my way out. My parents never made it out."

Maddie looked up at Adam. Tears were streaming down her face again. He pulled her closer to him and wiped her tears with his hand.

"It was never determined whether or not the fire was arson or accidental. No suspects were ever identified. Justice was never served.

"Orphaned and alone at age fifteen, I had nowhere to go. A Spanish gentleman who had emigrated from South America and amassed a great fortune as a prominent cattle rancher took pity on me. Pablo de Alvarado, known as Paul by those closest to him, was well-known and well-respected in the town. He took me in as a hired hand at his ranch. I was the cook in the main house.

"Paul was very kind. He employed a lot of people who were down and out on their luck. His staff included other immigrants, people who were freed after the war and needed work, and members of some of the friendly, local Pueblo Indian tribes. He believed in treating everyone with equality, which helped him to develop many loyal friendships and allies. But because tensions were still high following the war, he also had enemies.

"Over the course of the year that followed, Paul and I fell in love. Almost exactly a year to the day that he took me in, we were married. I was sixteen and Paul was twenty-nine. Back in those days, official marriage licenses were not required. We had a small, elegant ceremony in the church with a few of our closest friends. We were very happy together for a while."

Adam's eyebrows furrowed and his eyes narrowed. "You got married at sixteen?"

"You have to realize that people married at younger ages back then. They also didn't live as long as people do now."

Adam was not enjoying this part of the story at all, but his need to know kept his rapt attention.

Chapter 22

AS IF IN A TRANCE, Maddie stared blankly at the wall and continued her story. "I truly loved Paul. He was kindhearted and very handsome. In fact, I guess I have a type, because he looks a lot like you, except his eyes are so dark brown they are almost black. There was such warmth and depth in his eyes that I often found myself lost in his gaze—captivated. My love for Paul helped me to recover from my parents' deaths. I had a very good life with him."

Adam didn't like being compared to Paul, but he didn't want to interrupt, so he didn't say anything.

"Shortly after we were married, some of the Mexican immigrants who worked on Paul's ranch, and who had become some of our best friends, began teaching Paul and me about RTP. We'll call them Mel and Sancha, and their family members were masters of RTP. They believed in freely sharing the knowledge with family and friends.

"Over the next couple of years, we practiced what had been taught to us. Our teachers had warned us that it could take many years, even decades, to truly master RTP. And some people could never open their minds enough to learn it. But Paul and I both seemed to have a gift for it, and we learned very quickly. Eventually, we became masters of RTP. We made a vow with those who taught us, and with each other, that we would only use RTP for good, and never for evil or illegal activities."

She looked down at her hands and paused for a moment. Adam felt as if he was listening to a fairy tale, or a story made up by a crazy person, but he didn't dare to ask her any questions. He was afraid that if he interrupted her train of thought, she would have second thoughts and he might never get to hear the entire story. He waited patiently.

She sighed heavily and said, "I haven't spoken aloud what I'm about to tell you in a very long time, Adam. This part is very hard for me."

He remained silent and held her hand for reassurance.

"You have to understand that back in those times, seventeen was considered childbearing age. When I was seventeen, Paul and I were blessed with our first child, a beautiful son. A year later, we were blessed with our second son."

Adam swallowed hard. "Can I have another beer, please?"

Maddie pointed to the table and a cold Shark Fin materialized. Adam grabbed it and took several swigs.

So she expected him to believe she was married and had two sons over 150 years ago? The story was getting more unbelievable by the minute. He wanted to believe her—*had* to believe her. What other logical explanation was there? He had nothing. He rubbed his eyes and raked the fingers of both hands through his hair. He wasn't sure how much more of this he could take.

Her tears were flowing again and her voice was raw with emotion as she continued, "For the next ten years, we worked the ranch and prospered as we raised our sons and taught them to use RTP. Life was great, and I had never been happier.

"It was around that same time when we also learned of the ability to use RTP to prevent aging. It truly was the fountain of youth. We didn't have to age any more if we didn't want to. And who would want to?"

She laughed halfheartedly through her tears.

"Paul and I made a pact to stay young together forever, and to teach our sons to do the same. We would be young and happy forever.

"But as I said, Paul had made some bitter enemies during the war, and while fighting for territory and land over the years. He had been involved in battles where people were killed. Back in those days, there was often lawlessness and vigilante justice, and even Paul—who was good to the core—had been forced to kill during the war, and while defending his property and his family. Because of this, there were people who sought revenge on him.

"When the boys were eleven and twelve years old, we decided to allow them to go with Paul and some of the ranch hands on a cattle drive to Texas. Children were given more responsibilities at an earlier age back then, and we felt like they were old enough to help out with the family business. Both boys were excellent riders and ropers, and they were anxious to travel and see other parts of the country.

"They had only been gone for a few days when they were ambushed by a gang of ranch hands from a rival cattle company. A fight ensued."

Her words trailed off. Adam could hear her breathing rapidly, as if she might hyperventilate. Her face was contorted in a mask of anguish as her lips began to tremble. She barely managed to choke out the next words, "Our sons were killed."

An uncontrollable sob rose out of her throat as Maddie collapsed into him, pressed her face into his chest, and unloaded all of her grief and pain.

He held her tightly, rocking her and stroking her hair, allowing her all the time she needed to release the pent-up grief. He thought of all of the tragedies Maddie had faced in her lifetime. First the death of her parents, and then her sons. How could one person be expected to handle so much loss? It was remarkable she hadn't gone completely insane.

Or maybe she had.

If what she was saying was true, it was clear that she grieved for her sons as much now as she had back then. Adam felt as if he was on the verge of tears himself, and he fought to maintain his composure. This story was too much for him to comprehend. He was glad she couldn't see his face. It probably would have only upset her more.

After a while her sobs quieted and her breathing returned to a more normal rate. She pulled away from him and wiped her tears away with the backs of her hands.

Adam handed her a tissue and said softly, "You don't have to tell me any more."

She shook her head and said, "I have to do this. I have to finish what I started."

She paused as if weighing her words carefully, and then continued, "People who have never had children cannot understand what it feels like to lose a child. We were devastated.

"Paul fought desperately to save our boys, and he barely made it out alive. He was badly injured. He blamed himself for their deaths because he had failed to save them. Later, he confided in me that he wished he had died that day, rather than trying to live with the loss.

"I completely fell apart. It was the worst thing that I had ever gone through—and have gone through since. It felt as if my whole life had been taken from me, as if my soul had been ripped from my body. I became a lifeless shell. I sank into a deep depression, curled up on my bed for a month, unable to cope, unable to eat, and unable to talk to anyone. I refused any help that was offered.

"I wasn't capable of comforting Paul or helping him heal from his physical and emotional injuries. At first he mourned in the same way I did, removing himself from interaction with the world. But then the anger began to fester within him like an infected wound.

"Of course, we both hated the people who had done this to our sons. It was a normal reaction to want to kill them to get revenge. I thought about that often, even going as far as developing a plan of how I would carry it out without getting caught. But I knew deep down that I never would have been able to go through with it.

"But it was different for Paul. He had killed before, and as the rage and hatred continued to devour him on the inside, the very essence of him changed. I could see it in his eyes. The kindhearted Paul that I knew and loved was gone. All I could see in his eyes from then on was rage, hatred, and desperation.

"Paul began to use RTP to cause bad things to happen to the people who he believed were responsible for the deaths of our sons. He convinced some of his ranch hands to help him dispense vigilante justice by finding and killing everyone who had participated in the raid. But he didn't stop there. He declared that he would not stop killing until he took out the entire families of the guilty parties— even innocent men, women, and children. And he used RTP to help him carry out his evil justice.

"He began drinking heavily every day. He drank himself to sleep every night, crying, cursing, and swearing to never stop his quest for revenge on those who had murdered our sons. It was terrible to see him that way.

"For the first few months, he left me alone to mourn. I was in my own little world, and he in his. We should have been there for each other and helped each other get through it, but it seemed like neither of us was capable of it. I could barely find the will to live another day, much less help someone else overcome their own grief.

"It was during that time that our best friends, Sancha and Mel, became determined to help Paul and me overcome our depression and get on with our lives. They came to me daily and reminded me of RTP. They encouraged me to eat, bathe, and go through the motions of daily life. They tried to convince me that even though my sons were gone, life was still worth living. They used RTP to send positive and encouraging thoughts to me. And slowly, over time, I began to emerge from my depression enough to function normally again. I tried to move on with my life in a positive way and recover and be an active, productive member of society again.

"They tried to help Paul as well, but he pushed them away. He also pushed me away. He sank further and further into the depths of despair and alcoholism. He became mean and took out his anger on his field hands and friends. And then he turned his anger on me.

"A vast chasm had come between us. I didn't blame him for the deaths of our sons, but I couldn't look at him without seeing them. They looked so much like him. It got to the point where I couldn't stand to look at him. And I think the same happened when Paul looked at me. I was a daily reminder of his sons, and of his failure to save them. He hated himself for it, and he grew to hate me too. We were no longer husband and wife in more than name. We were merely two strangers existing in the same household.

"The abuse was verbal at first. He berated me daily and told me I wasn't worthy of being anyone's wife. Over time, the abuse became physical. It started with a slap here and there, and eventually got worse to the point where he even threatened to kill me on a few occasions. There were times when he would catch me by surprise and hit me hard enough to cause large bruises and swelling. But I never told anyone. Instead, I used RTP to heal my wounds and suffered in silence."

Adam could feel himself bristling inside at the thought of anyone hurting Maddie.

"I tried to stick it out and stay with him for almost a year, but he only got meaner and the attacks became more brutal. When I used RTP to shield myself, it would only make him angrier. I didn't know what to do. The situation seemed hopeless, but then I realized that I could use RTP to accomplish anything I wanted. I finally admitted to myself that I needed outside help.

"Eventually, I confided in Sancha and Mel. They told me they had suspected I was being abused, but I had hidden it well. Sancha and Mel observed the escalation of the violence, and realized that there was no way Paul was coming out of his downward spiral anytime soon. They were fearful that he would take his own life, or mine, or both. They realized that they needed to get me away from him before he killed me because they truly believed that he would eventually. I began to believe it too.

"Sancha and Mel secretly made arrangements for me to move out of state to live with some friends of theirs in San Diego, California—Stan and Mary Baker. They felt it was imperative that I made the move without Paul knowing. They were convinced that if he suspected me of trying to leave, he would kill me before I could get away. And I was fearful that he would kill Sancha and Mel if he ever found out they helped me escape. They had been his friends at one time, and he would see it as betrayal. I didn't know it then, but it was the beginning of a lifetime of hiding my identity."

Chapter 23

MADDIE CONTINUED HER SORDID TALE. "It was going to be extremely difficult for me to permanently leave my life in New Mexico and all of my friends. It was all I had known since my parents died. But I also understood that if I wanted to protect Sancha and Mel, and myself, from Paul's wrath, I had to go through with it.

"Sancha and Mel had never spoken to Paul about their friends in San Diego. They were certain he would never be able to trace me back to them—if he cared to try. We weren't sure if he would even bother to find me if I just disappeared. I doubted he would miss me at all.

"One night when Paul was passed out from his drunken rage, Sancha and Mel put the escape plan in motion. They didn't take the chance of traveling with me and being spotted. Instead, they arranged for me to travel with a wagon train that was passing through on the way to California.

"I didn't know a soul in the group, so I stayed quiet and kept to myself, trying to draw as little attention to myself as possible. They were kind and left me alone for the most part. The trip was long and treacherous, and mentally and physically exhausting. It took us about a month to reach our destination. By then I had grown accustomed to being alone.

"The Bakers were very kind and wonderful people. They took me in and made me feel welcome in their home. They respected my privacy, never pried, or asked me to divulge any information unless I offered it. We quickly grew comfortable with one another.

"I assumed a new name and a completely new identity. I never spoke of RTP, or Paul, or my children, or anybody else I knew, for that matter. It was as if my old life had never existed. At first it was very lonely and difficult. I absorbed myself in reading, and soon I began writing poems and works of fiction. I discovered that I loved writing. It was my muse, my escape from reality and the past.

"Eventually, the Bakers encouraged me to get a job at a local library, where I could further pursue my interests. When I wasn't working, I devoured all of the information I could on the subjects of writing and English literature.

"I started submitting articles to local newspapers under a male pen name, and eventually they started printing my work. When I wasn't working at the library, I spent time volunteering at the newspaper printing press so I could learn all aspects of the paper production.

"Over time I began to develop friendships with people at the library and printing press, and with other writers in the area. Each step forward in my new life put my old life a little further behind me."

Chapter 24

MADDIE PAUSED FROM TELLING HER story, her focus seemingly coming back to the present as she looked at Adam and said, "Have you heard enough, or would you like me to continue?"

Adam looked down at his hands and noticed they were tightly clenched into fists. He said, "I was afraid there was more. I want to hear more, but I think I need another beer first."

Maddie nodded, and yet another Shark Fin appeared out of nowhere.

Adam shook his head, still unable to believe what his eyes were seeing.

She shrugged and said, "No need to keep up the facade now that you know."

Wide-eyed, he said slowly, "Thank you? It may take me a while to get used to this."

Maddie snickered and smiled. This made Adam smile too. The mood was lightening up. It was so good to see her smile.

He picked up the beer, chugged about half of it and said, "Better. Now, please continue."

Maddie reclined back on the couch and rubbed her eyes. She sighed heavily and continued her story.

"While I was in California, James Mackay, the owner of the newspaper printing press, took an interest in me. He was a brilliant writer and took me under his wing. We started spending a lot of time together. At first, I thought he was only interested in my talent as a writer because he was almost twenty years older than me. But he soon admitted that he was attracted to me and wanted more than just a friendship.

"I cared for James. I even grew to love him, but not in the same way that I had loved Paul. It wasn't a love at first sight, or all-consuming, overwhelming passion. He was my mentor, my confidant, my best friend. I grew to love him gradually.

"The Bakers and some of my new girlfriends encouraged the relationship, and we became romantically involved. James was a gentleman, and we had a long courtship. He proposed to me two years later, and I agreed to marry him.

"Since Paul and I never obtained an official marriage license, I didn't have to go through the pain of filing for a divorce."

Maddie turned a few pages in the photo album and pointed to a picture of herself in a beautiful wedding dress with a distinguished-looking man in a tux that Adam assumed was James. She looked radiant and happy. He felt a little hint of jealousy, even though he knew it was silly. She was obviously not with him now. Or was she?

She continued. "James was fifty-two when we were married. He wasn't interested in having children, which was fine with me. I couldn't bear the thought of having more and possibly losing them. We made a good life together, and I was finally happy again.

"Eventually, I confided my story to James and tried to teach him about RTP. I tried to teach him how to use it to prevent aging. He believed my story, and he believed in RTP because I freely used it in the privacy of our home. He believed I had a special ability, but he never believed he could do it. And because he didn't *think* he could do it, he never mastered it.

"I couldn't understand how he could believe that I could use

RTP, but that he couldn't. Some people have a hard time believing in things they cannot physically touch or explain with science or logic.

"He did believe in the power of positive thinking in general, and he reaped the rewards in his career and in life in general. But he couldn't manifest things the way I do. And he never believed he could stop the aging process with his thoughts. So James grew older and I remained ageless.

"At first he liked the idea of having such a young-looking wife. He enjoyed watching the envious stares of other men when we appeared in public together. But as he aged even more, and the difference in our ages grew more apparent, he became uncomfortable with it.

"Some of our friends had also started to notice that I wasn't aging. I got countless questions from women asking me what my secret was. They wanted to know how I stayed so young-looking. I started to grow uncomfortable with the questioning. I knew that I could never reveal my secret to them. I didn't know if Paul had ever looked for me, but I didn't want the word to get out, just in case.

"So when James retired, we traveled constantly. When we traveled to places where no one knew us, he introduced me as his niece or his daughter. He was worried that he would look like a dirty old man if he told people I was his wife. I told him it didn't matter what people thought, but it didn't change his mind.

"I watched him age before my eyes, and nothing I could say or do would convince him otherwise. The longer I lived, more and more of the people I knew aged and passed away. It was difficult watching the people I loved and cared about disappear from my life.

"And at age seventy-five, James suffered a massive heart attack and was pronounced dead by the time the doctor arrived."

Adam gazed at Maddie, wanting to believe. She stared at the

wedding picture with sadness in her eyes, but no more tears came. He thought she must have been all cried out.

Was her story possible? Had she already gone through an entire cycle of life?

That would explain the maturity beyond her years and her old-fashioned ways. It would explain why she had wanted to take things slowly in their relationship. Now it was all making sense to him in a bizarre and unbelievable way. Like James, Adam wanted more than anything to believe her story because the converse story would mean she was completely out of her mind.

He stroked her cheek and said quietly, "What did you do after James passed on?"

"Once James was gone, and many of my acquaintances and friends that I had known in California had grown old or passed away too, I saw no reason to stay. I moved often from city to city. I never stayed long enough to put down roots."

Adam said, "What about Paul? Did he ever find you?"

"Not at that point," she said. "As far as I know Paul never came looking for me while I was in San Diego. He was probably glad to let me go. I'm sure it took some of the pain out of his life. I never heard from him.

"I did manage to stay in contact with some of my dear friends from New Mexico, like Sancha and Mel. They kept me informed about the activities of Paul and the KTP. Over the years, the membership grew, and the organization became more formalized and secretive.

"Paul knew the knowledge of RTP gave him even greater power. He used it for political gains, which afforded him a certain degree of protection in his illegal activities. He used his political contacts to get whatever he wanted, no matter what the cost.

"He didn't want just anybody knowing about RTP. He felt it was more valuable to him if he controlled who learned and could use it.

He decreed that all existing practitioners of Refined Transcendent Power must join the KTP or be put to death.

"It was terrible. Some of the people I knew from New Mexico, who were practitioners of RTP, were sought out by the members of the KTP and given the choice of membership or death. Those of questionable character gladly joined the order. Those who refused were killed. Still others fled and went into hiding before Paul and his henchmen could find them.

"Those who went underground became known as the Keepers of the Peace. They jokingly called themselves KOTP, in mockery of Paul's organization, although it truly was no laughing matter. They managed to form a remarkably sophisticated network of communication to keep in touch with each other and gather intelligence. They frequently sent out reconnaissance teams to watch the KTP's every move. They even formed an underground food and supply system to support all of the members. Even Sancha and Mel, the very people who had taught Paul and me about RTP, had to go underground and change their identities."

Chapter 25

MADDIE STARED STRAIGHT AHEAD AGAIN, remembering. She continued, "A few years after I had learned about the KTP, I happened to be living in San Francisco, California. I had only been there a few months when I was out walking around in the Bay Area and doing some sightseeing on a beautiful summer day. I liked the anonymity that was afforded to me by living in big cities. Public restaurants were a fairly new concept back then, so I decided to check one out.

"I chose a quaint seafood restaurant that had been highly recommended to me by a local. I was deciding what to order when I heard a hauntingly familiar voice coming from behind me.

" 'Madeline, is that you?'

"Instantly, chills raced down my spine. My eyes widened and I stiffened, staring straight ahead for a moment afraid to move.

"I felt a hand rest gently on my shoulder, and I fought the urge to shudder. I slowly turned around in my seat to face the person who was addressing me. Even though I already knew it, I was horrified to see it was Paul. I would have known that voice anywhere, even after all of those years. I tried to appear calm and collected, even though I was panicking inside.

"It was so strange to see Paul after so many years. He didn't look like the drunken, depressed shell of a man that I had left behind. His eyes were clear, not bloodshot and red like that of an alcoholic. He had cleaned up. He was wearing a nicely tailored suit, and he looked very handsome. He hadn't aged a bit, and for an instant, I saw the Paul that I had fallen in love with. I stood to face him, still speechless.

"His smile was warm as he hugged me in a big bear hug—the way you would hug a long-lost friend. I didn't move. When he sensed my rigidness, the look on his face changed ever so slightly as he released me. It was as if a switch had been flipped, allowing me a glimpse of his true intention. His smile remained, but his eyes gave him away. There was no warmth there, only cold darkness. I could sense that his hatred for me was still there. He was putting on an act. Paul discreetly looked me over as he said in mock pleasantry, 'So, what are you doing in the area, Madeline?'

"I didn't know how to answer. I didn't know if I should act nonchalant or make a scene and run out screaming for help. Mentally, I reasoned that he was not an immediate threat. I mean, we were in a public restaurant, after all. So I focused on keeping my voice steady and said, 'I'm just visiting the area and doing some sightseeing. What are you doing here, Paul?'

"He grinned slightly, humoring me, but I could tell he didn't believe me. He said, 'What a coincidence. I'm in town for the same reason—just sightseeing.'

"I glanced around to see if any of his cronies were with him. It appeared that he was alone. But I couldn't be sure. I had heard that the KTP traveled in numbers and that Paul never went anywhere without his bodyguards. Paul's henchmen operated similarly to the Secret Service. They could be in plain clothes and strategically placed throughout the restaurant to avoid detection.

"He brought me back to focus when he said, 'Do you mind if I join you?' as he nodded toward the table.

"My first instinct was to decline and get the heck out of there, but at the same time, I was curious to see where he was going with his little charade. So I nodded and held my hand out to the empty chair across the table from me.

"It was the strangest meal of my life. We chatted with small talk and neutral subjects. Neither of us brought up any of the events from the past. We both acted like we were just business acquaintances meeting for the first time. But seeing him in person reminded me of our sons. All of the pain and sadness that I had suppressed for so long was bubbling back up to the surface. And I was sure that seeing me again was having the same effect on him. Still, we went on with our act throughout the entire meal.

"Toward the end of the meal he leaned forward, reached across the table, took both of my hands in his, and gently pulled me toward him as his eyes met mine. I had gradually lowered my guard, but his gesture caught me by surprise, causing my unease to return.

"He had my full attention when he said, 'Madeline I've missed you so much. I never stopped thinking about you. For so long I've wondered about you and what had become of you. I have to confess that I've been trying to use Refined Transcendent Power to summon you to me, and here you are right before me. Apparently it worked.'

"Chills ran down my spine. If he could use RTP to summon me, what else was he capable of?'

"I said, 'You were always strong in your use of RTP.'

"He nodded slowly and said, 'Madeline, do you think there's a chance that we could forgive each other? Maybe we could get back to the way we were when we loved each other.'

"My fear was suddenly forgotten. I was incredulous and angry. I looked him directly in the eyes and said, 'No, Paul. I don't think that there's a chance in hell.'

"His smile faded as he put his hand to his chest and feigned being hurt. Or maybe he really was hurt at some level, but I didn't believe it. And I didn't care. I saw the dark anger flash in his eyes when he said in a cold voice, 'Pity. Well then, let's get down to business. I understand that you're not a member of the Keepers of Transcendent Power.'

"That was a known fact. There was no need for me to deny it. So now we were getting to his true intention.

"I said, 'And I never will be. You broke the oath that you took when you learned about RTP. You were taught to never use RTP for evil.'

"He laughed sarcastically and said, 'Whoever made that rule never had to deal with evil in their life. They were living in a fantasy world to think that there is no evil and that RTP would never be used for evil.'

" 'But you took the vow and you are using RTP in a way that was not meant to be, Paul.'

"He shrugged. 'I've never seen it make much of a difference one way or the other. Whether it is used for good or evil, RTP works the same way. But now that I think of it, I think it may be even more powerful when it's used for evil.'

"He grinned and stared at me in a way that made my fear return. I said, 'Well, I was taught that a positive, good thought is several hundred times stronger than a bad thought. And I still believe it.'

"He snorted. 'You would,' he said dismissively.

"I ignored his comment.

"He said, 'Well, even though you have turned me down flatly after I've done nothing but be nice to you, I still want to give you the chance to join the KTP of your own free will.'

"He stared at me, waiting for an answer. I didn't respond. I was trying to stall to give myself time to think of my next move.

"After several moments of silence he said, 'I'm growing impatient, Madeline. You know your options. You join the KTP, we reconcile, I let you live.'

"I grew even angrier. The gall of him! Through clenched teeth, and in the firmest voice I could muster up, I said, 'I would rather die than join your order.'

"He put both hands over his heart and pretended to be taken aback. He was just playing with me like a cat plays with a mouse. What an asshole. He knew all along what my answer would be. And like the proverbial cat, he was getting ready to pounce.

"He knew if he had shown any aggression to me earlier, I would've bolted out of that restaurant. So instead, he lured me in by treating me kindly and getting me to let down my guard. He had planned this all along so that he could make the proposition.

"I knew that if I refused to join him, he would kill me that very night. I scanned the room for any of the familiar faces that I had seen in the 'wanted' posters the people underground had circulated so we would know what the bad guys looked like if our paths ever crossed. I didn't see any familiar faces, but that didn't mean that they weren't there. I just couldn't see them.

"I suddenly grabbed my stomach, doubled over, and said, 'I feel like I'm going to be sick. Will you excuse me for a moment?'

"He studied me, trying to determine whether I was telling the truth.

"I wrapped my arms around my stomach even tighter and began rocking back and forth. 'I think I am going to be sick right on this table.'

"As I stood, he stood too and grabbed my arm tightly as he said, 'Let me help you to the ladies' room.'

"I felt like he was on to me. He knew that I was faking it, and he was going to make sure I didn't escape the ladies' room when he wasn't looking. He stood post outside of the door as I ran in.

"Once inside, I began making the most obnoxious vomiting sounds. I wanted to make sure he could hear me through the door. While I did this, I scanned the room for an escape route. There were no doors or windows leading to the outside. The only way out was the same door I had come in—where Paul was standing guard.

"But he underestimated my power of manifestation. In between making vomiting sounds, I summoned up all of RTP I could and visualized a window on the wall that would lead to the outside. I continued making vomiting noises and coughing loudly as I opened the window and climbed out of it. I emerged in an alley, and I wasn't sure what street I was on. I ran to the main road and merged in with a group of people who were out walking. I focused on blending in.

"Paul must have grown suspicious when the vomiting noises stopped and sent someone inside the ladies' room to check on me. I figured that I only had a few moments before he realized I was gone. I kept glancing behind me as I scurried down the sidewalk, weaving in and out of the crowd, trying to conceal myself. When I was a couple of blocks away I looked back and saw Paul and a few other men running out of the restaurant. I could see them frantically scanning the area, searching for me.

"At that moment I saw a covered wagon coming up the road. When no one was looking, I jumped out of the crowd and sneaked under the wagon cover. I peeked from under the cover and watched Paul and the others running in my direction. I wasn't sure if they had seen me or not. I started thinking positive thoughts.

" 'I am safe. They are not going to find me. I am safe now.'

"I didn't know the full extent of Paul's power at that point. I didn't know to what lengths he would go to stop me. But I felt certain that if he really wanted to, he could have used RTP to capture me. I tried to put those thoughts out of my mind. I just ducked my head and focused on escaping safely. I didn't look out again.

"I didn't return to my apartment that night. Instead, I hunkered down in the wagon until it stopped near a hotel that I had never been to before. I manifested a man's outfit, hat, fake mustache, and a suitcase. I quietly changed and the placed my lady's clothes in the suitcase. When I was certain no one would see me, I quietly sneaked out of the wagon and checked in using one of my false identities. I stayed holed up in the hotel room for two days and did not leave. I ordered room service and had them leave it outside of my door so that nobody would see me. I focused all of my thoughts on being safe and remaining hidden. Nothing happened. There was no sign of Paul, or anyone from the KTP.

"Every two days or so, I would move to a different hotel under a different identity. I repeated this pattern until I felt there was no chance Paul would find me. Eventually, I abandoned my apartment in San Francisco with everything in it except for one thing—the very thing I came back to New York for tonight."

Chapter 26

MADDIE STOOD SUDDENLY AND WENT to the bookshelf. She pushed several books to one side and then removed the back panel of the bookshelf, which had been painted the color of the wall for camouflage. Adam would have never known it was there if he hadn't seen her remove it. Behind the panel was what appeared to be a secret safe with a cipher lock and a biometric fingerprint lock. She pressed some buttons on the cipher lock, then pressed her finger on a green, glowing panel and opened the safe. She removed what looked like a very old, leather-bound book contained in a plastic, airtight case.

Maddie returned to sit beside Adam and held it close to his face so that he could look at it. He stared at the strange symbols or words that were engraved in the leather and written in a language he was not familiar with.

"What does it say?" he said.

She said, "This book is centuries old. It's written in Hebrew. The title translates to "The Power Within." It was handed down to me by the ones who taught Paul and me. It is the oldest-known instruction manual for teaching the use of Refined Transcendent Power. It is the one thing the KTP would love to get their hands on and destroy. It proves that the knowledge of RTP has existed for centuries, and if it were to ever be mass-published, it could potentially increase public awareness to the point where the KTP is rendered powerless. I promised to keep this book safe at all costs, and I intend to keep my promise."

She handed the encased book to Adam. He held it gingerly, staring at the cover, afraid to be holding something so old and valuable.

Maddie continued her story.

"I didn't think Paul knew that I had the book. That is why it was sent with me when I first escaped from New Mexico. The intention was that the book and I would disappear and never be found. But I couldn't take a risk and leave the book in my apartment in San Francisco. That's why I risked being caught to retrieve it.

"I was so shaken up from my encounter with Paul that I felt the need to isolate myself for a while. Instinctively, I knew he would continue to try to find me. I also knew he would never give up, and if he ever found me again, he would not let me go. I traveled the country, only staying in locations for short periods of time. And, as I suspected he would, he did manage to track me down a few other times.

"KTP membership has greatly increased, and with modern communication methods such as computers, cell phones, and GPS, he has perfected his methods for tracking people. I have become one of their most-wanted fugitives. Thankfully, the Keepers of the Peace have also developed an elaborate communication system, and we have managed to stay one step ahead of the KTP—so far.

"I have found that large cities are the best hiding places. So recently, I decided to move back to New York City. New York is one of the better places in the world to live anonymously. Needless to say, I have lived a lonely existence for quite some time."

She paused and looked at Adam. Tears were welling up in her eyes again. He felt so powerless. He wanted to know what to say or do to make it all better, but he didn't fully comprehend all she was telling him. It was too much to process at once. His heart was breaking for her.

As if reading his mind, Maddie touched Adam's cheek and gently turned his face toward hers so that she could look into his eyes. She sighed and smiled, even as her eyes were filled with sadness, and said, "Until one day when an angel with jet-black hair and gorgeous blue eyes knocked on my door to deliver my package."

She stroked his cheek and said, "I was attracted to you from the moment I saw you, Adam. And I had not felt that way for anyone in over a century. It terrified me and excited me all at the same time.

"So now you know my story. Maybe now you can understand what I was trying to do when I left you in the hospital that night. I think Paul used RTP to summon the fire in the nightclub and the storm that almost killed us, just by sending thoughts about deadly events to happen wherever I might be. His power has grown very strong, and we are almost certain he can cause things to happen to me even when he doesn't know where I am and then use internet searches and news headlines about the events to pinpoint my location.

"Don't take this the wrong way, but I should have never gotten involved with you in the first place. It would have been the right thing to do to keep you safe. But I was selfish and weak, and I wanted to have a normal life like everyone else. I let myself believe that everything would be okay and I could have a relationship with you.

"It wasn't fair that I didn't tell you the truth up front. But you wouldn't have believed me anyway. You would have thought I was off my rocker and ran for the hills. I thought I was protecting you by keeping you in the dark. You see, the KTP won't mess with people who are innocent and unaware of Refined Transcendent Power. They are only interested in recruiting the existing practitioners of

RTP. And they don't want to draw any unwanted attention to their order for fear of being exposed.

"I had suspected that Paul had caused the fire in the nightclub, but I wasn't sure. So, against my better judgment, I decided to continue seeing you. I had fallen for you by then and I needed you. I needed to feel love again. I desperately wanted it to work out between us.

"But after the blizzard and avalanche occurred, I was almost certain Paul was behind it and he would soon find my whereabouts but I still had hope that he did not know about you. I was afraid that if the KTP found out that you and I were seeing each other, they would assume I had told you about RTP and you would be in even more danger.

"Unbeknownst to you, your association with me has already almost gotten you killed—twice. I couldn't let it continue. My only hope for your safety was to get out of your life before they found out about you and our relationship. Plus, I'm not really sure how Paul will react if he finds out I am seeing someone. I can't even let myself think about what he might do.

"Leaving you like that was one of the hardest things I've ever had to do. I do love you, Adam. I hope that you believe me. I hope you can forgive me. But because I truly love you, the right thing to do is to keep you safe by disappearing from your life forever."

As crazy as her story was, Adam was starting to believe her. He felt he had no other choice. He loved her. He had to believe because he couldn't accept any of the alternatives. The feelings of anger and hurt toward Maddie had been replaced with a mixture of relief and sadness and a newfound anger aimed at Paul and those who had persecuted Maddie and all of the Keepers of the Peace.

He had so much to think about, so much to process. But at that moment, he took comfort in knowing she did truly love him. If what she said was true, she had tried to do what she thought was right, even if it meant sacrificing her own feelings and her own life to keep him safe. He understood and truly appreciated it.

After a few moments, Adam took Maddie's hand in his and said, "Maddie, I love you too. I do believe you and I understand why you did what you did. I forgive you. But you shouldn't have to live your life in fear. Why hasn't anything been done to stop the KTP?"

She shook her head and said, "Because we want to keep the peace. We don't want a war, and that is what the result would be if we provoke them."

"But it isn't fair to you, or any of the other peacekeepers," he said.

She shook her head again and said, "The KTP has grown in number. It would be very difficult to overtake them."

"Exactly how large of a number are you talking about?"

"We're not exactly sure. Thousands, maybe close to five thousand, maybe more in the U.S. alone."

"And how many peacekeepers are there?"

"We're not sure about that either, especially with many people in hiding and using assumed names. We believe it could be in the thousands as well."

"But the KTP is like a bully," he continued. "If all of the peacekeepers worldwide could organize and unite to stand up to the KTP, they might back down. To me it seems worth trying, rather than continuing to live in hiding."

"It's not peaceful to fight, Adam. We don't want to use RTP for evil or bad purposes."

"But using RTP to win your freedom is not using it for evil or bad purposes," he countered.

"Fighting against the KTP would mean certain death for the peaceful ones," she explained. "When members of the KTP attack and kill peaceful practitioners, they don't fight back. They don't believe in violence."

Adam felt his anger and frustration at the situation growing. He said, "But they should fight back. That's why the KTP will continue to harass you all and make your lives miserable until somebody fights back."

"It's not that simple, Adam," she said patiently.

She turned away from him and looked down at her hands. Adam thought she might be getting frustrated with him. Then she quietly said, "So now you know why I believe we can't be together."

At this, Adam grew angrier. He couldn't be quiet anymore. He had to think of a way to convince her that she didn't need to protect him and that they could be together. It should be as much his choice as hers. And then he thought of a new angle.

He said, "You're right about one thing, Maddie. Now I know the truth. And now I know why we *have* to be together."

Chapter 27

MADDIE COCKED HER HEAD AND looked at Adam incredulously.

He said, "You just said that the KTP would not attack the innocent. You left me in hopes that they would not attack me because I was ignorant of RTP. Right?"

She turned to face him, nodding slowly and looking at him suspiciously.

"Well, now I know about RTP," he continued. "I'm no longer innocent. And you don't know for sure that they don't already know about us. So if you leave me now with the knowledge of RTP but without training me on how to use it, you are essentially leaving me defenseless."

She started to say something in protest but quickly closed her mouth, realizing he had found the loophole. Her eyes narrowed.

"You can't leave me defenseless, Maddie," he said matter-of-factly. "That would definitely not be the right thing to do. I know too much now. Now you have to teach me to use Refined Transcendent Power. I know I can learn it. And then we can be together."

She stared at him for a long moment and softly said, "What if you are like James and you never fully master RTP? What if I have to watch you grow old and die while I remain eternally youthful? I don't think I can go through that again."

"At least give me a chance," he said. "Give me a couple of years. If I don't master RTP within two years, you can walk away. But at least give me the chance. Teach me. I know I can do it. I won't be like James. I promise I won't let you down.

"I should have a choice in this matter. I was in pure hell when you left me. I don't think I can handle it if you leave me again. This is our second chance. I would rather risk dying so that I can be with you than to live without you. Without you, my life is meaningless. I'm begging you to teach me about RTP."

Adam could tell by the look on Maddie's face that she was unsure. She said, "Let's just suppose I decide to stay. If the KTP was on my trail, I have probably thrown them off by coming back. I don't normally return to a place after I have left it. It's not my pattern."

She was considering it. She didn't flat-out say no. His hopes lifted ever so slightly. He nodded encouragingly and said, "Yes, that should buy us some time. Right?"

"Possibly. But even if it buys us a month or two, or even six months, what happens if they find me and I have to leave? That would be even worse than if we part ways now."

"Simple," he said. "I would go with you."

Her eyes grew wide and she said, "Think about what you're saying. Are you willing to just give up everything in your life to leave with me—your band, your friends, and your life as you know it?"

"Absolutely," he said without hesitation. "That's what I've been trying to tell you. Before I met you, I thought I wanted fortune and fame and the rock star life. I thought I wanted to go on tour, get a recording contract, and live that life for as long as possible. But now I know none of that matters if I don't have you in my life."

Still incredulous she said, "You're willing to leave Zach, Claire, and the band and uproot your life to go into hiding and follow me around the country? You're willing to take the chance that you might have to watch your back every day of your life because somebody might be trying to kill you?"

Adam looked her dead in the eyes and said with conviction, "Yes. That's what I want. I want you to stay and I want you to teach me RTP. If Paul finds you and you have to leave, then I want to go with you. You said you couldn't live with yourself if something happened to me. Well, how will you feel if you leave me defenseless now and the KTP finds me and something bad happens to me?"

He could tell she had no counter-argument. She narrowed her eyes and said, "That's not fair."

"All is fair in love and war, darling."

Before she could respond, he leaned over and kissed her. This time she didn't resist. He wanted her to feel the passion and love between them. He kissed her as if this was going to be their last kiss—so tenderly, so passionately. She responded with the same tenderness and passion.

Adam knew she could still get up and walk out the door at any moment. And he would never try to force her to stay. If she stayed, it would have to be of her own free will. He could talk tough and act like he wasn't going to let her go. But if that's what she truly wanted, he would let her go. He would be miserable and crushed, but he would not try to stop her. He would never try to force her to do anything against her will. All he truly wanted was for her to be happy.

They kissed for a long while. The months of separation made it even sweeter than Adam had remembered. Their hands and tongues explored each other in a familiar way. She wasn't stopping him, and this encouraged him. He decided to take a chance. He figured that it was now or never. He wanted to show her how much he loved her.

Adam stood, took Maddie by the hand, and gently pulled her

to her feet. He took her by the hand and led her to the bedroom. As he turned to face her, he pulled her close to him, pressing her body against his. She put her arms around his neck and leaned farther into the embrace. He kissed her even more passionately as his hands began to caress her face, her neck, her back, and her breasts. She ran her fingernails up his back and through his hair, igniting the passion between them.

Adam pulled back and took his shirt off. Her eyes admiringly scanned his body as she ran her hands up his sculpted abs and chest.

He moved toward her, pulled her shirt over her head, and tossed it on the floor. Her chest rose and fell from her rapid breathing. He unfastened her bra, gently slid the straps off her shoulders, and let it drop to the floor. He cupped her large, soft breasts in his hands and leaned down to kiss them. She moaned softly as he slowly circled her nipples with his tongue.

She unfastened his pants as he helped her pull them down so he could step out of them. Then he helped her do the same. Her unclothed body was even more beautiful than he had imagined. He wanted her more than ever, and he knew he was going to have her.

She was willingly giving herself to him. He hoped this was her way of confirming that she was planning to stay and teach him RTP, and never leave him again.

Adam gently laid Maddie on the bed as he kissed her neck, her chest, her breasts, her stomach, her thighs, until his tongue found her sweet spot. He heard her moan as he tasted her, his tongue circling and circling, her hips gently rocking to the rhythm. He cupped her breasts in his hands as she ran her fingers up his arms and through his hair, her moans steadily growing in intensity until, panting, she finally begged, "Take me now, Adam."

Unable to hold back his desire for her any longer, he slid into her as he took her hands in his and parted her lips with his tongue, an involuntary moan escaping his own lips as their bodies joined together, rocking in the fevered rhythm of lovemaking. In ecstasy, they became one as the pleasure surrounded them, enveloped them, united them as they simultaneously reached climax, both crying out in uninhibited abandon.

They made love several more times that night, falling asleep for short periods of time in between. They couldn't get enough of each other. Afterward, they lay spent in each other's arms, Adam on his back with Maddie's head resting on his shoulder while she slept. Although he was physically exhausted, Adam lay awake. He guessed it must be around three o'clock in the morning, but he willed himself to stay awake, partly because he loved holding her and wanted to savor the moment, and partly because he was afraid that if he fell asleep and let go of her, she would sneak out while he slept.

Even though he had no idea what he was doing, he tried to use RTP by thinking positive thoughts about her staying with him. He visualized the two of them having happy times together in the future. Eventually, he couldn't keep his eyes open any longer. He wrapped his arms around her tightly, so that he might feel it if she tried to sneak out, and drifted off to sleep.

He slept fitfully. He kept waking up in a sweat from wild dreams—all about him being lost and lonely in one way or another—only to find her sleeping soundly beside him. Each time he awoke and she was still there, he breathed a sigh of relief. Maybe things would work out between them after all. He could only hope.

Chapter 28

ADAM BOLTED UPRIGHT IN BED, panicked and angry at himself for falling asleep. He was immediately relieved to see that Maddie was still there, looking surprised by his sudden movement. She rolled over, smiled at him with her beautiful smile, kissed him, and said, "Good morning, sexy."

Those three little words were all it took to arouse him again. He pulled her close to him, and they made love again. Afterward, he held her tightly. He was hoping she had made up her mind to stay and teach him how to use RTP, but he didn't dare to ask her at that moment. He didn't want to push her too hard. He was hoping her actions were speaking louder than words, and that the mere fact that she was still there meant she intended to stay. Seeing the light streaming in through the shutters, Adam said, "What time is it?"

Maddie rolled over, looked at her phone, and said, "Would you believe it's almost noon?"

As he leaned over to kiss her again, his stomach growled rather loudly. She giggled and said, "I'm hungry too. Let's see if there's anything edible left in my apartment."

They rummaged through her kitchen but since she had been gone so long, the food offering was scarce. They managed to find some frozen dinners that weren't expired and decided to make a meal out of those.

He didn't want to leave Maddie's side, but he knew it was Saturday and Night Fury had a gig that night. Eventually, he would have to leave to get ready. And he would have to ask her the question he had been avoiding: *Are you planning to stay?*

They watched TV while they ate and talked about the good times they had together before she left. Adam kept an eye on the time, and debated whether or not he should even go to the gig. He knew that it wouldn't be right for him to skip out on his friends. He also knew he wasn't going to be able to stay with Maddie every second of every day. Eventually, he would have to trust her.

When he couldn't prolong the inevitable any longer, he said, "I have to go get showered and ready for the gig tonight. Are you planning to come with me?"

He held his breath and braced himself for her answer. He expected the worst. But she didn't hesitate when she said, "Sure. I'd love to."

"Really? You're sure?"

She smiled and nodded. Adam knew it was Maddie's choice to stay or leave. He was going to have to learn to trust her and be willing to let her go if she chose to, and he would have to start soon. So after they finished eating, he kissed her and reluctantly said, "I guess I better go get ready."

"Yeah, I need to get ready too," she said. "What time are we leaving?"

"I'll be back at seven-thirty to get you," he said.

"I'll be ready."

He tried to smile a genuine smile, but it didn't quite reach his eyes. He hoped she couldn't detect his anxiety. If she did, she didn't let on. And even though they were neighbors, when Adam walked out of her door, fearing he would never see her again, he forced himself to go anyway.

Chapter 29

I T TOOK ALL OF ADAM'S willpower to stop himself from calling Maddie or knocking on her door every five minutes. He had told her he would be back to get her at about seven-thirty, but somehow he managed to get ready a lot faster and found himself pacing the floor, waiting for the time to pass.

What seemed like an eternity later, he grabbed his guitar and amp and knocked on her door at precisely seven-thirty. He counted to thirty slowly. She didn't answer. He tried the doorknob. It was locked. He felt his heart start to beat a little faster.

He needed to get a grip—she always kept her door locked.

He pressed his ear to the door, listening for any sounds or movements. Nothing. He stood back and rubbed his sweaty palms on his pants.

Maybe she hadn't heard him knocking.

He knocked really loudly and listened again. A few seconds later he heard footsteps approaching the door. He closed his eyes and breathed a sigh of relief.

When she opened the door, he hastily took her in his arms and hugged her tightly. She was still here.

When he finally released her, she looked at him curiously as she searched his eyes. He knew she could sense his apprehension, but certainly she had to understand. He hoped she would be patient with him for a while until he calmed down some and quit acting like such a clingy freak. Who could blame him?

He took a moment to check her out. She was wearing tight skinny jeans with rips in the knees, a t-shirt with a plunging neckline, a denim jacket, and black, high-heeled boots.

"You look beautiful."

"Thank you," she beamed. "You're looking pretty good yourself."

He kissed her firmly on the lips. He thought about scooping her up in his arms, carrying her back to bed, and making love to her for the rest of the night. But he was reliable, if anything, and he wouldn't leave the band hanging. So instead, he kissed her gently one more time and took her arm in his to escort her to his truck.

Adam opened the passenger door for Maddie and then began to load his guitar and amp in the back of the truck. As he did, he had a realization. He had been so caught up in the events of Maddie's return that he hadn't had time to think about what would happen if he showed up with her at the gig with no warning or explanation.

It suddenly occurred to him that Zach, Claire, and rest of the band might not be so happy to see her. Zach and Claire were very angry at Maddie for what she had done to him. In fact, Adam thought Zach might even hate her. He had said some really nasty things about her, his way of showing his support for Adam. Adam knew that Zach meant well. He had his back. Zach couldn't understand how anyone could do that to someone they supposedly loved, especially when the victim was his best friend.

Adam also realized there was no way he could tell them the truth about why Maddie had left and how they had reunited. His friends would think Adam had lost his freakin' mind. How could he expect them to understand and believe Maddie's story when he wasn't sure he understood or believed it himself?

He knew that when he walked in the door with Maddie that night it was going to be a shock to all of them. He worried that they might tell her off. And he also knew they were going to think he was an idiot for taking her back. He didn't care about that, but he didn't want to alienate his friends.

Adam got in the driver's side of the truck. Maddie was sitting in the middle, right next to him, like she had always done in the past. She put her head on his shoulder and held his free hand as they headed for the nightclub.

After a few moments of silence Adam said, "You do realize that Zach and Claire and the guys are pretty angry about you leaving me?"

Without hesitation she said, "I imagined they would be. I don't blame them. I know they really care about you. They also don't understand."

"No shit," he said. "That might just be the understatement of the year."

Realizing his words sounded harsh, he laughed to try lightening the mood. She didn't laugh.

"They could never understand what has transpired between us," he said. "I'll never be able to explain it to them—at least not anytime soon."

She nodded somberly. "You're right. I'm sorry. I don't have to go if you don't want me to."

"I'm not asking for an apology, Maddie," he said gently. "I absolutely want you to go. I have already forgiven you. I just want you to be prepared and know they might not welcome you with open arms."

She winced and said, "I wouldn't expect any less. I know they will think I deserve it. They care about you. They're angry that I hurt you. I get it. I'm angry at myself for hurting you, but I truly believed I was doing the right thing. They don't know the truth, and they never will. I can handle it."

Adam began to think that maybe it was a bad idea to take her so soon. He should have eased everyone into her reappearance over time. It might have been better if they had more time to come up with a believable story about her return, but he didn't voice that opinion. They were already en route and he didn't want to let her out of his sight—not yet, anyway. Eventually, he would have to come clean with Zach and Claire and the rest of the band about being back together with Maddie anyway. They wouldn't be able to hide it for long.

And yet, if he were to be totally honest with himself, he was still a little hurt and wanted her to feel some discomfort for hurting him—just a little bit. He would've never admitted it to anyone, but a small part of him thought she should face the consequences of what she had done. He knew it was mean-spirited. But why should he be the only one who had suffered? Even though he knew that it must have been very hard for her to leave and he understood now why she had done it, he wanted to drive his point home to her that leaving him was the wrong decision. So he reasoned that now was as good a time as any to break the news that they were back together.

Adam said, "We've got to come up with a story about where you've been and why you're back."

"Well, as you know, I've gotten pretty good about making up stories about my life and hiding the truth. Let me think."

Wincing, Adam said, "Well I may have made matters worse when I told them that you broke up with me because you had to leave for a job assignment and you didn't know how long you would be gone."

"Really?! A job assignment?" Maddie said incredulously. "They think I broke up with you and left you in the hospital because I had a job assignment? Wow. That really makes me look like the girlfriend of the year."

"I was a mess," he said quietly. "They put me on the spot, and I couldn't think quickly enough. It was the best I could come up with under the circumstances since I had no idea why you really left."

Now it was Maddie's turn to wince. She paused, squeezed his

hand, and said, "Okay, so we can say that I was really traumatized after the accident and I couldn't stand to see you in pain. And then I found out that a close relative with cancer was given only a couple of months to live and was being put in hospice care, and my family needed my help. So, with all of the stress and being torn between staying with you and helping my family, I freaked out and made up the story about having writing assignment because I needed to escape reality. The first part wouldn't be a lie." She kissed his cheek and squeezed his hand tighter.

"And why are you back?" Adam said, playing along with the story.

"Because while I was gone I missed you terribly and realized how much I love you."

It melted his heart to hear her say those words. But he knew that was not really why she came back. She came back to get the book, and he caught her in the act. Otherwise, he probably would've never seen her again. He chose not to point that out at the moment. He wished that he could just trust her again. He was really going to have to work at it. He had built up walls around his heart to protect himself from the possibility of her deceiving him again, and he didn't like it. He didn't like that they no longer had complete trust between them. But how could it be otherwise? She had lied about her entire life to just about everybody.

But now he understood why. It wasn't because she was a bad person or because she was a liar at heart. She was a good person who lied to protect herself and the people she loved. He understood it, but he didn't think his friends would. They couldn't understand RTP. They would think Adam and Maddie were both crazy if they told them the truth.

He said, "Well, I can't think of a better story. If they ask, we'll just have to go with that and see if they buy it. Otherwise, it might be better not to explain it at all."

Chapter 30

WHEN MADDIE AND ADAM ARRIVED at the club, he held her hand as they walked in the backstage entrance. He sensed her apprehension when she squeezed his hand just a little too tightly. He could feel his own heart beating rapidly with dread about what was about to happen. Although he had originally wanted her to feel some discomfort when she had to face Zach and the others, he had since changed his mind. He didn't want her to feel any pain. He knew his friends could be brutal when they were standing together to protect one of their own. He wished that there was a way he and Maddie could be together and he and Zach could remain best friends. He wished the band could go on as usual, and no one would have any hard feelings.

But what if they never accepted her back into the group? What if he was forced to choose between her and his friends?

Adam knew what he would choose. There was no doubt in his mind. He had expressed it to Maddie the night before. He would be willing to give up his life as he knew it to be with her. It would be the hardest thing that he had ever done, but he would do it.

Still, he knew Maddie would not want him to give up his friends, the band, and his dreams. She would probably rather leave him again than to make him choose. He knew deep down that if his friends never accepted her, she would eventually leave. He didn't want to give her a reason to leave. So he tried to think positive thoughts. He didn't know a thing about RTP yet, but he visualized the outcome that he was hoping for. He knew it might take some time, but he hoped it would all work out somehow.

When they arrived at the club, Adam entered the backstage room first with Maddie close behind him. The room was filled with the usual people buzzing around, getting ready for the performance—the band members, some friends, stagehands and the rest of the crew. Everyone was busy setting up, testing their equipment, and going about the normal routine.

In an attempt to hide his nervousness, Adam casually delivered his usual greeting. "Hey, guys."

At first none of them paid much attention to their entrance as they said 'hey' back. But after a few moments, Adam saw some head-snaps and double-takes in their direction. No one said a word. He saw Claire and others staring at Maddie. The looks of surprise and shock on their faces said it all. He felt Maddie grip his hand even more tightly. Claire's gaze went from Maddie to Zach, who still hadn't seen her. Then she looked at Adam questioningly.

Zach was busy plugging his guitar into the amplifier and hadn't looked up yet. He started to say, "I didn't think you were going to make..."

But before he could finish his sentence, he looked up and froze when he saw Maddie. His mouth dropped open. At first he had a look of incomprehension, as if he couldn't believe what he was seeing. Then his eyes narrowed and the look turned to that of realization and anger. He glared at Maddie with a look that could kill and growled through gritted teeth, "What the hell is she doing here?"

At that point, everyone in the room stopped what they were doing and stared at Maddie and Adam. Adam and Claire exchanged glances. Inside, he cringed like a child being punished. Outside, he met Zach's gaze and tried to appear calm.

Adam pulled Maddie a little closer and said, "Maddie's back."

Well, that was brilliant.

He didn't know what else to say. Zach's eyes widened as he looked at Adam. The look said it all. Adam could tell that Zach thought he had gone completely crazy, and that he was an absolute dumbass. Incredulous, Zach said, "You've got to be fuckin' kidding me. Right? Is this a joke? Are you punking us?"

Adam locked eyes with him and slowly shook his head.

Zach looked at Maddie with disgust and hatred. She moved slightly behind Adam, as if he were a shield.

She said quietly, "Maybe I should go."

Adam shook his head and said, "No. Don't go. It'll be okay."

And with that, Zach threw his guitar down and stormed off, which was a very bad sign because he normally treated his guitar like his precious baby.

Adam looked back at Claire again. She gave him a disapproving look. Maddie stood there, her face blank, silently absorbing all of the scrutiny. She just took it. She knew it was her doing, and she was willing to accept it. But Adam still felt bad for her. He wished this moment did not have to happen, but there was no way around it. All he could hope for was that Zach and the rest of them would eventually get over it.

Maddie leaned close and whispered in his ear, "I can leave. You go talk to Zach."

Adam shook his head and said, "Please don't leave. I'll be right back."

She nodded and stepped back into a corner of the room and leaned against the wall. As Adam was leaving the room in the direction that Zach had gone, he noticed that Cristy—who had befriended Maddie when she first started attending the rehearsals—motioned for her to come and sit down in the empty chair beside her. Maddie slowly made her way over to Cristy and the other ladies and took a seat.

Adam was relieved to see that at least some people were welcoming Maddie back without question. The rest of band members had stayed surprisingly silent during the exchange between Zach and Adam. But still the tension in the room remained. Adam knew that Zach was pissed. But who could blame him? It was hard for Adam to put him through this. But he knew that even if he tried to explain, Zach could not accept it. Adam hoped maybe someday he would be able to tell Zach the truth. But for now, he could only hope Zach could forgive Maddie enough to accept that she was going to be a part of Adam's life, hopefully for a long time to come.

As he walked out the backstage door that led to the alley, he saw Zach pacing and puffing heavily on a cigarette. Zach only smoked when he was extremely drunk, stressed, or angry. When he saw Adam approaching, he stopped pacing and turned his back. Zach stared straight ahead and said, "What the hell is going on?"

"I know what you're thinking, and I don't blame you for being pissed," Adam said. "But it's a long story, and I can't even explain it to you. You've just got to accept that Maddie and I are back together."

Zach spun around to face Adam. Anger and disbelief flashed in his eyes. "You want me to just accept it? Just like that, huh? I was the one who watched you suffering and pining away over this girl who heartlessly left you while you were in the hospital after a near-death experience. Did you forget that? Did you forget that she left you in your greatest moment of need? She disappeared just like that and crushed your heart. Did you forget that, Adam? And suddenly she waltzes back into your life and you just take her back with open arms. Have you lost your fucking mind?"

Adam tried to remain calm and said, "I know it looks like that, Zach, but it's not that simple. We've had a really long talk and

Maddie apologized for leaving. She feels awful for what she did, and I don't think she will do it again."

Zach shook his head and said, "I bet you didn't think she'd leave you the first time either, did you? She said she loved you and then walked right out the door. How could you ever trust her again?"

That was a good question. Adam didn't know for sure that he could trust her again. Only time would tell. He didn't respond.

Zach didn't wait for a response. He continued, "The bottom line is you can't trust her. And you know it. When did she get back here, anyway? How long have you been hiding this from us?"

So that was part of the reason for his reaction. Zach thought Adam had been hiding something from him. One of the reasons their friendship was so strong was that they were always honest with each other—sometimes brutally honest.

Adam said, "I haven't been hiding it from you. She just got back into town."

Zach looked skeptical. "Well, where the hell was she?"

This was the part Adam was dreading the most. The story he and Maddie had made up on the way to the club didn't sound too convincing to him, but it was all they could come up with in a pinch. He sure as hell didn't think Zach would buy it. He sighed and told the story he and Maddie had rehearsed.

Zach snorted and said, "Bullshit. And she couldn't even answer your calls? That's called common courtesy."

He had a good point. Adam had to think quickly on his feet. He wasn't good at lying to Zach. He knew Adam too well. Adam said, "She just freaked out and didn't want to hurt me by giving me any hope."

Zach tilted his head and narrowed his eyes. "And she didn't think she would hurt you by leaving you and never talking to you again?"

"It was a bad decision," Adam said. "She made a mistake, and she's really sorry for it. Plus, she feels a little bit responsible for me getting hurt on the mountain, and the guilt kept her away."

Zach's eyes narrowed as he said, "Really? Why would she feel responsible for that?"

Adam realized he had said too much. Damn, but he was a terrible liar.

"Look, Zach, I don't really want to go into that right now. It's a very long story. Trust me. Someday I'll explain the whole story to you. But for now, you just have to understand that I love her and she's going to be a part of my life, hopefully for a long time. I've forgiven her, and I hope that you can too."

Zach tossed his cigarette on the ground, snuffed it out with his foot, and said, "I'm sorry. I can't forgive her just like that. I saw what she did to you. Claire and I were the ones who had to pick up the pieces. I don't know if I will ever be able to forgive her for that."

Adam pleaded, "Man, you're my best friend. You're like a brother to me. I really hope this doesn't come between us, but I love Maddie and I have to give her a second chance."

Adam could see the disappointment and sadness in his best friend's eyes, and he felt horrible. But he hoped Zach realized that he wasn't going to change his mind.

Zach stomped on the cigarette again, looked Adam in the eyes, and said, "Well, when she does it to you again, don't come crying to me."

He turned and walked back inside. Adam stood silently for a moment and then followed him. It had actually gone better than he had imagined. At least they hadn't come to blows. But still he feared their friendship had been permanently damaged. When Adam was a young boy, his mom liked to use the saying, "Time heals all wounds." He could only hope that in this case, it would be true.

Chapter 31

Z ACH AND ADAM DIDN'T SPEAK to one another for the rest of the night. The same went for Claire and some of the band members. But most people welcomed Maddie back. Adam thought it was nice having her there again, just like it had been in the beginning.

After the performance, Maddie and Adam went back to his place. She spent the night and they made love over and over. It was in moments like that when Adam wished he could freeze time and they could stay in the moment forever. They were just two people who were madly in love. All of the complicated, outside events of the world around them melted away when they were alone. They could simply be happy together.

In the morning, Adam woke before Maddie. While she slept, he gathered up some things and put them in his truck. When she stirred, he kissed her gently and said, "Wake up sleepyhead."

She yawned, stretched, and smiled as she put her arms around his neck and kissed him.

He kissed her for a few lingering moments, pulled back and said, "Get up and get ready to go. I've got a surprise for you."

"A surprise? I love surprises. Tell me. Tell me."

"Not tellin'," he said playfully.

She stuck out her lower lip, making her best pouty face.

"Come on," she whined. "At least give me a hint."

He shook his head and said, "All I'm going to tell you is that I'm taking you somewhere special."

"Do I need to dress fancy?"

He shook his head. "Nope. It's a casual kind of place. I hope you like it as much as I do."

She rolled out of bed and headed toward the bathroom. Over her shoulder she said, "If you like it, then I'm sure I will too."

He smiled. He really hoped so.

They finished getting ready, had a quick breakfast and some coffee, and prepared to leave. As they approached his truck, Maddie noticed fishing poles sticking out of the bed. She smiled and said, "Are we going fishing?"

Adam smiled slyly and said, "Maybe."

They headed north of New York City to the place where he and his family had gone fishing a lot when he was a kid. He thought that during the two or so hour drive it would be a good time to talk.

Shortly after they got on the road, Adam said, "Will you explain more about Refined Transcendent Power to me? How does it work? How does one go about learning to use it?"

Maddie thought for a moment and said, "Well, basically, it boils down to this—we all have the ability to imagine and dream and create, and if we can envision a thing or a state of being, focus our energy on it, and truly believe we have already received it, it will happen."

"Certainly there's more to it than that or more people would be doing it," said Adam.

"Well," she said, "it's simple and it's not. We could go into the modern principles of quantum mechanics and the 'Observer Effect,' which states that at a subatomic level, energy responds to our mindful attention and becomes matter. We are all connected to energy and a divine, infinite intelligence beyond space and time. Our conscious thoughts, feelings, and state of being can influence all probabilities in the quantum field to become reality. There's a ton of material about it all over the internet. We could talk about it and analyze it for days. But trust me, you don't need to be a quantum physicist to understand it. The ancient practitioners of RTP mastered it without knowing anything about subatomic particles or quantum physics. The basic principles are simple. Just know that your inner being is unconditional, infinite, unlimited, connected, and powerful. Our thoughts become things."

"Then how come I haven't ever seen anyone do what you do?" he said.

"Sadly," she said, "partly because Paul and the KTP have successfully ensured that the knowledge of RTP has been kept a secret, and partly because people simply don't believe it. It really depends on the person. Some people have an easier time believing and they learn to use it faster than others. Children are very good at learning to use RTP because they don't have any preconceived notions about what they can and cannot do. They just believe wholeheartedly and it works for them.

Some adults have a more difficult time mastering RTP. Many overthink and overanalyze it. Others have been let down in life, or they have lived a hard life, or bad things have happened to them. This causes them to have difficulty believing in what they cannot see. Adults are more skeptical. They can't believe they can use their thoughts to change their lives. Therefore, by the very nature of RTP, it doesn't work for them because they *think* it doesn't work for them. Since they believe it doesn't work or they can't do it, then it must be so. But don't let that discourage you. Many people, old and young alike, have had great success in mastering RTP."

"You make it sound so simple."

She turned to face him and said, "That's the beauty of it. It *is* simple. Basically, you can practice by thinking a sustained thought about something you desire. Then you must focus all of your energy on it and truly believe you have already received it. You must feel the feelings of thankfulness and gratitude for what you have received, even if you haven't received it yet. And then you simply release it into the quantum field, go on with your life, and eventually it will manifest."

Adam furrowed his brow and said, "But you seem to be able to manifest things instantly. It seems that you have a special superpower that most people don't have."

Maddie shook her head. "I don't have a special superpower for using RTP—no more than you or anyone else. It's just that I've been practicing using it for so long. I have trained myself to have absolute faith that I can manifest anything at any time. I truly believe that the possibilities of what I can think and create are limitless. Some people have a hard time mastering this belief. It is a mind game to some. Even I, as easy as I may make it seem, have my mental limitations at times.

"When I first started learning about RTP, it would take weeks, and sometimes even months, for me to manifest things. I would doubt that RTP even worked. I would doubt myself. But once I saw that it worked, my faith grew stronger and stronger. And as I saw more and more positive results, I got to where it would only take days or hours to manifest what I desired. I was elated the first time I instantaneously manifested something. And once that happened, my faith in RTP was cemented forever.

But for many, like James, belief in RTP is elusive. Some people cannot wrap their minds around the concept. I have seen cases where it took someone over a year to manifest a single thing. Sometimes it takes a lifetime. I have even seen some that never believe and it doesn't work for them. But again, I don't want to discourage you. I've also seen people master it very quickly."

Adam said, "It is hard to wrap my mind around it because in my entire lifetime you are the only person with this ability I have ever met. I mean, I remember my parents used to tell me that I could do anything in life if I believed in myself. But they don't have any knowledge of RTP. I thought that was just something parents tell their kids to encourage them to chase their dreams. And I do believe that to some degree. But I've never seen anyone materialize things the way you do. What you do seems miraculous and out of reach for us mere mortals."

She nudged him and chuckled as she said, "I know it's hard to understand at first. But that's just it, Adam. You can only manifest things instantly if you *believe* you can. Many people can't believe it because they have been taught that they have to work hard to get what they want. So they end up working hard all of their lives and never seem to be able to break out of the pattern. Many people have been led to believe that no matter what they do in life, they can expect to experience disappointments and failure. They focus on negative thoughts instead of positive thoughts. Most of us are taught that failure is something that happens to everybody. But you can only fail if you *believe* you can fail. What people don't understand is that they can change their entire life by changing their thoughts. The first step to learning to use RTP is learning to change the way you think."

She held out her arm and rubbed the area where the gash from her avalanche wound had been. There was no visible sign of a scar. The skin looked perfectly healed and smooth.

"Take my arm, for example," she said. "We have all been taught to believe it takes a long time for a wound to heal. And we have also been taught to believe a wound that is big enough to require stitches will cause a permanent scar. This will only happen if you believe it will happen. I don't believe it. I choose to believe that wounds, no matter the severity, can heal quickly and that scars are not permanent. And by the nature of Refined Transcendent Power, that has been my experience.

"You probably know the old saying: 'You're only as old as you feel.' Well, I believe that is somewhat true. I don't feel over 150 years old. So I changed the saying up just a little. I like to say: 'You're only as old as you believe you are.' If you think about aging, you worry about aging, and you believe aging is inevitable, you will summon aging to you. Why would anyone want to do that? Because they do not believe it can be otherwise.

"We have been taught and conditioned to think certain ways. Many people have limiting beliefs in their capacity to act and to create in this world. Suppose you believe that everyone cheats in relationships. That is what you will experience in your life. People are skeptical by nature and they've been taught to only believe in what they can see, or what they can physically touch, because that's how it's always been done, or that's how it's always been taught, or that's what they have experienced in their lives so far. The hardest part, and at the same time simplest part, of learning to use RTP is learning to change your thinking. Ironically, that is the part that some can never get.

"My teachers taught me to start with 'little things,' even though there is no difference in the process for manifesting 'big things.' There's no difference in the process for manifesting one dollar or a million dollars. The only reason that it is sometimes easier for people to start with manifesting little things is because people *think* it is easier to manifest little things, like a penny. And they *think* it is harder to manifest big things, like a mansion. But in reality, there is no difference. If you can think it and truly believe you have received it, and you are truly grateful for it, you can manifest it."

Maddie paused for a moment. Adam supposed that it was to give him time to let it all sink in.

"Are you telling me that I have to start monitoring all of my thoughts?" he said. "Now that's a scary thought in itself. I must have several thousand thoughts a day. And many of them I would definitely not want to manifest. How can I manage all of those thoughts?"

She said, "Don't worry about it. Most people get overwhelmed when they first realize that what they are thinking is creating what they are experiencing in their life. We all have good and bad thoughts, positive and negative thoughts, and personal thoughts that we wouldn't want anyone else to know about. And when people start to realize that their thoughts are forming their lives and that they are manifesting things, whether they are aware of it or not, it scares them. People believe it can be a daunting task to manage their thoughts, and then that becomes what they experience.

"So you've got to get in touch with how you're feeling. Feelings are how we gauge what we're thinking. If you're feeling good, you are having good thoughts. Likewise, if you're feeling bad, or anxious, or angry, or sad, then you are having negative thoughts. When you find yourself feeling bad, try to think about positive thoughts or things that make you happy. Try to get back on the positive thought wavelength. I was taught that a positive thought is hundreds of times more powerful than a negative thought. That is a comforting concept I like to keep in mind. Only persistent, negative thinking can manifest the bad, unwanted things in your life. By monitoring your thoughts and turning negative thoughts to positive thoughts, you can stay on track.

"Paul uses negative thoughts for his evil purposes. He uses RTP in a way it was never intended. And he has become quite adept at it."

Adam said, "Isn't there some way you can use RTP to stop what Paul is doing?"

Maddie stared out the windshield and sighed as she said, "I wish there was a way. You see, we can't control other people's thoughts. Nobody can manifest things for you. And likewise, you cannot manifest for another. If I was psychic and I knew in advance what Paul was going to do, I could protect myself from it. But I can't stop him from trying to harm me.

"No one else can determine your path. We're the masters of

our thoughts only. Sometimes other people's thoughts can cause unforeseen things to happen to us—like the avalanche or the fire. These things were not a result of our thoughts, but they intersect with our lives nonetheless."

She turned to look at him again and continued, "You know, I believe you are already good at using RTP to get what you want and you don't even know it."

Surprised, Adam said, "Really? What makes you think that?"

"Well," she continued, "you have a successful career. You are currently in the process of living out your dream of being a rock star. You have lots of friends, a nice place to live, and a nice truck. In general you are a positive person. You set goals and reach them. I've often wondered if you summoned me into your life or if it was the other way around. Maybe you summoned the package to my mailbox, or maybe we summoned each other subconsciously. You certainly summoned me back into your life even as I tried my best to disappear."

Intrigued, Adam said, "You mean you don't know if you summoned me into your life? Does that mean that, even after all these years, you don't have complete control over your thoughts?"

"Nobody ever gains complete control of their thoughts, Adam. I still think negative thoughts, just like everybody else. I still manifest and summon people, things, and events into my life inadvertently. I'm far better at controlling my thoughts than most people are, but it still happens occasionally. Our subconscious minds can be very powerful.

"I'm afraid Paul has learned to channel RTP and summon events and occurrences to happen to other people from afar, which would explain how he caused the fire in the nightclub and the avalanche. I don't know if he knows where I am or not. I suppose he could have had his cronies watching my every move and causing the events to occur. But somehow I don't think they have found me again yet. If they knew where I was, they would've tried to capture me by now. But hiding underground has always been my sanctuary. If he can inflict that much damage upon my life without even knowing where I am, then living in hiding may not even be safe anymore. That is one thought I am trying to put out of my mind. That's why I have never voiced this concern to anyone but you. And I am only telling you because now that we are together, it affects you too. I am holding firm to the belief that Paul does not know about you yet. Maybe that will provide you with some form of protection."

For the rest of the drive, Maddie continued her teachings about Refined Transcendent Power. She told Adam success story after success story, and he started to actually believe he could do it. He still couldn't believe it was that simple. There had to be more to it than what she was telling. But then he would catch himself thinking negatively and tell himself that he *could* do it. He tried to convince himself he was stronger and more determined than the people who had failed at it before him. He surmised that they were probably weak-minded or weak in their faith. He was determined to master RTP. If that was what it would take to stay with Maddie for the rest of his life, and protect them both, that is what he would do.

Chapter 32

WHEN MADDIE AND ADAM ARRIVED at their destination, Adam parked the truck in a small gravel lot near a trail that led into the woods. It was an unusually warm day for the time of year, and the brilliant sun made everything seem more beautiful and vibrant. He gathered the fishing gear and cooler out of the back of the truck and motioned for Maddie to follow him. As they walked, he told her funny stories about the times his family had come to that exact location when he was a kid.

Adam was a little worried about the short hike that was ahead of them because he still had the walking cast on, although he didn't mention his worry to Maddie. He had learned to maneuver fairly well in the cast and most of the time he didn't even notice it anymore. But he had only covered relatively short distances with it on. He couldn't remember exactly how far it was to the location, but he knew it was at least a quarter of a mile or more. Still, he was fairly confident he could make it.

He estimated that he and Maddie had walked about a half mile on the path when he started to wonder if they were going in the right direction. He had been confident he could remember the way to his family's favorite fishing spot, but it had been so many years since he had been there that he was now starting to second-guess himself. The trail seemed both familiar and unfamiliar at the same time. He hoped he wasn't getting them lost.

Just when he was about to suggest that they had missed a turn and should turn around, they rounded a bend and the trail opened up to a clearing. Adam could see the riverbank glistening in the sun just beyond the grassy area. It looked exactly as he had remembered it from his childhood. He was relieved that he had found the right spot after all. It brought back so many memories. He froze in place and took in the view while he remembered his past.

Maddie interrupted his moment of nostalgia when she said, "Adam, this is beautiful!"

She walked past him into the grassy area, stretched out her arms, and spun around slowly.

Watching her there in the nature setting with the sun illuminating her blond hair and causing a slight flush to her face, he had to agree with her.

"Yes it is beautiful," he murmured softly as her eyes met his and she smiled at him.

He knew then that it was going to be an awesome day. He laid a blanket down in the grass about ten feet away from the riverbank and proceeded to set up the fishing poles and cast them into the water while Maddie watched with interest. He was careful not to get too close to the water and get his cast wet.

Maddie said, "I can't remember the last time I went fishing. It has been so long."

"I can't either," he admitted.

They sat on the blanket near the bank of the river while they watched the fishing poles and waited for bites. Adam opened the cooler and took out the special bottle of wine he had packed. It was the same brand Maddie had brought to their first date. She smiled in appreciation. He poured the wine into two plastic cups, and they sipped while they chatted about random things. It was very peaceful and relaxing.

The fishing was slow. They got a few small bites here and there but nothing really to speak of. After about a half hour of catching nothing, Maddie said, "Do you want to see how I was taught to fish?"

This amused Adam for some reason. He wondered just how many ways there could be to catch a fish. He was curious to see what she was going to do.

"Sure," he said. "This should be interesting."

She stood up and nudged him playfully as she said, "Watch and learn." She then proceeded to strip down to her bra and panties.

Adam's eyes widened. She grinned at him slyly like the Cheshire Cat.

She had his full attention now. Yes, this was going to be very interesting.

As she walked toward the water she said, "Remember, you didn't tell me what we were doing today, so I didn't dress appropriately. I don't want to get my clothes wet."

Adam said, "I like your method of fishing already."

Still grinning, she proceeded to walk into the water, about mid-thigh deep, without any hesitation. This surprised him because he knew that, even though it was a sunny day, the water was still very cold this time of year.

He said, "Isn't the water a bit too cold for swimming?"

She laughed and said, "It's only too cold if you *think* it is. I think the water is very warm today."

He noticed she wasn't shivering or showing any signs of being cold. He was amazed.

She said, "Tell me what would be considered a prize fish in this area."

He thought for a moment and said, "Well, a six-pound bass would be considered a very nice prize fish in these waters."

She nodded, leaned over, put her hands into the water, and said, "I'm thinking of a prize fish, a six-pound bass or bigger."

She stood very still for a few moments, and then Adam saw a big splash in the water. Her hands move quickly and grasped onto something. To his astonishment, she lifted a huge bass out of the water and held it over her head triumphantly.

He didn't know why it amazed him so much because he knew she could do these things, but he still hadn't gotten used to it. He guessed he might never get used to it. He felt like a young boy watching a magic show unfold right in front of him. She was a master magician, and he was her captive audience.

Adam suddenly became aware that his mouth was gaping open and closed it. He jumped to his feet and almost shouted, "Holy shit! I think that's the biggest bass I've ever seen."

Maddie beamed.

Adam walked to the edge of the riverbank to get a closer look at the fish. He was already mentally calculating how he was going to fit it in the cooler, along with everything else, so he could show it off to the guys. They would never believe it. He reached for his cell phone so he could snap a picture for proof. But before he could get the shot, she was already lowering the fish back into the water.

He shouted, "No!" and almost ran into the water to stop her, but stopped short when he remembered that the walking cast was still on his leg. Before he could say or do anything else, she had already released the fish.

"Why did you do that?" Adam whined disappointedly.

"Because he is a very old fish, and we're probably not going to eat him."

Still a little miffed, he said, "Well, somebody we know would have eaten it. I wanted to show it off to the guys. They will never believe me now."

She tilted her head ever so slightly and raised one eyebrow, like a mother who was about to scold a child, and said, "And just exactly what were you going to tell them? That I caught it with my bare hands? Like they would really believe that."

She had a point, but he wouldn't admit it. He countered, "I could've told them we caught it the normal way. You know…with a fishing pole."

She shook her head. "I don't believe in fishing for sport and killing the fish if we're not planning to eat them. I was taught to fish for food and survival. Otherwise, I catch and release."

She washed her hands and began walking toward the shore. Adam watched her walk toward him with the sun shining on her hair and the water dripping off her scantily clad body. She looked so sexy walking out of the water like that. In that moment his annoyance with her vanished.

He met her at the water's edge, pulled her close to him, and said, "Well I do have to admit that was the sexiest fishing I've ever seen. You can fish like that in front of me anytime."

She smiled as she wrapped her arms around his neck and kissed him. They stood like that, kissing and caressing each other for several minutes, before he led her to the blanket. They made love there in the grassy clearing with only Mother Nature as a witness.

Afterward, they lay on their backs in the sun, dozing and just enjoying being together. After a while, they got dressed and had a picnic lunch of cold cuts, cheese, grapes, and other snacks Adam had thrown into the cooler.

He was still thinking about watching Maddie catch the fish in her underwear when he said, "So when do my private lessons on how to use RTP start? I think I'm ready to learn."

She considered it for a moment and said, "How about now?"

"Let's do it," he said.

She began to look around at their surroundings as she said, "Let's start with something small."

She stood and walked around in the grassy clearing where some wildflowers had started to bloom and butterflies fluttered around her.

Her eyes lingered on the butterflies as she said, "How about we start with a butterfly?"

Adam shrugged. He was game for anything, but he wasn't sure what she meant.

"A butterfly?"

She nodded and said, "Yes. That will be a perfect thing to start with. Think of a butterfly, but not just any butterfly. You have to think of a butterfly that is unique. Make it your own, with distinct markings and colors. It must be a butterfly unique enough that you would know it if you saw it again later. It can't look like any of these common butterflies. You have to be able to know without a doubt that it is the butterfly you manifested."

Adam lay back on the blanket, closed his eyes, and tried to think of a unique butterfly. He didn't know anything about butterflies. He had never really paid any attention to what they looked like or what was common or uncommon. So he just made one up in his mind. He didn't even know if the butterfly he imagined really existed or not. But in his mind he pictured a neon-blue butterfly with thin black lines outlining the edges of each wing, and even thinner black lines sort of spider-webbing throughout the wings like veins. In the bottom quadrant of the wings, he pictured a yellow circle with black markings inside of the circle that almost made it look like an eye on each wing. He held the thought of that specific butterfly in his mind for several minutes. Then he sat up, opened his eyes, and said, "Okay. I've got it."

Maddie said, "Now keep thinking of that butterfly. You must believe that the butterfly already exists and that you will see it soon. You must believe you have already received it, and be thankful for it, and know without a doubt that the butterfly will appear."

Adam looked around the grassy meadow and noticed that all the butterflies in the vicinity were yellow. He didn't see any neon-blue butterflies anywhere. He wondered if he had pictured a butterfly that didn't even exist. He tried to put that negative thought out of his mind immediately. He tried to keep visualizing the butterfly in his mind—his butterfly.

The sun was starting to set and it was getting dark, so they packed up their things to go. Adam never did see his butterfly that day, but Maddie assured him that it would come. He just had to believe. She told him to think about the butterfly every chance he got so that it would materialize. He was determined to make it happen. As they drove home that evening, and in the following days, Adam thought of the butterfly often.

Chapter 33

MADDIE AND ADAM SETTLED INTO a routine in the days following the fishing trip. Adam was beginning to quit worrying about Maddie leaving. It appeared that she had truly made up her mind to stay. So he relaxed a little bit about letting her out of his sight. Even so, they were pretty much inseparable when they weren't working.

About four days after the fishing trip, Adam went to the farmers market to get some fresh herbs for the gourmet meal that he was planning to prepare for Maddie that evening. As he was walking down the street, he passed a sidewalk newsstand. A *Rolling Stone* magazine caught his eye. One of his favorite musicians was on the front cover, and he stopped to look at it. As he reached for the magazine, his hand froze in mid-air. In that instant, a butterfly landed on the corner of that very magazine. And it wasn't just any butterfly. It was a neon-blue butterfly with black outlining the wings and black spider webbing through the wings like veins. On the lower half of each wing was a yellow circle with black markings that made it look like an eye. It was *the* butterfly. It was *his butterfly*—the butterfly he had pictured in his mind.

Adam's heart was beating fast. He could hardly contain his excitement. He had manifested something! He needed proof.

His first thought was to swat it, kill it, and take it back to show Maddie. But he figured she probably wouldn't be happy about that. So instead, he held his breath as he slowly took his cell phone out of his pocket and snapped a few pictures of it before it flew away.

He had done it. RTP had actually worked. He had manifested the butterfly. Sure, it took him four days to do it, but he had done it nonetheless. He was so excited. He texted the picture of the butterfly to Maddie. She responded almost immediately.

"I knew you could do it!"

Adam couldn't wait to get back to the apartment and tell her all about it and show her more pictures. It was the greatest feeling. It was at that moment that he knew beyond a doubt he could master RTP. It might take some time and a lot of work, but he knew he could do it. And by the nature of RTP, that was all he needed—to believe he could do it. He realized that was what it would take. And now he was a true believer.

Chapter 34

THE NEXT FEW MONTHS WENT by with no major incidents, no natural disasters, and no near-death experiences. There was no sign of Paul or his cronies. Maddie still suspected that breaking her usual pattern and returning to New York City had thrown them off. She and Adam also theorized that maybe the KTP thought they had succeeded in their mission by killing her in the avalanche. Whatever the case, they were just glad the KTP seemed to be leaving them alone.

Adam and Maddie decided to make the most of every moment together. They tried to put Maddie's past out of their minds. They were inseparable. Maddie went to every rehearsal and every gig with Adam. They spent so much time together that Zach and Claire and the others gradually began to trust Maddie again. They, and Adam, began to believe she was back to stay and would not hurt Adam again. And even though Zach couldn't bring himself to completely forgive her, at least he tolerated her and treated her with respect, if only to preserve his friendship with Adam.

Adam had been practicing using Refined Transcendent Power daily, and he was getting pretty good at manifesting what he called "little things," like the butterfly, or getting a gig at a certain venue, or making a good call on a stock market trade, or getting random things in the mail. He couldn't make things happen instantly like Maddie did, but he was able to manifest things more quickly. Instead of the four days it took for the butterfly to appear, he could now make some things happen in a day or two, or even sometimes in a few hours. But he had yet to manifest what he considered to be a "big thing," like a new sports car, or a large sum of money, or a major-label recording contract. He realized that the limiting factor was himself—or his mind, to be more specific. He still had a hard time believing that he could manifest a mansion or a million dollars or anything big like that.

One evening Maddie and Adam were talking over dinner about his progress in learning to use RTP. She sensed that something was bothering him and asked, "What's on your mind? You don't seem like yourself tonight."

He said, "Well, I was wondering if you could give me some pointers on how I can materialize the 'big things.' I'm having a hard time believing I can do it."

She put her hand over his and said, "You're doing everything right. There is no difference in the process of manifesting 'little things' or 'big things.' It's the same method. It is just as easy to manifest a one-hundred dollar bill as it is to manifest a one dollar bill. The only difference is your belief that it's easier to manifest a one dollar bill."

"I hear what you're saying, and I understand," he said. "I'm just having a hard time. It's such a mind game."

"It's only a mind game if you believe it's a mind game," she reminded him.

"I really want to believe. I mean, I want to believe I'm not going to age. I want to believe I can have or be anything I can imagine in life. I want to believe in it all. But you have to understand that, other than you, I have never known anyone who can manifest the 'big things.' "

Maddie tilted her head and looked at the ceiling as she pursed her lips. Then she looked at him and said, "How can I explain this? You see, sometimes it does take longer to manifest what you call the 'big things.' But it isn't because it is harder to do. It's just that sometimes the things we want in life require action. Take getting a recording contract, for example. It is very unlikely that you could get a recording contract without ever practicing an instrument or singing a day in your life. It doesn't work that way. The goal of getting a recording contract takes time and practice. Granted, it happens more quickly for some people than for others, but still there are certain steps that have to be taken to attain it. Do you understand what I mean?"

"I think so," he said, nodding.

"Okay," she continued. "Take a million dollars, for example. It is possible to manifest a million dollars quickly, perhaps by winning the lottery or by getting a large inheritance suddenly. But for some, there are actions that are required to obtain a million dollars, like working hard, making wise investments, and saving money. There is no right or wrong time that it takes to manifest something big. There is just the belief that it is possible. And if you truly believe that you are not aging, then time is not so important anymore because you've got an endless amount of time. So what if it takes five years to manifest a million dollars or a world tour."

"I think I know what you're trying to say," he said. "But I'm impatient. I want to be like you and be able to manifest everything I want instantly."

"Well, if you want it bad enough and you believe it with all your heart, you too will be able to do the things that I do someday. Besides, what makes you think you haven't already manifested everything you could possibly want?"

"Well, not to sound totally materialistic, but I've been thinking about abundance, wealth, a huge, sprawling mansion, a Harley Davidson Cosmic Starship, and maybe, just maybe, a 1962 Shelby Cobra 260 CSX2000 or two—to be exact."

Maddie chuckled and rolled her eyes. "That's not materialistic at all. Men and their boy toys."

"Well, when you tell a guy the sky's the limit, that's what you're going to get."

"So what makes you think you haven't manifested those things already?"

Adam wanted to say something sarcastic but decided on, "Well, um, because I don't see any of those things in the near vicinity."

"O ye of little faith."

Adam was perplexed. What the hell was she talking about?

Maddie put her hand to her mouth and appeared to be deep in thought. Then she sat up straight, pointed at him, and said, "I think I know a way that might help you."

"I'm all ears."

"Do you think you could take a week off from work?"

She had piqued his curiosity. "Yeah," he said. "I think I could do that as long as I have my laptop with me."

She was in full planning mode now. "We could leave on a Sunday and return by Friday so you don't miss any of your gigs."

"Sounds good. Where are we going?"

"It's a surprise. Just leave everything to me," she said as she winked at him. "This is so exciting!"

Chapter 35

MADDIE TAPPED HER FINGERS ON her desk as she waited for someone to answer the phone. Once she had her mind set on something, even she could be impatient. She had made sure Adam was showering at his apartment when she made the call so he couldn't hear her conversation. She made up an excuse, saying that she needed some things from her apartment, so she could keep everything a surprise. She knew she might only have a few minutes before he came to see what she was doing. He had been snooping and begging her to tell him what she was planning every chance he got. It had become a sort of game between them. She was determined to keep it all a secret until the last-possible moment.

She heard a click on the line and a familiar voice said, "Hey, Maddie. How are you, chica? How are things with your man, Adam?"

"Hey, Sancha. I'm wonderful! Everything is going so well that I have to pinch myself every day to make sure I'm not dreaming."

"Oh, Maddie, I'm so happy to hear that!"

"How are you and Mel doing?"

"We're fine. We just sold another house and we've been really busy with the closing and all. Business has really picked up lately. It's a buyer's market, you know."

"That's great. I'm glad to hear it. In fact, I think I want you to tell me all about it in person."

"What was that? I think there's something wrong with the line. I thought for a minute that you said you want me to tell you about it in person."

Maddie laughed. "There isn't anything wrong with the line. You heard me right. I think I want to bring Adam to meet you and Mel."

"Oh my god! We would love to meet him. Please come."

"Well, you said you're really busy and I don't want to impose. It can wait until another, less-busy time."

"No! No! We're never too busy for a visit from you. How long has it been? I can't even remember the last time we…" Her voice trailed off.

"I know. It's been too long," said Maddie with a hint of sadness in her voice.

Sancha's voice sounded like she was on the verge of crying, which also made Maddie want to cry. She missed her best friend. They tried not to dwell on the fact that they hardly ever got to see each other in person.

Sancha cleared her throat and said, "So there is no more discussion about it. You and Adam are welcome to come and visit any time that you want to. You know that."

"I know." Maddie hesitated and said, "Do you think it's safe?"

Sancha sighed and said, "I don't have to tell you that there are no guarantees. It's as safe as anywhere you go, I suppose. We've been safe here for several years now. Nobody knows where we are except for the people in the underground. So there's no reason to believe you would be in any danger. The KTP would probably never suspect you would come back to this part of the country anyway."

Maddie tried to keep the sarcasm out of her voice as she said, "Well that's real comforting."

"You know what I'm trying to say, Maddie. I wouldn't tell you to come if I didn't think it was reasonably safe."

"I know. I know."

"We really do want to meet Adam. And I would love to see you again, my friend. I miss you so much."

"I miss you too, and I really want you to meet Adam as well. I also wanted to show him what RTP has done in our lives. He's trying to learn to master it, and he's having trouble believing that he can manifest the 'big things.' "

"So many people have that same problem. It's settled, then. When are you planning to come?"

"Is Sunday too early?"

"No, that's perfect. We'll prepare for your arrival."

"Don't go to any trouble. I know how you can be. Don't knock yourself out cooking a bunch of food and making a big fuss over us coming. Just getting to see you all will be enough."

"You know I love to entertain guests. This is going to be so much fun. I can't wait!"

"Me too!"

"Send me your itinerary with your flight number and arrival time when you get a chance."

"Will do. We'll see you Sunday then!"

"See you Sunday!"

Maddie clicked off and began making all of the flight and rental car arrangements. If she was lucky, she could get it all done before Adam came looking for her.

Chapter 36

MADDIE DEFTLY REMAINED SECRETIVE WHEN she made the arrangements. The only thing she did tell Adam was that they were flying out early Sunday morning, and they were headed to Albuquerque, New Mexico. She had only agreed to tell him the destination so he could look at the weather forecast and pack accordingly. Even when they got the rental car at the Albuquerque airport, she still wouldn't tell him exactly where they were going, so he tried to relax and just go along for the ride.

As they left the airport, Adam admired the New Mexico scenery. It was different than anything he had ever seen—a strange mixture of mountains and high desert, beautiful in its own way. The view of the rolling foothills with the silhouette of the Sandia Mountains was awesome. They were enormous, imposing, and beautiful all at the same time. The strange yucca plants, prickly pear, and saguaro cacti made him feel like they were visiting an alien planet. Adam had never traveled far from the East Coast. This was all very new to him. Maddie explained to him that New Mexico is known as "The Land of Enchantment." Indeed, it was an enchanting and fascinating place.

After they drove for a while, it appeared to Adam that they were heading toward the outskirts of the city. They came to a neighborhood with enormous adobe-looking houses spread out on spacious lots across the foothills. Many had flat roofs, thick, light-tan walls, and rounded entryways to doors and courtyards. The landscapes of various cacti, desert willows, lavender, yarrow, pampas grass, and agave looked foreign to Adam, but somehow seemed perfect, even beautiful, in their environment.

Maddie said, "These homes are built in the Pueblo Revival style, designed to mimic the appearance of the Spanish Colonial West. This architecture style merges home-building concepts from Spain with the local materials and styles of Native American tribes, particularly the Pueblo and Hopi in the Southwest."

"Fascinating. I've only seen houses like these on TV. I didn't think I was a fan of adobe houses, but these homes are beautiful."

It didn't escape Adam's attention that all of the cars in the driveways were Lexus, Mercedes and various other expensive cars. Adam couldn't stand the suspense much longer, but she wouldn't tell him anything, so he just sat back and quietly observed.

Finally, they pulled into a driveway that led to a security gate. Maddie lowered the window and pushed the intercom button. Through the static a voice answered, "How may I help you?"

"It's Maddie and Adam. Please let them know we're here."

The voice on the other end indicated confirmation and the gate opened. As they wound up the driveway, Adam got his first good look at the house. From the outside, aside from being Southwestern-looking, it didn't seem like anything special. It appeared to be about the size of any average, ranch-style home.

Before they could even ring the doorbell, the large, curved timber front door flew open, and a beautiful woman who looked to be around Maddie's age ran out and threw her arms around Maddie's neck so hard that they both almost fell over. She had long, black, straight hair, dark-brown eyes, and the dark complexion of a person of either Italian, Spanish, or Mexican heritage. Adam guessed she might have been of Native American descent. Both women were laughing and crying tears of happiness at the same time.

The woman said, "Maddie! It's been so long. I can't believe you're here."

Through her tears of joy, Maddie said, "I can't believe it either. It's so wonderful to see you again!"

They hugged for a little while longer before turning their attention to Adam. Maddie wiped her eyes, took him by the hand and said, "Sancha, I'd like you to meet Adam."

So the beautiful woman was Sancha, Maddie's best friend. She was the one who had taught Maddie to use Refined Transcendent Power and counseled her, the one she called when she needed advice, the one that she'd known for over a century, the one who had saved her life. Adam instantly liked her.

Sancha gave Adam a warm, welcoming hug and said, "Adam, I am so glad to finally meet you! You know, I put in a good word for you. If it weren't for me, Maddie might not have even given you a chance." She smiled and winked at him.

Maddie shot Sancha a look.

Adam said, "It's nice to meet you too. Thank you for going to bat for me."

Sancha laughed, motioned toward the front door, and said, "Please come in."

As they entered the house, Adam realized that the front entrance didn't give a clue to the grandeur of the home. The adobe vestibule led them across a covered outdoor pathway to the main house and into a grand living room with windows from floor to ceiling that displayed one of the most amazing mountain views Adam had ever seen. He gasped as he stared at the majestic Sandia Mountains framed by the brilliant blue sky.

It was then that Adam realized the majority of the house had cleverly been built into the side of the foothill. It wasn't a single-story, ranch-style house after all. It was a sprawling, luxurious mansion.

He said, "Sancha, your home is beautiful."

"Thank you so much. I'm glad you like it."

"Like it? From what I've seen so far, I love it."

"Would you like a tour?"

"Absolutely," he said.

As they turned to follow Sancha, a tall, stocky man appeared. He looked to be around Sancha's age, maybe a little older, and he was muscular and well-built. He had a look on his face that Adam couldn't read. He got the feeling that this man didn't easily trust people, and one wouldn't want to cross him. Yet there was a softness around his eyes that suggested he could also be kind and caring. He had the same dark hair as Sancha, but cut short, and the same dark eyes and complexion. Adam assumed that he was Mel, Sancha's husband.

`Maddie confirmed this when she ran to him and hugged him tightly. "Mel!"

He easily lifted her off the ground as he hugged her back. "Madeline, it is so good to see you."

He gently put her down and looked at Adam disapprovingly, like the look a father gives a boy who is taking his daughter on a first date. It was a look that said, 'I don't know you and I don't trust you. You better take care of my girl or else.' Adam knew he would need to treat Mel with respect.

Maddie said, "Mel, I want you to meet Adam."

Mel stepped toward Adam, extended his large hand and said, "*Miguel Ángel, a tu servicio*. My friends call me Mel. Nice to meet you, Adam." He did not smile as he gave Adam a hard stare.

Adam looked him in the eyes, shook his hand firmly, and said, "It's nice to meet you too."

Mel squeezed Adam's hand a little too hard. It was only for an instant, but Adam got the message. He felt as if Mel was sizing him up and trying to see into his soul. He was trying to determine Adam's intentions and if he was worthy enough to be with Maddie. Adam had to fight the urge to shrink away from his intense gaze, but he did not look away. He stood firm. He wouldn't let Mel intimidate him.

Sancha interrupted their moment of machismo as she said, "Ahem. Now let's go for that tour."

As they toured the grand house, Maddie said, "This is what RTP can do for you, Adam. You can have anything that you want, anything that you can imagine, and anything that you can dream. If you believe it, you can receive it."

Sancha led them through not just one, but two large living and dining areas while pointing out the Southwestern Pueblo architecture-inspired tile floors, "Vigas," or large cracked wood beams spanning the width of the home across the ceilings, and the many tall, flowing "Kiva" fireplaces, that looked to Adam like clay ovens. They also toured a massive, state-of-the-art kitchen, a theater room, a huge game room, and an exercise room.

All the while Maddie kept glancing at him, smiling knowingly at his look of wonder. He had only seen houses like this one in magazines and on TV. This house could have easily been his dream home. None of the people that he knew could afford or even dream of living in such a place. A house like this seemed so far out of his grasp that he could not even imagine owning it. Hell, he couldn't even imagine visiting a house like this, and yet here he was.

Maddie said, "Sancha, tell Adam how you and Mel came to own this house."

"Simple. It's our dream home. We manifested it."

This blew Adam's mind. He said, "So you guys want me to believe that you manifested this house out of thin air like Maddie manifests corkscrews?"

Sancha laughed. Mel stared at him stoically.

Sancha said, "No, we didn't manifest it instantly. Mel and I are real estate agents. Over the years, we have traded up houses and made some very good real estate investments. We have flipped houses and purchased rental property. We worked hard to get this house. But we always knew we could do it. We never doubted it."

Adam could buy that. It seemed more realistic and achievable.

As the tour continued, they stopped by a wing of the house where Sancha and Mel's children's bedrooms were. The kids had not yet emerged to greet them. Adam wondered if they even knew they were there. The house was so big it wouldn't surprise him if they didn't.

Sancha knocked and opened the door to one of the bedrooms. A boy who looked to be about ten years old was playing a video game. Upon seeing them, he jumped up off his beanbag chair, ran to Maddie, and gave her a bear hug. "Maddie! Maddie!" he squealed with delight.

Maddie's eyes welled up with tears again as she put her hands on his shoulders and held him at arm's length, giving him a look-over.

She said, "Manuel! You've grown so much. I haven't seen you since you were a baby. How did you recognize me?"

"*Mamá* shows us pictures of you all the time so we would know you when we saw you. She tells us stories about you too."

Sancha said, "Mannie, this is Mr. Adam."

Mannie beamed at Adam and said, "Hi, Mr. Adam. I've heard a lot about you too." He smirked.

Sancha exclaimed, "Mannie! Don't be rude."

Adam held out his hand to shake Mannie's and said, "It's nice to meet you."

To Adam's surprise Mannie threw his arms around his waist and hugged him tightly. Adam smiled and patted Mannie's head. "We're going to be good buddies," he said.

"Awesome, dude!" Mannie exclaimed.

"High five."

Mannie released Adam and slapped his extended hand as hard as he could.

"Up high."

Mannie jumped and slapped Adam's hand high above his head.

"Down low."

Mannie went for Adam's hand again and he quickly moved it out of the way before he could hit it.

"Too slow!"

Clearly thrilled, Mannie giggled and said, "Again!"

Sancha interrupted their little game as she said, "Maybe later, Mannie. Maddie and Mr. Adam are probably tired from traveling. I'm sure they need some rest."

Mannie looked disappointed, but he nodded in obedience.

Adam said, "Maybe we can play some video games later or shoot some hoops or something."

Mannie was beaming again. "Sounds good, Mr. Adam. Catch ya later."

Sancha led them a few more doors down the hall. She stopped and knocked on another door.

A young male voice said, "Come in."

As they entered the room, Adam saw a young man who looked to be about age seventeen sitting at a desk, intently staring at a computer. He looked like a younger, thinner version of Mel. There was no doubt whose son he was. The teen looked at them with eyes that looked wise beyond his years. It made Adam wonder exactly how old he really was. Sure, he looked seventeen, but maybe he had already learned to use RTP. Maybe he didn't believe in aging and was much older than seventeen. Maybe even Mannie was older than he looked. Adam knew Sancha and Mel were older than Maddie.

So when did they have their kids?

A thought occurred to Adam. If Sancha and Mel were over a hundred years old and they had a ten-year-old, did that mean Maddie could still have children? And if she could, would she want to? He had always assumed he would have children when he got settled in life. But after hearing Maddie's story he wasn't so sure that would happen. Adam recalled Maddie saying she never wanted children with James and that James didn't want any, either. But would she be open to having children at all? He would ask her later when the time was right.

His thoughts were interrupted when Maddie said, "Luis! You're all grown up."

The boy smiled confidently at Maddie as he stood and hugged her. He was definitely more reserved than his younger brother.

Luis said quietly, "Maddie, it's so good to see you."

To Adam he sounded sincere.

Sancha said, "Adam, I'd like you to meet Luis, our oldest."

Luis looked at Adam for a moment, sizing him up. Then he held out his hand and said, "Nice to meet you, Mr. Adam."

Adam shook his hand firmly and said, "Likewise."

He sat back down and immediately began staring at the computer. That was it. No smile. No conversation. Like father, like son.

Sancha seemed to sense the awkwardness. She said, "Okay then. Let's move on with the tour."

Adam glanced at Maddie to gauge her reaction. She had a sad, distant look in her eyes. He wondered if she was thinking about her own sons. When she realized he was looking at her, she blinked and seemed to snap out of her reverie. She held his gaze for a moment and then looked away. Adam began to wonder if coming back here was such a good idea after all. It was forcing her to remember some very unpleasant moments from her past.

Sancha continued the tour of the house. Next, they walked through a corridor that led to the back base of the foothill and a grassy backyard, complete with beautiful outdoor living spaces, multiple decks, an outdoor kitchen, an outdoor Kiva fireplace, a resort-style swimming pool with a built-in waterfall and swim-up bar, and a pool house that was bigger than Adam's apartment. Adam guessed they could easily entertain at least thirty people comfortably. He would love the opportunity to cook and entertain there. It was luxury at its finest.

The tour ended in the guest wing, where Sancha showed them to their room.

"Why don't the two of you rest for a little while and freshen up. I'm preparing a traditional meal for dinner. I hope you like Mexican food, Adam."

Before Adam could answer, Maddie said wistfully, "I haven't had good Mexican food in so long. Adam, you're going to love it."

Chapter 37

MADDIE WAS RIGHT. ADAM HAD never tasted such delicious Mexican food. Sancha promised to share her recipes with Adam, but he doubted he would be able to duplicate them exactly. He figured she had over a hundred years to practice and perfect them. How could he measure up to that?

The conversation remained light for most of the meal, with Maddie and Sancha doing most of the talking and catching up. They talked about old times, and things that happened before Adam was even born. He listened in wonder. They never mentioned Paul, or Maddie's children, or anything hurtful from the past. Sancha's boys piped in every now and then, especially Mannie. Mel said very little. His silence made Adam feel uncomfortable.

At the end of the meal, Sancha served a dessert wine and flan, a creamy, rich, orange-scented custard with a golden, syrupy topping of caramelized sugar. Adam had never eaten anything like it. It was divine.

He said, "Sancha, Maddie was right. Dinner was delicious. Thank you for sharing your culture with me."

"Thank you. I'm glad you enjoyed it. We're so happy to have you and Maddie as our guests."

"I had no idea where Maddie was bringing me until we arrived. It was a nice surprise."

He looked at Maddie and squeezed her hand. She smiled smugly, proud of herself for pulling it off without him figuring it out.

Sancha said, "So, Adam, Maddie told me that you've been working on learning how to use RTP. How's that going for you?"

Adam thought for a moment as all eyes turned to him.

"Well, okay, I guess. I mean, I have learned to manifest what I call 'small things' and I'm getting pretty good at it. But I'm having trouble with 'big things.' "

Maddie said, "That's one of the main reasons we're here. I mean, aside from visiting you all. I wanted to show Adam the possibilities."

Sancha said, "Just keep working on it and don't give up. Based on what I've heard, you're doing well and learning fast. You seem to be a natural at it."

Adam wished he felt that way about his progress, but it just wasn't happening fast enough for him.

After the boys were excused from the dinner table, the adults went on telling stories about how they had learned to use RTP and taught it to others. Adam listened intently, trying to learn all he could from these amazing people.

At one point, Sancha brought up something about the underground and how they had managed to stay hidden with their secret identities for so many years. Curious, Adam asked, "Are Sancha and Mel your real names?"

It caught Adam by surprise when Mel, who had been relatively silent for most of the night, spoke up and said rather firmly, "Yes, they are. But outside of this household and outside of the secure telecom methods, we do not refer to ourselves by our real names. The only reason we are telling you is because we trust Madeline's judgement about her decision to bring you here."

He gave Adam a warning look. Adam nodded his understanding. Their secrets were safe with him. He would never intentionally do anything that would endanger Maddie or her friends.

Sancha pulled two business cards out of her wallet and handed them to Adam. They looked to be laminated real estate licenses. The names on the cards were Sára and Mateo Gonzales—their aliases.

Sancha said, "We never have our pictures made, and we always send hired agents to meet potential clients and show houses. We take a commission on the sales. We also get a large percent of our income from our many rental properties. We don't take any chances. And we try every way possible to avoid falling into traps set by Paul or his people."

Adam shook his head in disbelief. It was so sad to him that these people had to live in hiding, always having to watch their backs. It made him angry when he thought of Maddie, and Sancha and Mel, and others having to live this way. They were peaceful people, and they were being forced into hiding.

Adam said, "I hope I'm not overstepping, but it's a shame that you all have to live like this. Somebody needs to stand up to The Order. You are entitled to live your lives freely like everyone else, without worrying about being discovered and having to go through all of these measures to hide. It's terrible."

Mel gave Adam a look he couldn't read. Adam hoped he hadn't insulted him.

Mel said, "Of course we have thought about that, Adam. Standing up to the KTP seems to be the obvious answer. But those who have tried to stand up in the past are either dead or part of The Order now."

Maybe that was true, but Adam refused to give up so easily.

He said, "But what if the underground could get organized? If there are enough peaceful practitioners of RTP, maybe as a group we could confront the KTP and reach a peaceful agreement. Sort of a like a treaty. If the KTP won't cooperate, then we declare war."

Maddie, Sancha, and Mel all looked at Adam with wide eyes.

Mel said, "We are a peaceful group of people. We do not use RTP for evil or for killing or for war. That is what prevents us from standing up to the KTP."

Adam figured he was treading on thin ice, and he didn't want to offend his hosts, so he said, "I understand your reasoning. But that doesn't make it any less unjust."

Mel gave a half nod. Adam didn't know if it meant he agreed with him or he was just ending the conversation, so Adam dropped the subject.

When the dinner was over, Maddie said, "I'll help you clean up these dishes, Sancha." They went into the kitchen, leaving Mel and Adam alone at the table.

Thanks a lot, Maddie.

Mel stared at Adam for a long moment, and then he said, "Do you like Mexican beer?"

Surprised, Adam said, "I don't believe I've ever tried one."

Mel stood up and motioned for Adam to follow. He led Adam to the back patio, where there was another Kiva fireplace and a fully stocked refrigerator. Mel pulled two Dos Equis beers out of the fridge, and handed one to Adam. They stood by the fire pit, drinking their beers and enjoying the unique Southwestern sunset in silence.

Mel looked thoughtful as he stared into the fire, then he looked at Adam and said, "Madeline has been hurt a lot in her life."

Adam said, "I'm aware. She told me her story."

"I consider myself to be like a big brother to her. I feel like I need to watch over her, protect her, and look out for her best interests. I want to make sure she doesn't get hurt anymore."

Adam nodded and said, "I understand. I would never hurt Maddie."

Mel gave him a hard look.

"That said, if you ever hurt her I'll kick your ass."

So much for 'peaceful people.'

Starting to get annoyed, Adam slowly emphasized the words, "I understand."

After that, Mel seemed to relax a bit. Maybe the beer was kicking in. Adam looked out at the horizon. He couldn't get enough of the view of the Sandia Mountains off in the distance and the lights of the city of Albuquerque as they lit up the night.

Mel interrupted his thoughts. "You know, Adam, you're right."

Adam turned slowly to look at him, trying to suppress his look of surprise.

"We shouldn't have to live in hiding. It has always been difficult to find the balance between keeping the peace and fighting for our rights. Those of us who have thought about revolting and standing up to The Order realize we cannot do it without fighting and bloodshed. The Order will never back down and resolve this peacefully. So there is no hope for a peaceful outcome."

It surprised Adam that Mel was the one who had brought up the subject again. Based on the dinner conversation, Adam thought Mel was completely against fighting back.

Adam said, "Maybe if enough of us join together, we could do something similar to what the late Dr. Martin Luther King Jr. tried to accomplish with his peace marches. He had strength in numbers, and they protested peacefully without violence."

Mel nodded and looked as if he was considering the idea. Just then, the back door opened and Maddie and Sancha came out to join them. Maddie walked up to Adam, put her arms around his waist, and gave him a quick kiss. The discussion about the KTP was over—for now. But Adam set an intention to broach the subject with Mel again when the opportunity next arose.

They spent the rest of the evening sitting by the fire, talking about good times, and making future plans for getting together. They talked late into the night until Sancha finally said, "We should probably let you guys get some sleep. You've had a long day of traveling."

Chapter 38

MADDIE AND ADAM SPENT TWO days at Sancha and Mel's house. It was a wonderful visit, and it gave Adam some insight into what RTP could do in real people's lives. He got to see for himself that regular people like Sancha and Mel could have whatever they wanted in life if they just believed.

Adam couldn't help thinking about the conversation that he and Mel had that night on the patio by the fire. He felt a stirring for action, but he didn't know what he could do. He was a newcomer, just coming into the ranks of the practitioners of Refined Transcendent Power. Who was he to get involved in their business?

On Tuesday they left Sancha and Mel's for a new destination. It was bittersweet. Maddie was excited to get on to their next destination, but she was sad because she was leaving her best friends. Adam was glad to have met the people who had made such a big impact in Maddie's life. After the initial rough start with Mel, Adam felt like he and Sancha had accepted him.

Their next destination was a secret as well. Again, Maddie wouldn't tell him exactly where they were headed. All he knew was that she insisted on driving again and they were heading to Santa Fe, New Mexico's capital city.

When they arrived in Santa Fe, they drove around sightseeing for a while. Maddie acted as the tour guide. She explained that Santa Fe had been founded as a Spanish colony in 1610 and sits in the Sangre de Cristo foothills. As he was in Albuquerque, Adam was amazed by the heavy influence of the Pueblo-style adobe architecture.

They drove around the historic district's crooked streets looking at the Palace of the Governors, Santa Fe Plaza, the Cathedral Basilica of St. Francis of Assisi, and the San Miguel Chapel. They stopped at Canyon Road, home to a slew of art galleries selling renowned artwork from famed artists and cultural treasures like hand-woven Navajo rugs and Southwestern wood carvings, where they admired the craftsmanship and dined on traditional New Mexico red and green chile enchiladas. Adam found himself falling in love with New Mexico.

Once they had fully exhausted themselves, Maddie excused herself and made a secretive phone call. When she returned, she was ready to head out. Again, she insisted on driving as they headed toward the outskirts of the city. Again, she gave Adam no hints about where they were going.

It was clear that Maddie knew exactly where she was going because she didn't use GPS. About fifteen minutes later they pulled up to a gated community. Maddie retrieved a plastic card from her purse, placed it on the scanner, and the gate slowly opened.

Maddie said, "This is the premier gated golf community in Santa Fe."

Adam was enamored with the views of sunlit meadows and graceful piñon pines under a canopy of clear blue skies with the mountains as a backdrop.

"It's amazing," he said. "I'm assuming someone you know lives here."

"You'll see soon enough."

They drove a little farther until Adam saw a golf course and an adobe sign that displayed the New Mexico sun symbol and the words "The Club at Las Campanas." It seemed so ironic to him to see so much lush green grass there in the high desert.

Maddie said, "Maybe we'll stop there later to check it out."

"That'd be great. Where are we going now?"

"Patience. Patience. We're almost there."

They passed several rather large homes that looked to Adam like pieces of functional art. They melded with the landscape so as to not detract from the natural beauty. He found himself wondering how much it would cost to live in one.

At last, Maddie pulled into a driveway and parked the car. The house looked larger and more contemporary than Sancha and Mel's, but still had some of the same Southwestern characteristics. She sat staring at the house for a few moments. Adam watched her face. She seemed to be deep in thought or remembering. Finally, she blinked a few times and said, "We're here. Let's go inside."

As they approached the immaculately landscaped entryway, a stout, middle-aged, well-dressed man with male-pattern baldness opened the door before they even knocked. He spoke in what Adam thought was a rather formal British accent.

"Madeline. So good to see you. Do come in."

Maddie gave him a loose hug and said, "Ian, it's so good to see you too."

She did seem genuinely glad to see him, but it wasn't as heartfelt as it had been with Sancha and Mel. Adam sensed that she wasn't as close to him since she hadn't mentioned him before.

A woman, who looked to be around the same age as Ian, with severe short, angled brown hair and strong facial features, walked up behind him and said in an equally British accent, "Well, look who we have here. It's so nice to see you, dear." The woman hugged Maddie.

Maddie said, "Adam, I'd like you to meet Ian and Helen."

Adam shook their hands politely and said, "Pleasure to meet you both. Your home is amazing."

Ian and Helen exchanged quizzical looks and then looked at Maddie.

Ian said, "Oh, I assumed you had already told him."

Told me what?

Maddie gave him her best dazzling smile and said, "Adam, this isn't Ian and Helen's house. It's mine."

Chapter 39

A T THAT POINT IN THEIR relationship, Adam didn't think anything Maddie said or did could shock him, but he was genuinely surprised.

Wide-eyed, he said, "Is this where you and James lived?"

Ian and Helen exchanged quizzical glances again.

Maddie shook her head and said, "No. I bought this house after James."

She gave Adam a look that made him think maybe she didn't want him talking about James or Refined Transcendent Power in front of those present.

She continued, "Ian and Helen are the caretakers of my home. They live here full time and take care of the house and grounds."

"We love it here," said Helen. "What a rare treat for Ms. Madeline to join us. Well, let's not just stand here, please do come inside."

Ian and Helen helped them carry in their luggage. Adam's mouth started watering as the smell of meat cooking wafted around him.

"Whatever you're cooking smells delicious," he said.

"Please tell me it's my favorite," said Maddie.

"How'd you guess, dear?" said Helen. "You know we always make stew and dumplings when you visit."

"It's been so long," said Maddie. "I've almost forgotten what it tastes like. Adam, have you ever had it?"

"No, I don't believe I have. I'm game for anything."

"Why don't you two drop off your belongings in the bedroom and get comfortable while dinner is cooking," said Ian. "Perhaps you can meet us in the sitting room for a gin and tonic in a half hour or so."

"Absolutely," said Maddie. "That will give me just enough time to show Adam around."

Ian nodded and said, "Ms. Madeline, you left your car parked out front. Would you mind if I move it into the garage?"

Maddie tilted her head slightly, and said, "No, I don't mind. Why?"

"It's only a precaution. Some new neighbors moved into the house up the street. We did the standard checks and have no reason to believe they are affiliated with the KTP, but I'd rather not draw any attention with an unfamiliar car parked out front."

So Ian and Helen did know about the KTP.

Slightly annoyed, Maddie said, "Ian, why didn't you mention this to me?"

"I didn't want to raise a false alarm and scare you. Like I said, we haven't found any connections to the KTP."

Helen chimed in, "They just moved in a few weeks ago, and sometimes we see them walking past the house. They seem like a pleasant-enough couple just out for their evening walks. We just thought we should be a little cautious about what we let them see."

Ian shot Helen a look that Adam couldn't read. He said, "I'm sorry. With all of the excitement of your arrival, I didn't think to tell you to pull the car into the garage right away."

The conversation made Adam feel uneasy, and he could tell by the look on Maddie's face that she felt the same way.

"I'll get the car," said Adam as he reached for the keys in Maddie's hand.

Ian put his hand on Adam's and said, "Maybe we shouldn't draw any extra attention to ourselves. It wouldn't be a good idea for them to see a stranger pulling the car into the garage. I'll do it."

Maddie knitted her eyebrows but proceeded to hand Ian the keys. She looked a little perturbed that they hadn't told her ahead of time about the neighborhood newcomers.

When Ian walked out of the room, Helen said, "Madeline dear, don't worry. I'm sure Ian is just being paranoid. They're probably just a nice couple."

Maddie snapped, "Well, some members of the KTP can appear to be the nicest people in the world. But then they'll kill you without thinking twice about it."

Helen pursed her lips but didn't say anything.

Adam couldn't help wondering if Ian and Helen were trying to protect Maddie or not. If they were, they weren't doing a very good job of it.

Maddie sighed and said, "Adam would you like a tour of the house?"

"Of course. Can't wait."

Helen said, "I'll check on the stew. You two enjoy your tour."

Maddie thanked her and motioned for Adam to follow her. Her house was larger than Sancha and Mel's. It was definitely more space than a single person would ever need. It looked like a museum, lavishly decorated with paintings, sculptures, and very expensive-looking art and furniture.

Maddie said, "When I used to travel a lot, I collected antiques, artifacts, and all kinds of treasures. I needed a place to display them, so here we are. Just think about it—I used RTP to manifest this house and everything in it."

Adam glanced sideways at her as she quickly added, "I might have gone just a little overboard."

He raised an eyebrow and gave her a sideways grin.

"OK," she said. "I went way overboard. But you get the point. I'm trying to show you the potential of what you can do with RTP in your life."

It was all so unbelievable, but Adam could tell she was really trying to drive her point home. He nodded in understanding. It wasn't that he didn't believe she could do it. He was way past doubting Maddie could do anything. The problem was believing *he* could do it. He had never imagined he would be dating a woman who lived in a mansion. She must've had wealth untold. It seemed like every time he started to feel like he knew Maddie well, she would reveal another secret part of herself. He wondered if her surprises were endless. It made the mystique of her even more appealing.

Chapter 40

MADDIE AND ADAM HELD HANDS as they walked from room to room in her gigantic museum of a house. They toured her billiard room, art room, library, and several of the guest bedrooms. The master bedroom suite was unbelievable. It contained a very large, king-sized, canopy bed with sheer bed curtains flowing around it. The suite also contained a large, lavish bathroom, complete with a full-sized hot tub and a balcony that provided a magnificent view of the mountains. Adam found it ironic that Maddie had amassed so much wealth and luxury, but she couldn't fully enjoy it because she was always on the run.

He said, "Maddie, do you realize how ridiculous it is that you can't live in your own house?"

Her back was to him as she drank in the scenic view. She seemed to freeze for a moment before she turned around to look at him. He thought he saw a hint of sadness in her eyes.

She said, "Yes I do. I haven't been here in ages, and coming back now really drives it home. It really is sad that I can't live in my own house."

He said, "Sancha and Mel managed to do it. Why can't you?"

She looked at him intently and said, "Because I am a primary target."

She paused to let her words sink in and then continued. "The truth is, while Sancha and Mel would be very desirable additions to the KTP, I would be Paul's most prized possession. After my meeting with him in San Francisco, he turned up the heat in the search for me. It was almost like it triggered something in him, and he decided he wanted to force me to join. I don't know if he wants me back as his wife, or if he just wants to possess and rule over me. Whatever the motivation, he has been relentless in tracking me down. So I haven't risked living here for many years."

"What about Ian and Helen? Are they practitioners of RTP?"

"They know about it. They're aware of it, but I don't think they're very strong in it. They seem to have aged since the last time I saw them, which makes me think of James. They know I don't age, but they've never questioned me about it. They've always protected the secret."

"Are you sure about that?"

She gave him a quizzical glance.

He said, "Have there ever been double agents who have infiltrated the underground and reported back to the KTP?"

Maddie said, "I've heard of it happening to others. To my knowledge, it's never happened to me."

He said, "Well, that was a careless mistake, letting you leave the rental car out front if he is unsure of KTP members living nearby."

Maddie looked conflicted. "I know. It did seem kind of odd, didn't it?"

He could tell that she wanted to trust Ian.

"Ian has protected me for many years. He has vowed to protect humanity."

Adam was still doubtful.

"If you haven't been in the house all this time, how would you know? Does he know your whereabouts when you travel?"

"No. But he does know how to get in touch with me if there is ever a problem with the house. He has contacted me on a few rare occasions—like when there was a water leak that caused a lot of damage—to ask me how I wanted to handle it, although I've given them a fund to take care of things like that."

"Just be careful, Maddie. I don't have a good feeling about this."

She stared straight ahead.

Finally she said, "Do you think you could get used to living in a place like this, Adam?"

"Are you kidding? This is my dream home. Twist my arm."

She walked over to him, put her arms around his neck, pressed her body against his, and kissed him tenderly.

She whispered against his lips, "That's why I brought you here. See what a powerful manifestor you are?"

Surprised, he pulled back to look at her.

"Me? What are you talking about?"

"I'm talking about our relationship and this house and everything in it."

"Please don't take this the wrong way, but our relationship started with a chance meeting. And this is your house, Maddie, not mine."

"There's no such thing as a chance meeting. You manifested it with your thoughts and you didn't even know it. And haven't you always dreamed of prosperity and wealth? Well, what's mine is yours. I love you and I want to share everything I have with you. You also manifested all of this."

Adam considered it.

"I think you manifested all of this, Maddie."

She shook her head.

"I tried to leave you, remember?"

"Um, yeah, that one's not easy to forget."

"You brought me back. Your thoughts and feelings were so strong that you manifested me coming back."

"But I didn't consciously think, 'I'm manifesting Maddie back into my life.'"

"Adam, our thoughts become things. What we focus intently on is what we manifest. Whether they are conscious or subconscious thoughts, they become what we experience. And you, my love, are a powerful manifestor."

Before he could answer, she pulled him closer to her and kissed him deeply. Her tongue explored his. His body responded to her immediately. He began to run his hands up under her shirt.

"Ahem," said Helen, appearing in the doorway. "Excuse me, but dinner will be ready soon. Would you care to join us for those gin and tonics?"

Startled, Adam and Maddie released their embrace and stepped apart.

"Thank you, Helen. We'll be right there," said Maddie as she straightened her shirt.

Creepy.

Dinner with Helen and Ian was different than dinner with Sancha and Mel. The conversation was superficial, even after a few gin and tonics. The food was delicious, but Adam was glad when Ian and Helen retreated to their wing of the house. He couldn't put his finger on it, but he just didn't feel comfortable around them.

Maddie said, "There are a few more things I want to show you. Follow me."

She led him down a dimly lit, concrete passageway that didn't fit in with the rest of the house. Adam thought it resembled the entrance to the Bat Cave. At the end of the corridor, there were shelves that contained various types of helmets, boots, and motorcycle gear, and a clothes rack where a few leather jackets were hung.

Light reflected off the large metal door as Maddie opened it. When they stepped inside, Adam got his first glimpse of Maddie's vehicle collection. He froze and covered his open mouth with both hands.

"You've got to be kidding me!" he said. "This is freakin' awesome!"

Maddie laughed and said, "Boys and their toys."

"Look who's talking. You're the one with a garage full of cars and motorcycles."

"They're investments."

"You mean to tell me you don't ever drive any of them?"

She looked down and said, "Um, rarely."

Realizing his blunder, Adam said, "I'm sorry. I wasn't thinking."

"It's okay. Take a look around. Try them out."

"You mean I can touch them?"

"Of course. Check out the interiors, too."

Like a kid in a candy store, Adam wove through the maze of rare Lamborghinis, Ferraris, Porsches, Mercedes, Kawasakis, Ducatis, and Harley Davidsons, pretending to drive each one. He had never seen any of them in real life. He couldn't believe it.

"I wish we could take them for a test drive," said Maddie, "but I don't think it's a good idea at the moment."

Adam got annoyed every time he was reminded that Maddie was not free to live her life out in the open. He wished he could do something about it. As he was thinking, he saw something that caused him to stop in his tracks. There before him was a Harley Davidson Cosmic Starship and, not one but two 1962 260 CSX2000 Shelby Cobras—one red and one blue.

Adam blinked, rubbed both eyes, and blinked again. His mouth fell open again as he covered it with both hands. Those were the exact models he had mentioned to Maddie when she was teaching him how to use RTP.

"Well, what do you think?" said Maddie.

"They're incredible. They're even more amazing than I dreamed they would be."

Maddie motioned for him to try them out.

"Seriously? I don't want to mess them up."

Grinning, she said, "I can fix them if you do."

He gingerly took a seat in the red Shelby Cobra, leaned back, and closed his eyes.

"Do you like them?"

"Like them? I'm in heaven. I love them."

"They're yours then. The motorcycle and both cars."

Adam blinked and looked at Maddie sideways, not sure if he had heard her right.

"Maddie, that's very generous of you, but I can't accept these."

"Why not?"

"They're way too expensive. I can't afford them."

"There's no cost. You manifested them. They are yours."

"I don't mean to seem ungrateful, but I didn't manifest them. They were already here. They've been yours all along."

"Don't you see, Adam? You stated that you wanted them. Do you think it was a coincidence that you just happened to perfectly describe a motorcycle and two cars I already owned? I don't think so. You thought about them, and no matter how they came to you, your thoughts became real things. You manifested them into your life, so therefore, they are yours. I told you that you are a strong manifestor."

"I can't take them, Maddie."

"I insist."

"I can't."

She crossed her arms and said more firmly, "I insist."

They stared at each other for a long moment, then Adam jumped out of the car, picked Maddie up around the waist, and swung her around.

"Have I ever told you how amazing you are, Madeline Smith?"

They both laughed like children as they spun around and around.

Almost falling over from dizziness, Adam steadied them both and pulled Maddie close. He kissed her, gently at first, and then more passionately. She leaned against the car door as she put her arms around his neck and pulled his body closer to hers. Their kissing became more frenzied as their hands explored each other's bodies. Maddie fumbled with Adam's pants button and zipper. Adam paused and looked at her questioningly.

"Here?" he whispered.

She kissed him deeper as her hands slid into his fly and pulled his pants down. He moaned as she touched him, and unfastened her jeans as well. He gently lifted her by the waist until she was straddling him. He carried her to the front of the car, gently lowered her onto the hood, and finished removing her pants. She lay back on the hood and put her legs over his shoulders as he entered her. They both moaned as he lowered and kissed her deeply while their bodies moved together in the rhythmic love dance. Enamored by the house, the motorcycles, the cars, the woman he loved, Adam had never experienced anything so exotic. Hell, he was making love to Maddie on the hood of a classic Shelby Cobra, which he was now the proud owner of. He exploded in ecstasy as he felt Maddie's body convulsing around him. This was a night he would never forget.

He and Maddie spent the rest of the evening in the master bedroom suite making love, relaxing in the hot tub, drinking champagne, and enjoying her luxurious home.

While they were sitting in the hot tub relaxing, Adam said, "I have to ask. What do you do when you're alone and you live in a house with all this space?"

She said, "That's just it, Adam. That's part of the reason I choose not to live here anymore. There was a time in my life when I thought this was what I wanted. When wealth and fortune and power were what motivated me. I wanted the mansions and fancy cars. I thought the material things would make me happy. And they did for a while—at least I thought they did. Then I realized that all these material things cannot make happiness. I would be in my house, surrounded by all of my material possessions, and I would feel so lonely. At times, it was overwhelming to be in here. So I decided to move out. It was actually a relief when I left. But it was also sad because I have so many memories here. This was my life for many years. It's my museum—my shrine to myself. I need to visit every now and then to remember my past life. Just being here a day or two is enough. Then I'm ready to go live in a little apartment in New York City."

She smiled at him and said, "I'm more comfortable there."

Adam tried to understand what she was saying. But at the same time he had never experienced what it was like to have the kind of wealth and power she had manifested. He still wanted a chance to experience those things and come to his own conclusion about whether or not material things could make him happy. He got the feeling Maddie would be open to either way of living as long as they were together, and he certainly hoped they would be. But deep down, he knew he was already beginning to understand what she was talking about. When she had left him, nothing else had mattered. Yes, the material things were icing on the cake, but the most important thing was to have her in his life. However, he decided that for now he would like to try to have his cake and eat it, too.

Chapter 41

MADDIE HAD ORIGINALLY PLANNED FOR them to stay two nights in her house, but the next morning she suddenly changed her mind and was ready to leave. Adam didn't know if it was because of the car-parking incident, or if she was just feeling unsure about Ian, Helen, and the KTP. She said they were going to Los Alamos, New Mexico, so he could see some of the historic sites, ancient ruins, and nature and wildlife areas. He didn't question her reasons for leaving so abruptly. She had been so secretive about the trip, she probably wouldn't tell him anyway. He just let her run the show.

As they were saying good-bye to Ian and Helen, Maddie handed Adam the rental car keys. He thought it was odd because she had always insisted on driving up until now. Again, he felt like it wasn't the time to question her. When they had finished saying their good-byes and it was finally time to back out of the garage, he noticed that Maddie had adjusted her seat as far back as it would go and slumped down out of any passerby's view. It made him feel uneasy. Maybe she really did believe KTP was nearby and watching. He looked at her, concerned.

She shrugged and said, "It doesn't hurt to be cautious."

"Cautious?" he said, furrowing his brow.

"I had a nightmare last night," she said. "You know, one of those dreams so vivid that it seems real? I know this is going to sound crazy, but it just made me feel uneasy about being here."

"What was it about?"

"Never mind. I don't want to speak it into existence. I'm trying to forget about it. Let's just focus on having an amazing time in Los Alamos. You'll love it."

The drive from Santa Fe to Los Alamos was about fifty miles by way of the Turquoise Trail National Scenic Byway along Highway 14. It started at Sandia Crest and went through the mining towns of Golden, Madrid, and Cerrillos. There were some breathtaking views along the way, with long stretches of nothing but desert hills covered with brush and cactus, and the mountains were always majestically looming in the far distance. For several miles there were no trees to be seen, at least not the kinds of trees Adam was accustomed to. Being from the East Coast, he had never seen such wide open spaces, and he still marveled at the unique beauty of the high desert landscape.

They were on a long stretch of road, with hardly any other cars coming or going, when Maddie started to doze off. Adam tuned to his favorite satellite station and sang quietly while Maddie drifted off to sleep.

A little while later, a flash in the rearview mirror caught Adam's eye—what looked like a police car in the distance, approaching rapidly with lights flashing. Their car was the only other car on the road at the moment, and he looked at the speedometer to make sure he wasn't speeding. He was only going about five miles over the speed limit, but slowed down just in case. In a place like New Mexico, with long stretches of highway and nothingness, the temptation to speed seemed inevitable. He figured that if people didn't speed, it would take forever to get anywhere.

He didn't alert Maddie to the police approaching because he was hoping they would just pass him by. There was no reason to wake her up. And besides, if they pulled him over, he figured she would know soon enough. The police car must have been going extremely fast because it caught up to them in no time. When it got close, Adam realized there was not just one, but two police cars—one right behind the other, both with their lights and sirens on. He wondered why they were in such a hurry. Had there been an accident somewhere?

When they got closer, he decided to pull over, even though he really didn't think they were after him. He was just going to give them room to pass. There happened to be a dirt road right off the highway, and he needed to take a leak anyway, so he made a right and drove until he felt he was out of sight. He stopped the car and looked at Maddie. She stirred and said, "Are we there?"

"No, I just have to take a leak. I'll only be a minute."

She adjusted her pillow and tried to go back to sleep.

As quietly as he could, he opened his door and stepped to the back of the car to relieve himself. As he finished zipping his pants, he heard the sound of sirens getting closer. He looked up and was surprised to see the police cruisers had followed him. He could see the New Mexico State Police logo on the front of the lead car. Adam looked back at Maddie through the rear window. Apparently, she had heard the sirens too, because she was looking back at Adam, appearing dazed and confused. Adam returned to the driver's seat.

"What's going on?" said Maddie, rubbing her eyes.

"I was speeding a little, but they were way back there. I don't know how they could have clocked me before I slowed down. And besides, I wasn't going more than five miles over the speed limit."

"That's strange," she said while she rummaged around in the glove compartment to find the registration of the rental car.

They sat in the car and waited for the police to get out of their cars and approach. Adam watched them in the rearview mirror. There were two officers in each car. Two of them got out of the car closest to Adam and approached the driver-side window. He noticed they were in full uniform with side arms. A man in plain clothes got out of the other car and was approaching on the passenger side, which was odd. He had never seen an officer approach on the passenger side like that. But he still didn't think much of it. He just figured that maybe there wasn't much going on that day and this was the only action the officers had to look forward to.

Maddie was still looking in the glove compartment for the information and hadn't seen the officers approaching the car. When she finally glanced up and looked in the passenger side-view mirror, she froze and uttered a single word: "Paul."

In that instant, Adam froze too as his blood ran cold. Maddie frantically tried to lock the door, but as she reached for the lock, the door flung open, and the man grabbed her and began pulling her out of the car.

Adam shouted, "Maddie!" and tried to get a hold of her to keep her from being yanked out of the car.

She was kicking and fighting, but Paul quickly pinned her arms and almost had her out of the car. Adam frantically grabbed for her feet, or anything that he could reach, to stop him, but he couldn't get a good grip. He started to panic. If Paul got her into his car and took off, Adam may never see her again. They would disappear and she would be his hostage—or worse. Adam shuddered at the thought.

In the next instant, Paul put a cloth over her nose and mouth. She suddenly quit fighting him as she lost consciousness and her body went limp. Paul finished jerking her out of the car.

Adam was in full panic mode now. He started to jump out of the car and run after Paul, but the other two men were waiting for him on the driver side. Paul picked Maddie up, cradled her in his arms like a baby, and pulled a concealed weapon from under his shirt. He held the gun to her head as he carried her back to the car, where the driver waited.

Adam didn't know what to do. He was defenseless out in the

middle of nowhere. There were no other witnesses around and Maddie was unconscious. He managed to lock the doors before the other men were able to get his door open, but he knew that they had guns too, and he wouldn't be safe in the car for long. In his panic, he wondered for an instant if he should try to make a run for it, but he would never leave without Maddie.

Then something snapped in him. Just as suddenly as the panic had set in, an instant calmness came over him. He knew without a doubt that he was going to get Maddie back no matter what it took. He waited until the men reached for his door and then flung it open as hard as he could, knocking both of them to the ground. He jumped out of the car and ran toward Paul and Maddie as fast as he could.

Paul was laying Maddie's limp body in the back seat of the other cruiser. The other two men weren't down for long before they were up and running after Adam. One tackled him and brought him down hard, while the other jumped on top of him. They had him pinned to the ground. He tried desperately to fight them off as they began to pummel him. He felt no pain, only concern for Maddie.

He shouted in between blows, "No, Paul! Don't do this. You'll regret it."

Paul ignored him and jumped into the back seat of the cruiser beside the unconscious Maddie. The driver of the cruiser peeled out in the gravel as he spun the car around and took off. If ever there was a time to use Refined Transcendent Power, it was now. Up until now, Adam had only been successful at manifesting small things. He still doubted himself when it came to making things happen instantly. But he knew that if he didn't do something quickly, Paul would get away, leaving him with the other two men, who were intent on killing him, and he would likely never see Maddie again even if he managed to escape.

A sudden rush of anger coursed through his body. He decided

he was not going to let this happen. Still struggling to fight off the men, he focused all of his thoughts, emotions, and energy on stopping the car that was speeding away with Maddie in it. He visualized the car stopping and repeated the same thought in his head over and over, "*Stop that car. The car must stop.*" He felt RTP surge through him.

To his astonishment, the car started skidding out of control. It was almost as if it hit a patch of ice or something, but there was nothing like that out there in the desert. Adam wondered if he had actually done that, or if the driver had just lost control. The car skidded, turned sideways, and flipped over and over several times. It landed so hard that the front driver side of the car was crushed. The driver wasn't moving. A new wave of panic rushed over Adam. Maddie was in that car. What if she was hurt—or worse?

Adam screamed, "Maddie!" as he tried to get to his feet.

The two men jerked him up by his arms and held them behind his back. This was the first time he got a chance to get a good look at them. They both had stunned looks on their faces. One of them he had never seen before, but the other, he realized with a shock, was Ian—Maddie's caretaker. When Ian saw Adam's look of recognition, he looked away.

Adam snarled in his face, "You coldhearted bastard! I will kill you!"

Smirking, Ian said, "Try it."

So, he was a double agent after all, and he had turned Maddie in. Adam struggled to free his arms. He wanted to hurt Ian badly.

The other man looked confused.

He said, "Release him."

Ian stared at the other man for a few moments. Adam jerked his arm free and ran toward the other car to check on Maddie. The two men didn't try to stop him.

As he was approaching the car, he saw Paul climbing out of the shattered window. He didn't see any other movement.

With only concern for Maddie on his mind, Adam shouted, "Is she okay?"

Paul didn't answer. He was walking rapidly toward Adam. It was then that Adam saw that Paul had a gun in his hand. His dark eyes fixed on Adam, wild and dangerous. Adam stopped in his tracks. With about twenty yards between them, Paul pointed the gun directly at his face.

"So you're the new flame in her life?" Paul spat.

The hatred in his voice was unmistakable.

Adam ignored his question and growled, "Is Maddie okay? Let her go now, Paul."

Paul calmly said, "I don't think you're in any position to make demands. I should kill you, but I do find it interesting that you have mastered RTP so quickly."

Adam didn't respond. He was trying to look around Paul at the wrecked car to see if he could spot any sign of Maddie.

Paul looked back at the car then back at Adam with an evil grin. "My sources tell me you've only been learning about Refined Transcendent Power for a few months. Very impressive. She has taught you well."

"Paul don't do this. She doesn't want to join you and she never will."

Paul's grin widened. "Perhaps you're right. But now that you're also a master of RTP, we have something to discuss as well. I was just going to dispose of you out here in the desert, but someone who can master RTP as quickly as you have might be valuable for the KTP. Apparently, you are a natural, and I could train you to do great things. But you've seen too much and you know too much. I'll only give you this choice one time—join the KTP or die."

"Maddie and I will never join the KTP," growled Adam through clenched teeth. "I would rather die than join you."

Paul laughed. "We'll see about that. If you want to save Maddie, you'll join us. That greatly narrows your choices. If you refuse,

I'll kill you, and then I'll have Maddie here defenseless, without anyone to protect her. If you join the KTP, I'll take you and Maddie back to The Order. You'll both be safe."

Adam shook his head and said sarcastically, "Yeah, I'll take your word for it. For some strange reason, I'm finding it really hard to trust you."

Paul feigned being hurt and said, "Oh, so harsh to judge me without even getting to know me."

Adam's anger was starting to boil over. He fought to keep his voice steady as he said, "Like I said, we would rather die than join your Order. I know Maddie feels that way too. So you might as well go ahead and kill me now."

The thought of leaving Maddie defenseless was killing Adam inside, but he knew that what he was saying was true. She would refuse Paul's request, just like she always had, and she would want him to do the same. He tried to think of what Mel and Sancha would do. Would they just stand there, refuse to join, and let Paul kill them? Perhaps, but Adam had already decided he was not going down without a fight. He knew the Keepers of the Peace would disapprove, but he believed it was time somebody stood up to the KTP.

Paul stood there, watching him carefully. Then he said, "My patience is wearing thin. Make your choice. What will it be?"

As Adam faced Paul, Ian and the other man stepped back. Still, they stayed closed enough to attack if Paul gave the command.

Adam repeated coldly, "I already told you my answer. We would rather die than join the KTP."

Paul shrugged nonchalantly and said, "What a shame. Such a waste of talent. Have it your way, then."

He raised the gun and pointed it directly at Adam. Adrenaline flowed throughout Adam's body. His heart beat so hard he thought he was going to have a heart attack. He focused his thoughts on surviving so he could save Maddie. He had to save Maddie.

Adam felt more hatred for Paul than he had ever felt for any other human being. All he could think of at that moment was killing him—to eliminate him. Paul was the obstacle that stood between him and Maddie. Adam focused all of his thoughts and energy on killing Paul.

He thought about being invincible and envisioned it in his mind. And then he watched helplessly as Paul pulled the trigger. After that, everything seemed to be in slow motion. Adam heard the loud bang of the gun as the bullet came racing toward his head. He braced himself for the impact and hoped it would be quick and painless; at the same time his arms reflexively moved in front of his face in a blocking motion.

I am invincible. Paul is going to die.

To everyone's astonishment, the bullet, which was coming directly for Adam's head, looked as if it ricocheted off his blocking arms and flew back toward Paul so quickly that he had no time to react, hitting him right between the eyes. He fell to the ground in a heap, blood pouring out of the gaping exit wound in the back of his head.

Adam stood there stunned for a moment, letting what had just happened sink in. He glanced behind him at the other two men. They were just standing there with shocked looks on their faces and their mouths hanging open. When they noticed him looking at them, their looks turned to fear as they held their hands up in surrender and backed away. Adam took off toward the car to find Maddie. They didn't try to stop him.

When he reached the car, Adam could tell the impact had crushed the front driver side. It was clear that the driver was dead. He frantically scanned the back seat and saw Maddie's still body. He didn't see any visible signs of blood or trauma, but she wasn't moving.

He called through the broken window, "Maddie! Are you okay? Wake up."

She didn't respond.

He yanked the door open and gently shook her leg. She didn't respond. He didn't want to move her too much in case she was injured internally. He gently pushed her hair out of her face and stroked her forehead and cheek.

He whispered in her ear, "Maddie, baby. It's me. Please wake up."

To his great relief, her eyelids fluttered a little and then she opened her eyes.

"Adam? What's going on?" she said weakly. "What happened? Are you okay?"

Relief flooded through him as he said, "Shhh. Don't worry about me. Are you hurt? Can you move? We need to get the hell out of here."

Chapter 42

MADDIE HAD BEEN UNCONSCIOUS DURING the crash, which was probably a blessing in disguise, because she didn't appear to have suffered any major trauma.

Adam said, "Do you feel pain anywhere?"

She thought for a moment and said, "I don't think so. I think I'm okay."

He exhaled the breath that he didn't realize he had been holding.

He kept glancing out the window and looking back at the other two men. They were huddled over Paul's body, checking his pulse and listening to his chest for a heartbeat.

Maddie sat up and started to get out of the car.

"Whoa," he said. "Hold on a minute and let me help you."

She still seemed a little groggy. Whatever Paul had drugged her with was still wearing off. He helped her get out of the car and onto her feet. She looked around, taking in the scene. When she spotted Paul's body on the ground, she gasped and said, "Oh my god! Paul! What happened?"

She ran to where he lay.

"Paul!" she cried. "No!"

She looked at the two men standing over him and asked in a trembling voice, "Is he dead?"

They nodded somberly. To Adam's astonishment, Maddie fell to her knees, put her face on Paul's chest, and began to sob. That was not the reaction he had expected. He was completely shocked. He then remembered when she had told him that she had never loved anyone like Paul. Maybe she still loved him. Maybe she would always love him more than anyone—more than Adam himself. The self-doubt started creeping back in. Adam wondered if he had just killed the man Maddie loved. He didn't know what to do. He just stood there dumbfounded and let her grieve.

After what seemed like an eternity, she turned and looked at Adam, sad and bewildered, and quietly said, "Did you do this?"

He nodded. She closed her eyes and looked away.

"It was self-defense," he said. "He was trying to kill me. He was trying to kill us."

She hung her head. Adam felt a pain in his chest, and he thought he was going to be sick. He fought the urge to vomit.

Ian was standing off to the side, his face a mask as he looked off into the distance. He would not look at Maddie or Adam. Adam figured that Paul must have paid him a huge sum of money to carry this out.

The other man stood there beside Maddie, apparently not knowing what to do either. He looked at Adam and said, "What Paul said is true. You have mastered RTP in a short amount of time. That's very rare."

Was Adam imagining it or did he hear a hint of respect in the man's voice? He didn't know how to respond. Up until that day, Adam didn't think he had mastered anything. It was only when he was faced with a life or death situation that he was able to summon RTP on demand. He decided to keep that to himself. Not knowing how to respond, he simply nodded.

The man nodded twice. Adam wasn't sure what that meant.

The men didn't seem like a threat anymore. Adam took a chance and said, "It doesn't have to be this way, you know."

To Adam's astonishment, the man nodded again and said, "Not everybody in the KTP agrees with Paul's methods. There are some who would like a more peaceful way of life, who don't want to force people to be in the KTP or kill people that won't join. There are some who believe that Refined Transcendent Power should be widespread knowledge used for good, but they are fearful of Paul and will not speak out."

He looked at Paul's body on the ground and said, "Or they *were* fearful of Paul."

Adam said, "There's got to be a way we can work something out between the peaceful ones and the KTP."

The man nodded and said, "There are powerful people in the KTP who would be willing to hear your case. My name is Jeremy. Until just a few moments ago I was second-in-command. We'll discuss this further at a later time."

Maddie looked at Ian and said in a trembling voice, "Ian, how could you?"

Ian stared at her, unapologetic, but said nothing.

Adam moved to stand closer to her. Ian looked away.

She went back to crying over Paul's lifeless body. Again, Adam wondered if he had made a mistake that would damage their relationship forever. He wondered if he should've gone peacefully with them and not fought back. But it was too late now. He couldn't undo it. It was over. Paul was dead.

The three men stood there for a moment, no one having anything to say or making a move. Then Jeremy looked back toward the interstate and the cars passing by in the distance.

He said, "We'd better clean this up before the real law enforcement gets here."

Ian nodded. He walked to the back of one of the cruisers, opened it up, and pulled out a tarp. Adam gently tugged on Maddie's shoulders, trying to get her to let go and stand up. He almost had to pry her hands off Paul's body. Dazed, she reluctantly stood and blinked at Adam through her tears. She buried her face in his chest and continued to cry while Ian and Jeremy rolled Paul's body in a tarp and put him in the trunk of the police cruiser. They then focused on the car that was overturned.

Jeremy raised his hand toward the wrecked police cruiser and the car rose up off the ground, flipped over, and landed upright with a loud thud. Adam had never seen someone use RTP in that way. He was amazed. They gathered up the dead driver's body in the same manner.

Again, Jeremy raised his hand toward the crushed car, and the damaged parts of the car seemed to decompress and magically fix themselves. It was like watching a video of the crash in rewind with the shattered glass rising off the ground and forming back into unbroken windows, and the dents popping out as flecks of paint reapplied themselves.

The blood from Paul's lethal head injury had magically disappeared. In a few short moments, the scene had been transformed to the way it was before anything had happened. There was no evidence left. No one would ever be able to piece together what had happened.

Seeing this happen before his eyes gave Adam a new appreciation about what Maddie, Mel, and Sancha had been trying to tell him about RTP of the KTP and how it could be used for evil and illegal purposes. The KTP could make someone disappear without a trace and without ever being discovered by the police or prosecuted. And they had perfected their methods over centuries. Adam shuddered at the thought.

Without saying another word, Ian got in the driver's seat of one of the police cruisers as Jeremy approached Adam.

He said, "I'd like to arrange a meeting between the peacekeepers and the KTP leadership. I think some of our leaders would be interested in what you have to say. They might even consider a truce now that Paul is no longer in power. Some that were afraid to speak out may be willing to listen and compromise. How can I contact you to set up the meeting?"

Maddie looked at Adam; her eyes seemed to plead for him not to give them any information.

Adam said, "I am only speaking for myself. I'll need some time to speak to the others to see if anyone is even willing to meet and make arrangements. Let me contact you."

Jeremy studied Adam's face for a moment and then reached into the window of the cruiser. He retrieved what looked like a policeman's citation pad and a pen and scribbled something. Then he ripped off the sheet and handed it to Adam. Adam looked at the paper in his hand. Jeremy had written his name and a phone number.

Jeremy said, "You need to act quickly before the KTP has time to process what went down here today. To say that some people will not be too happy about what happened to their leader is an understatement. They may seek swift revenge. I can only hold them off for so long. So you need to contact me quickly, and we need to set up the meeting as soon as possible."

Adam said, "Give me a couple of weeks."

Jeremy looked as if that wouldn't do.

Adam said firmly, "Five days. I'll be in touch."

Jeremy nodded. Then he turned, got into the other police cruiser, and they both sped away.

Maddie and Adam stood there for a moment, not believing what had just transpired. They slowly walked back to their car. Adam held the passenger door open for Maddie. She started to get in, but paused and said, "Wait. Please open the trunk. I need to get something out of my suitcase."

After rummaging through her luggage for a few moments, she retrieved two New York Yankees ball caps and two pairs of aviator sunglasses.

She handed one set to Adam and said, "Here, put these on. I know they're not great disguises, but I had to pack light."

Adam watched as she swiftly arranged her hair into a tight bun on the top of her head, then donned the ball cap and glasses.

Adam never dreamed he'd be in a situation where he would have to wear a disguise. He stared at the ball cap and glasses in his hand and then back at Maddie. She stood with her hands on her hips, impatient. He obediently put them on.

Once he sat in the car, the adrenaline began to subside and the stress of what had just occurred hit him all at once. He was so exhausted, mentally and physically. He just needed to rest.

"Maddie, I'm going straight to the hotel."

She didn't speak. She only looked straight ahead and nodded. They didn't speak at all during the ride. Maddie was looking out the window away from him. From her profile he could see tears streaming down her cheeks. Occasionally, he could hear her quietly whimpering or crying. Adam found himself constantly watching his rearview mirror, wondering if the KTP would be coming for them. Images of the bullet striking Paul in the head, his lifeless body slumping to the ground, and blood soaking the ground where his head lay kept running through his mind. He had killed a man today.

Actually, Adam realized, he had killed two people—Paul and the driver. He had actually used RTP to stop a moving car, ward off a flying bullet, and kill people. Granted, it was self-defense. He was protecting Maddie. Had he not used RTP, they would probably both be dead by now or held prisoner by the KTP. But still, Maddie had taught him, as she had also been taught, to never use RTP for evil.

But was acting in self-defense evil?

He couldn't forget the look on Maddie's face when she had learned it was he who had killed Paul. It was a look of horror, or fear, or a mixture of both. He couldn't tell. It was as if she was seeing Adam in a whole new light. She was seeing him as someone who was capable of using RTP to do bad things.

Was he just like Paul? Did she think he would end up the same way? After all, was what he did that much different than what Paul had done?

Paul had used RTP to get revenge on the people who had killed their children. He used RTP maliciously and violently. He had killed bad people, and the innocent people who were not directly involved with the deaths of their children. But Adam knew that fundamentally he was not like Paul. He was not evil. He hadn't intended to kill anyone.

Or had he, in that moment? Still, did using Refined Transcendent Power to kill people in self-defense make it okay? Was it any less evil than what Paul had done?

Chapter 43

WHEN THEY ARRIVED AT THE hotel in Los Alamos, Maddie insisted they park in the back.

"Stay here," she said. "I'll be right back."

"Wouldn't it be better if you stayed here and I went in?"

"Well, Adam, I think you might have just surpassed me on the list of the KTP's most wanted. You don't need to be seen. This won't take long."

Having no valid argument, he nodded and looked straight ahead out the windshield as she closed the car door. He watched in the rearview mirror as she approached the back door of the hotel and wondered why she didn't have him drop her off at the front. Back doors of hotels were usually locked and only accessible to guests with keys. He saw her attempt to open the door. It didn't budge. She stood with her hand on the handle for a moment, then pulled again. The door opened, and she disappeared inside. He shook his head. He thought he'd never get used to witnessing her mastery of RTP.

While she was inside, Adam's mind started racing again. He couldn't quiet his thoughts. He worried that Maddie was now afraid of him, like she was of Paul. He couldn't deny that when Paul was aiming the gun at him, he was angry and he wanted him to die. He couldn't even say he regretted what he had done because he didn't. Adam was glad the bastard was dead. It was about time Paul got what was coming to him.

So did that make him no different than Paul? Was he the first person to use Refined Transcendent Power to stand up to the KTP? Is that why Ian and Jeremy had let them go without a fight?

Adam had stood up to the bully, and the bully had backed down. They let them go, and now they were willing to negotiate.

Or was it a trap?

Deep in thought, he jumped when Maddie suddenly appeared in the driver's side window. She raised her eyebrows as she opened the door.

"I know. Don't say it," he said. "I need to be more alert now. Let's get our stuff."

When they got to the room, Maddie triple-checked the locks to make sure the door was secure. Then she sat down on the bed and put her head in her hands.

Without looking up she said, "I need to call Mel and Sancha. We need to warn them."

She rubbed her eyes, pulled a cell phone that Adam had never seen out of her purse, and dialed Mel. She relayed the events to them, choking up from time to time, especially when she got to the part about Paul's death. Adam couldn't hear what Mel was saying on the other end. He worried that they might all turn against him. At least Maddie told Mel it was self-defense. She told them that, if he hadn't acted quickly and killed Paul, they would both have been captured or dead.

When Maddie got off the phone, she turned to him and said, "Mel is setting up a meeting with the leaders of the peaceful ones."

Adam was puzzled. "Leaders?" he said. "I didn't know the peaceful ones had leaders. I didn't think they were that well-organized."

She said, "Actually, the peacekeepers are very well organized. We wouldn't have been able to survive this long if we weren't. We formed an emergency plan and a group called 12 Leaders, or 12-L, many years ago just in case a situation like this should occur. Mel, Sancha, myself, and nine others, make up 12-L. 12-L is responsible for getting a warning out to all of the peacekeepers and organizing everybody. We never wanted it to come to this."

She looked down at her hands. Adam wondered if she was disappointed in him. The thought of Maddie being disappointed in him hurt terribly.

Would she rather he had died nobly? That he had let Paul take her?

He tried to put the thought out of his mind for the moment.

A text buzzed on Maddie's burner phone. She read it and said, "They want to meet first thing tomorrow morning. We probably won't be able to make it back home in time for your gig tomorrow night."

Adam was surprised that, in spite of everything that was happening, she was worried about him missing his gig. It made him feel slightly better.

He said, "I'll call Zach and let him know that I probably won't make it. He's had to cover for me a couple of times when I was sick, or had laryngitis, or was in the hospital..."

Maddie winced. He wished he hadn't said that last part. He also knew Zach would not be happy. It was one thing to ask Zach to cover for him when he was sick and truly couldn't help it. But he knew that he could never explain to Zach what had really happened. Adam could just imagine the conversation:

Hey Zach, I won't be able to make it back tomorrow night because I killed two people with my mind and possibly started a war. So tomorrow we've got to meet with the peaceful practitioners of Refined Transcendent Power. You know, 12-L, man.

Yeah, that would not go over well. He would think Adam had dropped some acid or gone crazy and was blowing the band off because he was having too much fun on vacation. Not to mention that Zach was still not Maddie's biggest fan. So instead, Adam would have to lie to his best friend.

Maddie said, "Where are the car keys? I need to run a couple of quick errands while you call Zach."

Adam didn't like the thought of them separating. "I'll go with you."

She shook her head. "The less we're seen together, the better. If they're looking for us, they'll be looking for a couple."

"Where are you going? I don't like the thought of you going out alone."

She sighed. "Adam, now is not the time. You're going to have to trust me on this. I've been doing this for a long time. I know what I'm doing. I'll be back in an hour or so."

With growing frustration, he rubbed his face with both hands. "Fine."

He handed her the car keys. "I really don't like you going out alone. Are you sure you'll be okay?"

"I'll be fine. Be sure to lock all the locks behind me. Don't open the door for anyone. I'll text you when I get back and I'm almost at the door. I'll knock once and say… 'butterfly.' That will be our code word. Do not open the door until you hear me say it."

With that, she turned, unlocked the door, and walked out without saying good-bye. Adam flopped back on the bed and covered his face with his hands. He shook his head in disbelief. His world had gone from stupendous to shit in just a few short hours. He was alone in a city he had never been to and without a method of transportation.

He hated to think it, but he wasn't even sure if Maddie would come back. With the way she was behaving, he didn't know where he stood with her. He didn't know if he felt more like crying or drinking heavily, or both, but none of those were options at the moment. He had to remain calm, strong, and clearheaded. He rubbed his eyes a few more times, then sighed heavily and rolled over to grab his phone.

"I guess I'll get this over with," he said aloud to the empty room.

He called Zach and told him their plans had changed and he wasn't exactly sure when he would be back. Zach reluctantly agreed to cover for him, but Adam could tell he was not pleased. He told Zach that he would make every effort to be back within a week, but he couldn't make any promises. He resisted the urge to blurt out the entire crazy story and ask Zach to come to his rescue. He knew that was not really an option, but he thought it nonetheless. Zach wouldn't believe it anyway. He would think Adam had gone mad.

When was this nightmare going to end?

When Adam got off the phone, he found himself pacing the room, replaying the events in his mind. He looked at his phone every five minutes. When an hour had gone by and he hadn't heard from Maddie, he grew more panicked. Where the hell was she?

He resisted the urge to call her and tried to think positive thoughts.

But even as he tried to force himself to think positively, he found himself doubting she would return.

After another half hour had passed, Adam couldn't resist any longer. As he picked up his phone to call Maddie a text came in: 'I'm back.'

He stopped pacing, closed his eyes, and let out a sigh of relief. A few moments later he heard a single knock on the door.

"Who is it?"

"Butterfly."

He quickly unlatched all of the locks and let her in. She held several shopping bags. Adam grabbed a few to help her in. He caught a whiff of French fries and fast food. He realized that he was starving.

As Maddie walked past him she said, "You should have left the swing latch on and made sure it was me before you opened the door all the way."

No greeting. She was all business. Adam wondered if she was being a tad bit too paranoid, but as she had said, she had been doing this a long time. She was accustomed to this way of life. He was only beginning to understand the full ramifications.

Maddie unpacked several wigs of various hair colors, various styles of hats and sunglasses, a couple of fake mustaches and beards, and bottled water and snacks. She handed him a bag of fast food and a soda then sat down to eat hers. Famished, they quickly devoured their food in silence.

Finally, the stress and exhaustion overcame Maddie and she lay down on the bed. Within moments her eyes were closed and she appeared to be asleep. Adam lay down on the other side of the bed and tried to sleep too. But, exhausted as he was, sleep eluded him. He dozed off a time or two. And when he did, he kept dreaming of a car flipping over and over, the crushed driver, and a bullet whizzing straight toward his head. He kept seeing the look on Paul's face when the bullet struck him between the eyes. He saw Paul's body slumping to the ground and blood pouring out of the wound in his head. He saw Maddie crying over Paul's dead body. And then he saw twelve people seated around a table in a meeting room. They were discussing Adam's fate. Each time he woke up, his heart was pounding and he was drenched in sweat.

Chapter 44

THE NEXT MORNING MADDIE woke Adam before sunrise. All she said was, "Adam, get ready. We've got to leave as soon as possible if we want to get all the way to Albuquerque by 10:00 a.m."

The tension between them was palpable. He hated it. He robotically went through his morning routine of showering, brushing his teeth, and getting dressed as quickly as possible, all the while wondering what the morning's events had in store for them.

As he was getting dressed, she handed him a blond wig with a matching beard and a fedora. She had donned a red, shoulder-length wig with bangs and heavy makeup. To Adam, she was one of those women who could be beautiful with any look. Still, he preferred her natural blond hair and understated makeup.

He tipped the fedora to her and said, "Mornin' Red," in an attempt to lighten the mood.

She smiled a half smile that didn't quite reach her eyes. She was tense. He hated seeing her that way. They quickly packed up their belongings and checked out. When they got to the parking lot, Maddie headed toward a car he didn't recognize. He stopped walking and scanned the parking lot, realizing that he didn't see the rental car anywhere.

"New wheels?"

The car near Maddie chirped as she clicked the remote.

"It's just a precaution. We can't be too careful at this point."

"This doesn't give me a warm fuzzy."

She didn't respond but, instead, looked at him sadly and opened the trunk. They stowed their things and hit the road.

Maddie remained mostly silent on the ride to Albuquerque. So Adam used the time to replay the previous day's events in his mind and to think about the way he wanted the meeting to go. Would his act of self-defense inadvertently open the door for the peacekeepers to take a stand? To his knowledge, he was the first person to defend himself from the KTP in a way that resulted in the deaths of two of their members. The end result was the classic bully effect. The KTP bully had backed down—at least temporarily. As long as the peaceful ones refused to fight, the KTP would continue attacking them. When Adam took down Paul with RTP, the two remaining KTP ceased their attack. Jeremy had even offered to meet and discuss a possible truce between the KTP and the peaceful ones, although it could be a trap. Jeremy was second-in-command under Paul. He could be planning to avenge Paul's death by luring them to meet.

But what if he truly wanted to try to work something out? What if he was telling the truth?

Adam felt like the peaceful ones had to explore this option. They couldn't back down now. They would miss their opportunity, and they would have to go on living their lives in fear and in hiding. And now, add on to that the fear of retaliation from the KTP for killing their leader. So he tried to use RTP to think positive thoughts about the outcome of the meeting. He hoped he could convince them to at least meet with the KTP to plead their case.

Maddie hardly said a word to Adam the whole ride, which worried him because he didn't know how she felt about what he had done. She had told Mel that he had acted in self-defense.

Adam wondered if she was angry with him and, if so, if she could forgive him. It frightened him to think that this might ruin their relationship. But he wasn't ready to push her or ask any questions. He felt like she needed some time to think.

When they arrived in Albuquerque, Adam recognized that they were approaching Sancha and Mel's house. He wondered why they were going back there. They followed the same long driveway to the back of the house. This time, Sancha and Mel were not waiting to greet them. Instead, they parked and let themselves in.

Maddie motioned for him to follow her as she approached an area of the house he had not seen before. They entered a room that looked like a study or a library, with shelves of books lining the walls. Maddie approached a section of shelves and slid a few books to the side, revealing a keypad. She entered a few numbers and then placed her thumb on the biometric reader. Adam heard the sound of a latch unlocking and watched in amazement as she pushed the bookshelf inward like a door. He followed her as she disappeared through the hidden entryway.

When they walked into the room, Maddie removed her sunglasses and wig, so Adam did the same. He saw Mel and Sancha sitting at a large computer console with a young man who looked to be of Asian descent. They looked up and nodded but did not smile. Adam nodded back. The atmosphere in the room felt somber.

They were intently watching a large video teleconference monitor as the young man's fingers raced over the keyboard as if he was taking a typing speed test. There was a phone console in the center of the desk. The large monitor screen was divided into eight equal-sized squares, some with people's images, some filling sporadically as people joined the meeting remotely. Maddie and Adam took seats next to Mel and Sancha. Sancha looked at Maddie with sadness in her eyes, which caused Adam to wonder what Maddie might have disclosed to her.

Adam felt strangely calm in the hidden lair, almost as if he belonged there. Although he did worry they might cast him out since he had used RTP to kill members of the KTP, albeit in self-defense. He tried to keep his thoughts on influencing the outcome of the meeting. He thought about a peaceful agreement between the KTP and the peaceful ones. He thought about the peaceful ones living their lives out in the open—no more hiding, no more fear. It would mean freedom for everyone.

The KTP could benefit too. They might actually get more members if they didn't force people to join and use RTP for evil or corrupt purposes. Jeremy had indicated as much when he told Adam that not all members of the KTP were bad or evil.

When all of the squares on the screen were filled with faces, Mel looked at the computer whiz and said, "Jonathan, is the room secure?"

The young man nodded and said, "Yes, sir. I've checked all of the phone and network lines. All clear."

"It's time," said Mel.

It was clear that he was leading the meeting.

He opened the meeting by saying, "I want to thank you all for joining us today on such short notice. As you know, we wouldn't have called this meeting if we hadn't felt that it was absolutely necessary. A situation has occurred that we hoped would never happen. Now all of our training and planning for such an event will be put to the test. I'd like you all to meet Adam Lancaster, the newest member of our ranks."

Mel motioned toward Adam. Not knowing exactly how to respond, Adam raised his hand and said, "Nice to meet you all."

Several responded similarly. Some sat silently. An elderly man cleared his throat and said, "If he's so new, why is he here? How do we know we can trust him?"

"Maddie has vetted him, Albert," said Mel.

"And so have we," Sancha chimed in.

Albert's eyes narrowed, but he seemed to be placated.

Mel continued, "For those of you who may not have heard, Maddie and Adam were attacked by the KTP yesterday, which resulted in two KTP members being killed. One was Paul, who as we all know was the leader of the KTP."

There were audible gasps and murmurs, and some very alarmed and shocked looks on people's faces. Maddie kept her gaze on Mel, her face a mask concealing her thoughts.

Mel raised his hands to restore order and said, "I want to make it clear to you that the KTP attacked first. Paul disabled Maddie by rendering her unconscious with what appeared to be chloroform. He attempted to carry her away while two other men attacked Adam. So, as I understand the story, it was in self-defense that Adam used RTP against the KTP to save Maddie and himself. Correct me if I'm wrong, Adam."

All heads turned to look at Adam. He saw expressions ranging from shock, to fear, to amazement, to disdain. Adam nodded his agreement.

Mel continued, "Adam used RTP to stop the car from racing away with Maddie in it. In the process, the car flipped and crashed, killing the driver. Maddie and Paul were in the back seat of the car when it crashed, and they were unharmed, although Maddie was unconscious. Paul climbed out of the car and, impressed by Adam's ability to quickly master RTP, he proceeded to invite Adam to join the KTP. When Adam refused, Paul pulled a gun and shot at him. Adam used RTP to block the bullet which ricocheted and found its mark by hitting Paul in the head, killing him instantly. So, in a sense, Paul shot himself with his own gun."

There were more gasps and murmurs. Adam swallowed hard. It was tough for him to hear the story told out loud. It made it seem more incredible. He knew that the events had actually occurred, but he still secretly wished that it was all a bad dream from which he would wake up soon.

"Order," Mel commanded.

Everyone went silent. All eyes were still on Adam. He wondered if he should say something. Just when the silence began to get unbearable the elderly man that Mel had called Albert spoke.

"Do you have any idea what you have done by killing the leader of the KTP? This is extremely bad. They will retaliate."

Mel raised his hand and said, "Don't jump to conclusions so quickly. The strangest thing occurred yesterday after Paul died. Instead of immediately retaliating, the other two armed men backed off and released Maddie and Adam. In fact, they had a civil conversation. One of the men claimed to be Jeremy, the KTP's second-in-command. Adam, please tell us what Jeremy had to say."

Adam wasn't expecting Mel to call on him. He was glad to be offered a chance to speak for himself. This was his opportunity to plead his case, the same case he had spoken about to Mel about on the night they met. He had a feeling Mel knew what he was about to say. He gave Adam an encouraging look.

Adam sat up straighter in his chair, cleared his voice, and began. "We didn't realize that Jeremy was the second-in-command until he identified himself. He was paired with Maddie's former caretaker, Ian, whom we recognized right away. From the comments Paul and Jeremy made, I'm convinced that they had been spying on Maddie for some time. They knew Maddie was training me to use RTP, but they were surprised when they saw what I was capable of in person. Hell, I didn't even know what I was capable of until I was put under the pressure of a life-or-death situation. No one was more surprised than I was.

"I told them that things didn't have to be the way they were between the KTP and those who want peace. Jeremy agreed. He told me there are also other people in the KTP who agree with me and are willing to talk about a compromise or truce.

"He also stated that many of the KTP members were afraid of Paul and would never have spoken out against him while he was in charge. Jeremy seemed to show no remorse that Paul was dead. He's in favor of meeting with you all to discuss a peace treaty. However, he did stress that we need to move on it quickly because he also fears that the hostile members of the KTP will try to retaliate soon. He doesn't know how long he can hold them off. He wants to meet within the week."

At this, people began shifting in their seats and murmuring.

A plump, middle-aged woman with tight, black curls and the name 'Wyndolyn' displayed at the bottom of her screen, spoke up.

"It's probably a trap. They want to get us together so they can kill us all at the same time. They don't have any mercy. I've never known a KTP member to be peaceful. It doesn't seem right."

Many people nodded their heads in agreement.

Adam said, "I agree it could be a trick. No one can know for sure. But I saw the look on Jeremy's face. He seemed sincere. And the fact that he backed off and didn't try to harm us makes me believe him even more. My gut feeling is that he is telling the truth. He let us go peacefully. Have you ever heard of that happening?"

The woman stared at Adam in disbelief. Several people shook their heads. It seemed as if some of them were beginning to believe it too. Mel nodded for Adam to continue.

"I believe that a bully effect has been going on for all these years," said Adam. "The peaceful ones have always backed down when confronted by the KTP. Maddie and I witnessed firsthand that, if you stand up to the KTP, they will back down. This might be our chance to form an alliance, not just for the twelve of you, but for all of the peaceful ones.

"If we show up in force, like Martin Luther King Junior's marches of peaceful resistance, at a time when the KTP is weakened from the death of their leader, I believe they will back down and listen to our pleas for peace.

"It will take them some time to mourn the loss of their leader and regroup. This might be the perfect opportunity for you all to be able to live in freedom—freedom from the oppression, freedom from having to hide and live under aliases, and freedom from having to wonder every day if and when the KTP will find you and enslave you or, even worse, kill you.

Maybe this is your chance to change things for the better so that you don't have to live like this. And although you've managed to do it well for so many years, you can't experience life to the fullest unless you are completely free."

Adam searched the group's faces to see if he was getting through to anyone. Some people looked down at their hands. Some had tears in their eyes. Some looked like they might be agreeing with him. Still others looked angry.

"It is against our beliefs to use Refined Transcendent Power for evil things," chimed in a hulk of a man who was built like a professional wrestler. "It can only be used for good."

Adam said, "Do you believe that a person who defends himself from evil is evil? Do you think that I am evil because I defended Maddie and myself and got us out of there alive? Yes, RTP was used to kill, but it was in self-defense. If people are killed in war, are the people who killed them evil? Or are they just defending their country, or their property, or their lives? If someone breaks into your house with the intent to harm you and your family, and you kill them, does that make you evil?"

Several people shook their heads.

"I'm not suggesting that we attack the KTP and try to kill them. I'm suggesting that we come out in full force and confront them and demand a peaceful agreement. We show them that we are not going to back down. We stand up to the bully. If they won't back down and we have to defend ourselves, then so be it."

A sinewy woman with short, spiky, rainbow-colored hair and several tattoos and piercings spoke.

"Isn't the act of demanding a peaceful agreement in itself provoking them?"

Adam was surprised when Mel spoke in his defense and said,

"Roxy, they've already been provoked—inadvertently—by Adam killing their leader. They are waiting on us to make a move now. I think Adam has a good point here. Maybe we have been doing it wrong all these years by allowing them to have power over us. They only have power over us because we let them. I don't think we should take it anymore. We should prepare to defend ourselves against them in mass numbers. We have more power than we think, and more power than they think."

A slender black woman said, "Their numbers are great. They probably have thousands among their ranks."

She looked so young that Adam guessed she couldn't have been a day over eighteen.

Mel gave a sly smile and said, "Think about it, Shannel. Worldwide, our numbers are greater. If we call all of the peaceful ones to action, we could have many more on our side."

Chapter 45

MEL HAD EVERYONE'S RAPT ATTENTION when he said, "I agree with Adam. This might be our opportunity to finally stand up to the people who have oppressed us for so many years."

Adam couldn't believe Mel was actually agreeing with him. He recalled the night when he had confided in Mel his thoughts about standing up for the peaceful ones. On that night, based on Mel's reaction, Adam had believed that Mel disagreed with him and was offended. He couldn't read Mel's reaction then. He wondered if Mel had changed his mind or if he had secretly agreed all along. Mel loved Maddie like a sister, and Adam knew he was deeply concerned about her coming so close to being the KTP's latest victim.

Maybe that was what finally changed his mind.

A middle-aged man with smooth brown skin, glasses, and a beard interjected. "But if we decide to take a stand, it could mean bloodshed. Are we all willing to use RTP to hurt or kill others in the name of self-defense?"

Without hesitation, Mel said, "I, for one, am willing to do just that, Tarek. We will not provoke or initiate violence. I propose that we meet with the KTP in hopes of a peaceful agreement. But we must be prepared to defend ourselves if necessary. This may be our best opportunity to free ourselves. We can no longer allow the KTP to oppress us. We've let this drag on for far too long, and we need to stand up for ourselves.

"If Adam had not acted yesterday, he and Madeline would be dead or KTP prisoners. If the KTP had imprisoned them or killed them, would we just keep our heads in the sand and not act? That would be the wrong thing to do. We can't wait any longer. Now is the time to act."

For the first time, Maddie spoke up and said, "Mel's right. We can gather our numbers and demand a peaceful resolution. Maybe, if enough of us stand up, we can reason with those in the KTP who have longed to change The Order but who have never had the courage to do so. They've been just like us all along, afraid to stand up for themselves. Adam said Jeremy wants to meet within the next week. We need to act before they have time to regroup and let their anger settle in."

Roxy said, "What if we meet with the KTP and it's a trap? What if we all end up being killed? Are we ready to ask thousands of people to possibly give their lives?"

Mel said, "We can only trust in RTP. We have to manifest positive results. We have all been taught that a single positive thought can outweigh a negative thought a thousand times over. And if thousands of people are thinking positive thoughts, there is no way the negative thoughts of the KTP could prevail. We have to believe without a doubt that there will be a positive outcome. Have we forgotten what we know about RTP? We can use it to achieve the desired outcome."

There was silence for a moment. Adam thought that Mel was getting through to them.

The hulk spoke up. "You have a point, Mel. It is fear that holds us back. So far, no one has been willing to give their lives for this cause."

Mel said, "Roman, have you forgotten that some have already

given their lives—the ones who were captured by the KTP? They were given the choice to join or to die, and many chose to die. They were martyred for the cause."

Roman clenched his jaw, narrowed his eyes, and said, "Of course I haven't forgotten."

Adam decided he would not want to be on the receiving end of Roman's wrath.

Mel said, "Adam surprised the KTP by being the first to defend himself against them. They probably think he acted as a lone wolf and not with the consent of the group. So if we did meet with the KTP, they would not expect us to defend ourselves. We can plan this to our advantage. I believe we can do this. This is a golden opportunity we may never get again. I am ready to act upon it now. Who will join me?"

To Adam's surprise, Maddie stood up immediately and said, "I will join you, Mel."

Sancha and Adam stood up, almost at the same time, and said simultaneously, "I will join you."

There was silence for a few moments, then slowly, Jonathan stood. On the monitor Roxy stood, followed by Roman and Shannel. Soon, others followed and stood. When it was all said and done and the final vote was cast, ten of the twelve council members agreed to take a stand. Two people, who hadn't spoken so far, declined. The majority was in favor of meeting with the KTP.

Mel handed Adam a cell phone and said, "Use this burner phone to contact Jeremy. It will only be used for this one phone call, and then it will be destroyed. Tell Jeremy we will meet with them five days from now at the Hummingbird Ranch in the Sangre de Cristo Mountains at 10:00 a.m. It's a holistic and spiritual place where people go to find spiritual enlightenment, an ideal place for a peaceful meeting. We know the owners and will reserve the place for a private event."

With everyone watching, Adam entered the number Jeremy

had written on the citation form and hoped and prayed it was a valid number. It rang and rang. Just when Adam thought no one was going to answer, he heard a male voice say curtly, "Jeremy speaking."

Adam mustered up as much authority in his voice as he could and said, "It's me. The one you've been waiting to hear from."

Jeremy was silent for a moment and then, without any pleasantries, said, "Were you able to arrange the meeting?"

"We want a peaceful meeting, Jeremy."

"And so do I."

"No tricks. No violence. Those are our terms."

"Understood. You have my word."

Adam gave him the meeting information Mel had instructed him to provide.

"I would prefer to meet at the KTP headquarters," said Jeremy.

"Hummingbird Ranch is a neutral location," retorted Adam. "We meet there, or we don't meet at all."

Jeremy was silent for a moment, considering. Adam held his breath.

"Fine. We'll be there."

Adam silently released his breath and gave Mel and the others a thumbs up. Without saying another word, Jeremy clicked off.

Adam laid the phone on the table. Mel touched it and, to Adam's amazement, the phone shattered into a thousand tiny pieces that dissolved into nothingness when they hit the ground. Mel's eyes met his again, and he said, "No one will ever be able to trace that call."

Still amazed, Adam nodded. Mel addressed everyone else at the meeting.

"We now have exactly five days to use RTP to summon all of the peaceful practitioners from around the world. Leave no one out. We will need everyone we can get—masters, apprentices, and even newbies like Adam. Use every method available to us—our thoughts, secure phone and email messages, secure websites, and blogs, social media, and any other method that proves useful. Just be extremely careful. The KTP may be anticipating this and may try to intercept messages and obtain our locations. They're just like the FBI in many ways. They have all the latest spying and tracking technology. We need as many peaceful practitioners of RTP as possible to stand with us. With all of the peaceful practitioners together in one location using their collective thoughts to control the outcome of the meeting, it can only be as we *think* it will be.

"I look forward to peace and freedom. I look forward to being able to live in this world without fear, without having to hide who we are and what we know, without having to keep RTP a secret from others who could benefit from it. For the next five days, until the meeting, summon as many people as you can. Focus your positive thoughts on the outcome of the meeting. Meditate on it as often as you can."

One of the people who had voted against the meeting—a woman with fiery-red hair, ivory skin, and striking green eyes—said, "I'm sorry Mel, but I can't join you on this. I can't put my family in jeopardy."

The other person who had voted against the meeting—a man who looked so similar to the red-headed woman that Adam thought they must be related—looked conflicted. He muttered, "I agree with Caragh. I'm sorry, too."

Mel said, "Callum and Caragh, no pressure. It's a lot to ask of anyone. You both have young children to consider. We will still consider you both trusted members of our council." They solemnly nodded their understanding, then their monitors went blank as they signed off.

Everyone remaining sat in silence until Mel finally said, "I won't keep you any longer. We will reconvene and begin our planning sessions soon. I thank you for taking the time to meet with us on such short notice. I wish you all health and happiness."

As the meeting adjourned, some people signed off immediately, while others remained connected. Some asked Maddie and Adam further questions about the events that occurred, particularly Adam since Maddie had been unconscious for most of the ordeal.

Adam noticed that Sancha took Maddie aside, hugged her, and comforted her. He was glad Sancha was there for her.

Mel shook Adam's hand and said, "Thank you for giving us this opportunity. We should have taken a stand a long time ago."

Not knowing what to say, Adam nodded. Even though he knew deep down that it was the right thing to do, he still didn't know exactly how he felt about the whole situation. It was getting to be a bit too much for him—too heavy of a burden on his shoulders. He was still wrestling with his conscience about killing two people. The authorities would never know. There would never be a trial. He would never pay any penalty in the American legal system, but he was now probably the KTP's most-wanted fugitive, and he imagined that the justice they would serve would be far worse than any he would encounter in the normal legal system. He feared his life would be in danger if the meeting didn't go well with the KTP. He wondered if his relationship with Maddie could withstand this trial if it all went down wrong. He wondered if everyone would be forced to go even further into the underground and it would be his fault. He would have to leave his life as he knew it—the band, his friends, and even his family. They wouldn't even know what happened to him. He would simply disappear, leaving them to mourn and wonder if he was alive or dead.

Then he thought about Maddie's life and all she had been through. She had lived a life of lies and fake identities for over a hundred years. It made his heart ache for her. It also made him very angry at the KTP and Paul, who had once loved her and had probably still loved her in some strange and twisted way. Adam was angry that Paul had done this to her and all of the others. He had taken care of Paul, but it also made him want to lash out at the KTP. He was conflicted. He wanted to join the peaceful ones and be a practitioner of Refined Transcendent Power so that he and Maddie could be together forever—eternally young, eternally happy. But he couldn't guarantee that future for them as long as the KTP existed and was still a threat. They would never be able to live their lives freely. It made him realize, even more so, that facing the KTP was the right thing to do.

Adam also knew that facing the KTP was dangerous, and there was a good probability that they would all be killed if the meeting went badly. With so many thoughts going through his head, he was really starting to feel stressed. He and Maddie hadn't been able to talk about how they both felt about the situation. He recalled when she told him the story of her sons being killed. The trauma had caused her to enter into her own little, mental world unable to function for months. Adam feared that the current events might do the same damage to her, and that it might be months before their relationship could be repaired. He feared that she was angry at him for killing Paul. He feared that she hated him. They hadn't kissed or been intimate, or even held hands, since the incident occurred. He feared that she was just tolerating him long enough to meet with the KTP. She hadn't told him to go to hell and leave, but she hadn't been affectionate either. He didn't know what to make of it. It hurt him to think they might not ever be the same again, because he loved her with all his heart. His life would not be worth living if she wasn't a part of it. So he decided that if she told him she didn't love him anymore, he would fight to the death if the meeting with the KTP went south. He hoped that, by fighting for freedom, eventually his death would give her a better life.

Suddenly, Adam became aware that his thoughts were those of fear and doubt. He reminded himself that he needed to get the negative thoughts out of his mind and only think positively. He told himself that she was just having a hard time dealing with Paul's death. Maddie had loved Paul. She bore his children—even though he turned out to be a monster. Adam could see why she might still care for him, if only somewhere in the recesses of her heart. She was probably also afraid of what the future held for her and Adam. Knowing her, she was more fearful for the lives of the ones she loved than for her own life. Adam knew they needed to talk, but he didn't know when the time would be right. So until then, he continued to give her space.

Sancha and Mel invited Maddie and Adam to stay at their house until the meeting was over, but they decided it would be best for all of them if they split up. If the KTP decided to go ahead and seek revenge, it would be better to be spread out in different locations. Maddie and Adam booked a suite across town. When they got to the hotel, Maddie was still not talking to him. She immediately started making phone calls and telling people about the upcoming meeting. Adam didn't know any practitioners of Refined Transcendent Power other than the ones Maddie had introduced him to, so he didn't have any phone calls to make. Instead, he got online, using the secure laptop and VPN connection that Jonathan had provided him, and started searching some secure websites that Maddie had given him for possible ways to contact people. He tried to think of positive thoughts of thousands of people from all over the world attending the meeting. He imagined people of all races, ages, and beliefs with one thing in common—they were all peaceful practitioners.

Maddie asked each person that she contacted to spread the word and ask their friends to do the same. Adam found a few interesting hits on the internet. He had never Google searched for "Refined Transcendent Power" before, but he actually found some groups, chats, and blogs that could possibly be visited by practitioners of RTP. He posted anonymous messages just in case KTP hackers were watching. If the KTP hackers did happen to intercept the communications, by the time they could figure out his location, he and Maddie would have already moved on. Worst-case scenario, he could leave the laptop in the hotel if they needed to leave in a hurry. That would throw them off for a little while. They continued trying to reach people for most of the day until they were both exhausted.

Adam found his thoughts wandering frequently. He couldn't clear his mind. He wondered if he would ever see the band members or his family again and what they would do without him if he got killed or had to go into hiding.

Chapter 46

ADAM TRIED TO REFOCUS ON thoughts of summoning all of the peaceful practitioners to the meeting. But try as he might, his thoughts would drift back to thinking about the implications of the upcoming meeting with the KTP. He thought of the possible outcomes: One, they would all end up in a battle and die; two, they would reach a peaceful resolution with the KTP that would free the peaceful practitioners; or three, they would all end up having to go back into hiding for the rest of their lives, with Adam being a wanted man for killing their leader.

He rubbed his face and eyes. He had to believe that he had already received the outcome he wanted and show sincere gratitude for it. He and Maddie were so intent on contacting the others that they didn't notice how quickly the day went by. They didn't even stop to eat. Adam didn't as much as glance at the clock until his stomach started grumbling and his eyes grew heavy. By the time he realized how hungry and sleepy he was, he didn't know which he wanted to do first—sleep or eat. He decided they should eat to keep their strength up. Neither one of them had eaten much in the past few days. Since they were still in their disguises, he took the liberty of ordering room service.

The food arrived but remained untouched, as neither one of

them wanted to stop what they were doing. Maddie continued calling, texting, and e-mailing. He continued searching the internet for possible leads and ways to alert others without alerting the KTP of their plans. Around midnight, when they were both finally exhausted, Maddie stopped what she was doing and lay down on the bed. She rolled on her side and stared at Adam. Feeling the weight of her stare on his back, he turned to look at her. It was the first time in several days she had actually stopped to look at him.

Although she smiled, her eyes betrayed her sadness as she said, "Adam, will you please hold me?"

Surprised, Adam returned her stare. He was so glad to hear her say those words. She didn't hate him. She needed him to comfort her. He lay down behind her and wrapped his arms around her, spooning her back to his chest. She turned her head to look at his face, her eyes searching his.

"I can't stand the silence any longer. I know you probably hate me, but I haven't had a chance to thank you for saving my life," she said softly.

Once again she surprised Adam. He didn't know how to respond. Was that how she saw it? That he hated her? He started to say something, but she cut him off.

"Please, let me finish," she said. "I truly believe that if you hadn't done what you did, we would both be dead right now. And I'm sorry if I haven't been coping well with this whole situation. I never dreamed our vacation to visit friends would turn out this way. I'm so sorry that I dragged you along and put you in danger—yet again."

It was then that the realization hit him. She had not been quiet and aloof for the last few days because she was angry at him or because she didn't love him anymore. She was, once again, blaming herself and feeling guilty for putting *him* in danger. She thought he was mad at her. She believed that she was the one who put him at risk, not the other way around. He almost laughed aloud at the irony of the situation. He released a sigh of relief.

Apparently, all this time, she had been beating herself up inside, worrying that she was putting Adam at risk and feeling guilty about it. He should have known. That was why she had left him after the avalanche. She had said she couldn't live with herself if something had happened to him. How could he have been so foolish?

He pulled her closer to him and said, "You don't know how relieved I am to hear you say those words."

She looked puzzled as if that was the craziest thing she had ever heard.

"You don't hate me?" she said.

"I thought you were angry at me for killing Paul and the other man."

She furrowed her brow.

"Angry at you for saving my life and for acting in self-defense? I could never be angry at you for that."

"Well," he said, "I could never be angry at you for bringing me here and introducing me to your wonderful friends. I love you, Maddie, and I'd rather die than for us to be apart."

Relief flooded her face as she said, "I love you too, Adam. And I will be putting you in danger once again at the meeting next week."

He winced and said, "You can't blame yourself for that one. I was the one who opened my big mouth and told them my ideas about meeting. So I could turn it around and say that I'm putting you at risk."

She smiled and even giggled a little. It was such a relief to hear her laughter and to see her smile a genuine smile for the first time in days. He pulled her closer. She rolled over to face him, hugged him tightly, and wrapped her legs around him. She pulled back and looked at him, her eyes searching his.

"You actually thought I was mad at you?"

"I couldn't help but wonder. You told me you loved Paul like you had never loved anyone before. I thought maybe you still loved him, and that you hated me for killing him."

Her eyes grew wide. "How could you believe that? When I said I loved Paul more than I had ever loved anyone before, I meant over a century ago. It was true then, and it is true at some basic level now. I do love him—well, did love him—but only in the way I would love a family member or a longtime friend. I haven't had any romantic feelings for him in as long as I can remember. I only love one person, and that person is you. I can truly say I have never loved anyone more than I love you, Adam."

Everything was right in the world again. Forget worrying about the outcome of the meeting. That was all Adam needed to hear to keep going. He would learn to deal with the guilt for taking the lives of two people. It would all be okay as long as he and Maddie had each other. Now that he knew the truth, he would face anything to protect the love between them. He became even more determined to summon a positive, peaceful result for the meeting.

He hugged her tightly and kissed her gently. They kissed for several moments, gently at first, and then the familiar passion overtook them. When he was with Maddie, Adam could be fully in the moment. He could believe that everything was going to be okay.

They clung to each other for the rest of the night, sleeping peacefully for the first time in days. Adam only woke up a couple of times with the hauntingly familiar nightmares. But this time Maddie was by his side in his dreams. We he awoke, he no longer had a feeling of dread.

Chapter 47

T HE NEXT DAY, ADAM, MADDIE, and what was now the 10-L, met in the secret lair to review the objectives and strategize. Everyone knew the main objective was to come to a peaceful agreement with the KTP. But they also knew they had to be prepared in case the meeting turned out to be a trap and took a violent turn. They all agreed that they would do everything in their power to avoid physical violence, but they also had to be prepared to defend themselves. If they did end up having to fight, it would not be because the peaceful ones provoked it.

As they were concluding the meeting, an incoming connection request from "Fire and Ice" appeared on the monitor. Mel looked surprised, as did everyone else in the room. Jonathan accepted the connection request.

A square on the monitor lit up with the faces of the two council members who had declined to join them—Caragh and Callum.

Callum said, "We've prayed and put much thought into your proposal. And, although we were fearful in the beginning, we've since realized that it is the right thing to do. We want to join you in the peaceful protest."

Caragh nodded her agreement.

Roxy said, "Yes!" and started clapping. Others followed suit. Everyone was smiling. This gave them even more confidence. They had a unanimous agreement. Mel quickly filled the two newcomers in on the plans and they all adjourned.

Chapter 48

THE HUMMINGBIRD RANCH WAS LOCATED in the Sangre de Cristo Mountains of northern New Mexico on almost 500 acres of lush land, high forested valleys, and meadows surrounded by trees, shrubs, and various other forms of vegetation. There was a large horse pavilion, and behind it, acres of grassy meadows with room enough for the number of people that they were expecting. The venue had been reserved for the private event with guards stationed at the entrances to ensure no access to the general public.

Adam's nerves were surprisingly calm on the morning of the meeting with the KTP. He had done all of the mental preparation possible, and he knew without a doubt that the outcome of the meeting would be a good one. They were as ready as they were ever going to be.

When Maddie and Adam arrived at the expansive gravel and dirt parking lot, they were encouraged to see that there were already a lot of vehicles. Adam hoped that many of them belonged to peacekeepers. They walked hand in hand toward the grassy meadow, looking for familiar faces.

Already, there were people everywhere, from all walks of life, all cultures, and all ages. It made Adam think of images he had seen of the 1969 Woodstock festival, with an estimated 400,000 spectators, and what he imagined it would have been like to attend. Although there weren't nearly that many people here yet, he hoped there would be—at least on the peacekeepers' side.

Since they had never seen many of the people they were expecting, the peacekeepers devised a way to distinguish between friend and foe. The 12-L decided that the signal would be a Namaste greeting with a slight bow and hands pressed together, palms touching and fingers pointing upward, thumbs close to the chest. Adam and Maddie followed a trail of people giving Namaste greetings until they saw a small group of familiar faces gathered around Mel on one end of the meadow. Across the meadow Adam noticed that the KTP had begun to arrive in full force—some in buses, some in large all-terrain, military-like vehicles. Their presence was unnerving.

As they approached the group, Jonathan ran up beside them.

"Hey guys. Big day." If he was nervous he didn't let on.

Maddie said, "Adam, let me do some quick introductions. You've met on the telecom, but I'd like you to meet them in person."

She pointed toward each person as she said their names, "This is Roxy, Tarek, Wyndolyn, Roman, Shannel, Caragh, and Callum."

Each person shook Adam's hand as Maddie said their name. He then hugged Sancha and shook Mel's hand. Adam was surprised to see their older son, Luis, with them. He shook Luis' hand and said, "Luis, thanks for joining us, man. We can really use your help."

Luis looked pleased at the comment. At that moment Adam heard a familiar voice say, "High five, Mr. Adam."

He turned to see Mannie emerge from behind his father with his hand held high. Adam glanced at Maddie. She looked just as shocked as he figured he looked himself.

Adam gave Mannie a high-five and said, "Hey, big guy. I'm surprised to see you here."

Mannie looked a little disappointed.

Sancha said, "This sly one was supposed to stay home. Imagine our surprise when we opened the trunk of the car to get our supplies and found this stowaway."

She made a fake mad face at Mannie and tousled his hair.

He shrugged and said, "No way was I going to miss out on the action."

Maddie and Sancha exchanged worried glances.

"Just stick close to all of us," said Mel. "You'll be fine."

"Where's Albert?" asked Maddie, using her hand for a sun visor as she scanned the area.

"He's over there being Albert," said Roxy sarcastically, pointing in the direction of the horse pavilion.

Adam turned in time to see Albert, who looked to be in his mid-seventies, wheeling a large cart with several cases of bottled water stacked high on it. Adam's manners kicked in, and he started to walk toward Albert to offer a hand. He felt a large hand on his arm and turned to look up into the face of Roman, the hulk.

"Trust me. He won't take kindly to you offering him help," said Roman with a slight grin on his face.

Adam turned back to look at Albert more closely. Although Albert's face was that of an old man, he didn't appear to be having any trouble pushing the heavy cart. In fact, the more he watched, the more he realized that Albert seemed quite fit and wasn't struggling at all.

As if reading his thoughts, Roman said, "I know. He's a strange old bird. Strong as an ox. He could appear any age that he wanted, but he likes his current form. Thinks it gives him an added advantage. People underestimate him."

Adam cocked his head. "Hey, if it works, power to him. I guess."

Roman laughed and gave Adam a single pat on the back as he walked past him toward Albert. Adam watched as he tried to take the cart from Albert. Albert shook his head, aggravated, and pushed

Roman away. Instead, Roman walked side by side with Albert until they both joined the group—Roman grinning all the way.

Adam glanced across the field again and saw Jeremy and at least twenty others huddled together.

This was like a giant football game with hundreds of players.

Based on the files that Adam had seen on the KTP, he recognized several of the top leaders in the group. He tried to focus his attention on what Mel was saying as he gave the last-minute game plans.

At precisely ten o'clock, Jeremy motioned for Mel and company to join them. By then, the field was lined with so many of the KTP that it gave the appearance of a military force—an army of sorts. There were thousands of them all over the field.

Some of the other peacekeepers followed Mel onto the field. Jeremy walked to the center of the field carrying a bullhorn. As Mel started walking to meet him, he motioned for Adam to join him. Jeremy shook both of their hands and announced through the bullhorn, "This is a momentous occasion."

Many on both sides of the crowd cheered. Mel and Adam nodded in agreement. Jeremy looked back and motioned for the other twenty or so KTP leaders to move forward. Mel motioned for the rest of the 12-L council to move forward as well. Everyone met in the middle and shook hands.

Mel extended his hand to request the bullhorn. Jeremy handed it over.

"We come in peace today," he said. "We don't want any violence."

Again, many on both sides of the crowd cheered.

Jeremy nodded as well. Adam couldn't tell by the looks on the faces of the other KTP whether they agreed with Jeremy or not. The peacekeepers would need more than just Jeremy's support if they were going to accomplish anything.

Jeremy looked at Mel and said, "We all know why we are here today. One of the newest members of your ranks has killed our leader. I have made it clear to the Keepers of Transcendent Power that this was an act of self-defense. Adam shielded himself when Paul shot at him. He didn't intend to kill him. Due to such an unprecedented event, I was willing to listen when Adam suggested that we call a truce so that none of us have to live the way we have been living. We don't have to live with this violence and persecution. We have decided to hear your case. There are many of us in the KTP who would like to find a peaceful resolution as well."

"Adam, please state your case to the members of the KTP," said Mel as he backed up to give him the spotlight.

Adam had expected Mel to do all of the talking. He was caught by surprise when he was asked to speak. He hadn't prepared a formal speech, but he knew exactly what he wanted to say and what Mel wanted him to convey to the audience. So he took the bullhorn and spoke from his heart.

"For more than a century the KTP has recruited members by way of force and has deemed that, if anyone is a peaceful practitioner of Refined Transcendent Power, they must join the KTP or die. Under Paul's command, the KTP would do anything to keep RTP a secret. Some in the KTP use RTP for violence, evil, and illegal activities, which goes against the teachings of your forefathers."

At this there were angry rumblings from both sides of the crowd—some angry at the accusation, some angry at the truth of the statement.

Adam swallowed hard, rubbed his sweaty hands on his pants, and continued. "The KTP has kept the knowledge of Refined Transcendent Power a secret from the rest of society. This has caused all of the peaceful ones, the ones who do not want to join the order and use RTP for illegal activities or for evil purposes, to go underground into hiding and lives of persecution of fear, never knowing when they might be confronted by a member of the KTP. I believe it does not have to be this way. We do not know how many peaceful practitioners there are for sure, but as you can see from the turnout today, our numbers are in the thousands, if not tens of thousands. If this is the case, then it stands to reason that, despite the best efforts of the KTP to contain Refined Transcendent Power and get all of the membership within its order, it has not worked."

Adam heard gasps and murmurs coming from the ever-growing crowd as he was speaking. He could see more peacekeepers in the crowd, but there were still many more members of the KTP. Some looked angry while others nodded their agreement. Everyone was listening intently.

"There is no containing RTP. It will be taught, no matter who tries to contain it. Therefore, since the KTP leader who strongly enforced these archaic rules is gone, we are here today to ask you all to hear our case. We believe many of you may disagree with the KTP policies regarding RTP, and this could be your chance to speak out for change. We believe that we can all live peacefully among each other and practice RTP without fear. We come here today to ask for a treaty. We ask you allow us to live peacefully. We ask that you quit forcing peaceful people to join your ranks. Let the membership be strictly voluntary."

Adam looked at the faces on the KTP side and saw many who looked as if they agreed with him. They were clapping, cheering, and nodding in agreement. He wondered if some of them were former peacekeepers who had been captured by the KTP and forced to join against their will.

"Paul was good at one point in time," he continued. "Terrible things happened in his life that caused him to turn to using RTP for evil. He let hatred fester inside of him. I wish we could have had the opportunity to show him that RTP can be used for good and for healing—spiritually, mentally, and physically. I plead with you to try to learn from Paul's mistakes and come to a peaceful resolution."

Jeremy stepped forward again and said, "It is obvious by our actions and our willingness to meet you here today that we also desire to find a peaceful resolution. Many of us disagreed with Paul's practices and rules. Many were afraid to speak out for the same reasons that you give."

As Jeremy was speaking, Adam turned around to glance at the peacekeepers. He was shocked to see that there were now several thousand people standing behind him. Many of them were standing in the Namaste pose. The KTP was well-organized and had arrived ahead of time and in full force. From what he could tell, the peacekeepers' numbers were getting close to matching, if not exceeding, the KTP numbers. The anxious feeling in his chest began to lift and was replaced by a slight, but growing hope.

He focused his attention back on Jeremy as he was saying, "I am now the leader of the KTP, and I decree a truce between the KTP and the peacekeepers. A peaceful agreement has been made."

Most of the audience—peacekeepers and KTP alike—erupted in applause and cheers. People were hugging and laughing. Some people from both sides stood motionless and expressionless, perhaps in disagreement with the arrangement.

"It is on our handshake, our honor, and our word that we reach this agreement," said Mel.

Jeremy went down the line and shook hands with all of the 12-L council members. The rest of KTP's leadership followed suit.

Just as the handshaking was almost over, Adam looked beyond the KTP leadership at the crowd. A few yards behind them, he caught a glimpse of Ian and Helen, Maddie's former caretakers, emerging from behind a tree at the edge of the meadow. Ian bellowed something similar to a military command, pulled an assault rifle out from under his jacket, and raised it above his head. Adam turned to look in the same direction that Ian was looking and was horrified to see several hundred additional KTP members dressed in combat fatigues emerging from the surrounding trees, also with assault rifles.

"No!" Adam heard himself scream in an otherworldly voice.

Time seemed to move in slow motion as the realization set in about what was happening. The 12-L and KTP leadership all turned to look at Adam, and then upon seeing the look of horror on his face, turned to see what was causing him such distress. At the same time, most people in the crowd looked in Ian's direction.

Upon seeing the armed KTP members, many people on both sides began to flee into the woods.

Mel grabbed the bullhorn and roared, "Stop! Ian, no! This was not our intention. Peacekeepers, hold your ground."

Many of the people who were running away stopped.

"It is *our* intention," said Ian in a loud, formidable voice. He looked at the crowd and screamed, "You betrayed Paul—all of you!"

"Ian, you have no authority here, and you will not speak for The Order!" Jeremy warned.

Ignoring Jeremy, Ian fired a single shot into the air, and the armed KTP began running toward the crowd with their guns raised in the ready position.

There was a brief moment where time seemed to stand still and no one dared to move. Then suddenly the backup plan kicked into full gear. Adam heard Mel's battle cry. The remainder of the peacekeepers, who had purposely remained hidden, began to pour out onto the field. They came running in fearlessly. There were men, women, teenagers, people of all cultures, races, ethnicities, and all walks of life. Adam estimated that several thousand people had materialized on the field in a matter of seconds.

Ian and his troops were momentarily startled, which gave the peacekeepers the few extra seconds they needed.

"Get ready!" Mel commanded.

About that time, Ian yelled, "Go!"

"Go!" commanded Mel.

The peacekeepers and KTP members raced toward one another and merged into a massive battle. Bullets began to fly all around them.

Jeremy looked at Adam and Mel, eyes wide, as he earnestly mouthed the words, "I swear, I had no idea," and took off running in Ian's direction.

Adam watched in amazement as an assault rifle appeared out of nowhere in Jeremy's hands as he ran, and then he panicked.

He was a novice at this RTP stuff. What the hell was he doing out here? He was going to die.

He spun around, frantically looking for Maddie. He spotted her a few yards away, flanked by several of the 12-L and KTP leaders alike. She, and many others around her, had manifested what looked like tactical riot gear. They were advancing toward the enemy, beating off attackers with shields and batons.

Adam saw Caragh and Callum standing back to back, each with both hands extended. When bullets or attackers came close to them, bright balls of energy burst from their hands, knocking back anything in their path.

He saw Roman donning a gladiator helmet and steel breastplate while swinging a steel sword so large that Adam doubted he could even lift it. Roman wore a determined smile. Was he actually enjoying this?

Adam heard Maddie yell, "Adam, watch out!"

In the same instant, he heard bullets whizzing by and felt a stinging, painful sensation in his bicep. He reflexively grabbed his arm and felt the slickness of blood. He pulled his hand back and stared at the blood in disbelief.

"Adam!" screamed Maddie. "Are you okay?"

She came to him and put her hands on his shoulders. It suddenly seemed like they were in a cone of silence as bullets ricocheted off an invisible force around them.

Dazed, he shook his head, looked at her and said, "I think so. It's just superficial."

Relief flooded her face. She covered his wound with her hand and it healed instantly.

"Either do something or take cover!" she yelled into his face. "I can't just stand here shielding you. We have to fight."

He inhaled sharply and remembered his vow to himself. He would die on this field fighting if it meant Maddie and the others could live free lives.

With a renewed sense of purpose, he grabbed her face with his hands, kissed her roughly, bellowed a battle cry and ran headlong into the crowd.

Wyndolyn and many of the peacekeepers were standing motionless in the Namaste greeting stance with their eyes closed. As Adam ran past them, he could hear bullets ricocheting off their invisible shields. He heard someone scream. It was one of the gunmen. The gunman fell. And then another. All around them the gunmen continued to fall from their own ricocheting bullets. All of the shielded peacekeepers remained standing.

As Adam ran, he envisioned himself being able to see bullets in slow motion. He focused all of his thoughts on blocking the bullets or any other form of attack. As he ran, time slowed down into a quantum moment. He was moving quickly, but the bullets were coming at him slowly. He imagined his body being made of steel. He swatted the approaching bullets out of the air like flies. He saw a punch coming toward his face. When the fist made contact, it bounced right off as the attacker screamed out in pain. Adam punched the attacker back, knocking him to the ground. He kept running. He had one target in mind—Ian. He would pay for this dearly.

Adam ran by Jonathan, who stood nearby with both hands outstretched. A few yards away was a heap of KTP attackers lying pressed together on the ground as if in a football dogpile. As other attackers advanced on Jonathan, they were pulled by an invisible, magnetic force into the human pile. Struggling only seemed to make the hold stronger.

Roxy and Tarek had joined forces, moving in what looked like a beautiful martial arts dance. Each flying in the air, spinning, kicking, flipping, punching, and blocking in ways Adam had thought to only be possible in the movies. They were so fast the attackers didn't know what hit them—but Adam could see everything vividly in slow motion.

Shannel had manifested nunchucks in both hands and was swinging them rapidly with the grace and expertise of a ninth-degree black belt. Everything that came into her path felt the wrath—bullets and body parts alike. Adam watched in slow motion as a bullet ricocheted off the nunchucks and struck the attacker in the heart, killing him instantly.

As he searched the crowd for Ian and Helen, Adam saw Albert limping along on the field using a stick for a cane. He started to head toward him to check on him but stopped short when he realized what Albert was doing. As attackers ran by, bypassing the seemingly harmless, injured old man, he would slyly trip them with the stick and then snicker.

The old bastard was enjoying this.

One attacker caught on to the game. After being tripped, he jumped to his feet and proceeded to throw a spinning heel kick aimed at Albert's head. Adam winced, expecting to see Albert get the total knockout. Instead, to his and the attacker's surprise, Albert's hand shot out and grabbed the foot in an iron grip an inch from Albert's face. He gave the shocked attacker a sly grin before he flung his leg with enough force to send the attacker hurling through the air and into a tree. TKO!

Adam continued to push his way through the crowd but stopped again when he saw a lightning bolt strike the ground and knock Sancha, Mel, and hundreds of other peacekeepers off their feet. The air smelled of ozone, scorched grass, and singed hair. The people on the ground weren't moving.

Adam screamed, "No! Sancha! Mel! No!"

He ran toward them, scanning the area as he ran to see if he could identify the manifestor who had caused the lightning. He saw Maddie and several others running to the downed people as well. He did not see Luis or Mannie. Where were they?

He saw Maddie crying and screaming. "Sancha! Mel! Oh my god!"

She got to them first, checked their pulse and listened for heartbeats. It was then that Adam spotted Ian standing about a hundred yards away with a smug grin on his face. Helen and a large group of KTP were with him.

Maddie placed one hand over Sancha's heart and one hand over Mel's as she closed her eyes in deep concentration. Adam felt like his own heart might stop as he ran toward them, waiting in suspense to see if they were okay.

Before he reached them, he heard a loud crackling sound and saw an orange flash out of the corner of his eye. Then everything went black.

Chapter 49

ADAM'S EYES SHOT OPEN WHEN he felt something heavy come down on his chest. He sat up, swinging wildly.

"Whoa! Whoa! I'm not the enemy, man," said Jeremy as he stepped back and held up his hands to show he meant no harm. "Ian almost took you out with that lightning bolt. Hurry, we have to catch him."

Adam whipped his head around.

"Where's Maddie? Where's Sancha and Mel?"

"There's no time. We have to take Ian out. Get up."

"Why should I trust you?" Adam spat.

Jeremy said, "Adam, I swear to you. I had nothing to do with Ian's attack. You have to trust me. Who do you think just saved your life? Now let's get the son of a bitch."

Jeremy pulled Adam to his feet. They both took off in Ian's direction.

Ian, Helen, and a few hundred of their cronies were still about a hundred yards away and ready for them. Ian and Helen both raised their hands and looked toward the sky. Clouds swirled around and lightning bolts began raining down from the sky. Jeremy and Adam dodged the lightning as they ran.

Adam saw a lightning bolt heading directly for Jeremy. His

anger and determination renewed, Adam relinquished all conscious thought and focused on saving Jeremy. In the next instant, he saw the lightning bolt bend in a sharp angle and head straight toward Ian and the KTP.

Wide-eyed, Ian and Helen barely had time to dive out of the way. A couple of their cronies were not so fortunate.

Jeremy looked at Adam like a proud father would look at his son.

When Ian got back on his feet, his mouth fell open in surprise as he was forced to dive again as another lightning bolt narrowly missed him. Then another lightning bolt hit nearby. A few more KTP fell while others scrambled to dodge them. All of the lightning bolts that Ian and Helen had manifested were now raining down upon them.

Adam looked at Jeremy, surprised. Jeremy looked at Adam, also surprised. Neither knew who was responsible for redirecting those last few lightning bolts. They simultaneously looked behind them and were shocked when they saw Luis and Mannie grinning widely.

"Great job, guys!" Adam shouted.

Behind the boys, Adam could see thousands of peacekeepers and KTP stampeding toward them. He saw Mel, Sancha, and Maddie leading the angry mob, now intent on demolishing Ian, Helen, and their cronies. Adam felt relief wash over him. They were okay.

Horrified, Ian's and Helen's faces fell as they realized that thousands of people were using RTP against them.

"Fire!" Ian screeched.

Ian's supporters opened fire. Bullets ricocheted as the peacekeepers held their ground, and several of the KTP dropped at once. Ian was knocked off his feet when a bullet struck him in the chest. Helen ran to him.

Adam held his breath. Was it over? Was Ian dead?

Helen and a couple of Ian's henchmen grabbed Ian by the arms and dragged him off into the woods. Someone hollered, "Retreat! Retreat!"

The rest of the KTP resistance started disappearing into the trees.

Without even thinking, Adam gave chase, flanked by Jeremy, and followed by the angry mob led by Mel, Sancha, and Maddie. They spread out in the woods, searching for the deserters. They searched for at least an hour, but there was no sign of them. It appeared that hundreds of people had disappeared without a trace.

Adam shouted, "Ian, Helen, if you can hear us, give up your fight now. You will never win against RTP. You are clearly outnumbered and we're not going to take it anymore. If we have to, we will hunt you down. If you approach us, we will fight back from now on. We will not join with the likes of you, nor will we go peacefully as your prisoners any longer. We will fight until the death, whether it be ours or yours."

Adam heard loud cheering all around him. Thousands of peacekeepers and reformed KTP were cheering, hugging, and laughing at the retreating traitors. He wanted to track Ian down and take care of him once and for all, but he had vanished. Now they didn't know if Ian was dead or alive. For now, they would have to be satisfied with their retreat and consider it a victory.

"We will take care of them later," Adam heard Jeremy say in a low, steely voice that raised the hairs on the back of his neck. He knew Jeremy meant it, and he knew he would not want to be in Ian's shoes, if he were still alive when Jeremy found him.

Maddie ran to Adam, threw her arms around his neck, and hugged him so tightly that he couldn't breathe. He picked her up and swung her around.

"You did it," she cried. "We did it! I'm so proud of you, Adam. You led us to this."

She planted a big kiss on his lips.

Mel approached him next. Adam thought he was going to give

him a handshake, but instead Mel threw his big arms around him in a tight bear hug and lifted him up off the ground, swinging him around the way that Adam had swung Maddie around.

Mel laughed and said, "I will consider you a brother from now on. We consider you a full member of the council as well—13-L."

Sancha also hugged Adam, followed by many others. Peacekeepers and peaceful KTP alike congratulated one another. When the congratulations and the cheers finally died down, it was a sobering moment when everyone looked around at the ground littered with blood and the bodies of the fallen KTP and peacekeepers.

Wyndolyn, followed by a large group of people, approached Adam. All of their faces were distorted in anguish and many of them were crying. Tears were streaming down Wyndolyn's face.

She simply said, "You said we would find a peaceful resolution."

Adam didn't know how to respond. He hadn't wanted anyone to die, but he had been prepared to die or kill if need be. All he could think of to say was, "I'm sorry."

Wyndolyn turned, shook her head, and walked away. The group of people with her followed.

"Wyndolyn, wait," said Roxy, chasing after her. Shannel went after her, too.

Adam hung his head. He suddenly felt responsible for all of the deaths.

He turned to Maddie and said, "Can't you do that healing thing? It worked on me and Sancha and Mel."

With sadness in her eyes, Maddie shook her head.

"I can only heal living people, Adam. To my knowledge, no one has been successful in using RTP for resurrection. Once the soul is gone..." Her voice trailed off.

At that moment, Jeremy approached the 13-L and said, "We will consider this a victory for peace and a truce between the KTP and the peaceful ones as long as I am in power. We will make sure that it is so."

He noticed Adam surveying the land where the dead bodies lay. He put his hand on Adam's shoulder and said, "Leave the cleanup to us. We never intended this outcome."

Adam said, "We didn't intend it either. We'll help."

Jeremy searched Adam's eyes, then nodded.

The bodies were carefully rolled up in tarps and removed. The ground was still covered with all of the guns and munitions. Everyone used RTP to pitch in to help. When all that remained were bloody pools on the ground, Jeremy and several others lifted their faces and arms toward the sky. Adam watched as clouds gathered and rain began to pour down, washing the blood into the ground and destroying all evidence that anything out of the ordinary had occurred.

When the rain started, some people began to leave. Many sought shelter under the horse pavilion and got to know one another. The KTP and peacekeepers mixed together in an unprecedented event. The 13-L—minus Wyndolyn—stayed, as did the KTP leaders. People brought out food and drinks. They played music, danced, and talked on into the night while the rain continued to downpour hard and heavy, washing away all traces of violence. It was reported the next day that a record-breaking rainfall had fallen in that part of New Mexico. Meteorologists hadn't seen it coming.

As they parted ways with Jeremy late that night, he promised they would meet again soon to continue getting to know each other and reinforce the peace treaty. He also promised to keep the peacekeepers posted on the progress of capturing the KTP who had mutinied.

Chapter 50

AS THEY PREPARED TO LEAVE, Sancha said, "Why don't you two stay with us tonight? We can all have a late brunch together tomorrow and you can make your travel arrangements on the secure network."

Maddie said, "Are you sure? Do you think we should still split up? I mean with Ian's group still on the loose…"

Adam thought it was ironic that, although the day's events were considered a huge victory, they still felt the need to be cautious. It saddened him. He had expected a better outcome.

Mel said, "I think it'll be fine for just one night. Besides, we need to talk about our next moves and our new normal."

Next moves? New normal?

Adam just wanted life to remain as it was before this trip to New Mexico. He was exhausted and wasn't ready to consider what the future had in store for them.

When they arrived at Sancha and Mel's house, everyone said goodnight and quietly adjourned. Alone at last and holding each other in bed, Maddie said, "Adam, I am so proud of you."

Adam had mixed feelings about everything. He didn't regret the trip to New Mexico. He had met Maddie's best friends and traveled to a beautiful part of the country he had never seen before. He had learned so much more about Maddie's past and the positive things that Refined Transcendent Power could do in people's lives. He had met some truly amazing people with incredible abilities and had begun to realize his own capabilities of using RTP. He had even led the movement for a peace treaty with the KTP. But the deaths and the escape of Ian's gang bothered him. He had hoped, perhaps naively, that this would be it—a peaceful treaty would be made, life would return to normal, and they would all live happily ever after. Had his positive thinking not been enough?

He said, "I'm glad we did it too. If only I had mastered my thoughts a little better before this happened…"

Maddie's eyes searched his.

"What do you mean?"

"Well, I was so sure of a peaceful outcome."

"And you got one."

"But it wasn't exactly what I was hoping the outcome would be. People died. And what about Ian's gang being on the loose? They're still a threat as long as they're out there. Where do you think they went? How did they disappear like that?"

"Adam, don't dwell on that now. They must have devised a way to hide or make a rapid retreat. Let's just be thankful for the positive outcomes. RTP doesn't always work exactly the way we expect it to when other people are involved."

"Why is that?"

"We can only control our own thoughts. We can't control the thoughts of others. So when several thousand people come together with thousands, or even millions, of different thoughts, the outcomes sometimes—directly or indirectly—affect our lives in ways we can't foresee or control. And sometimes when we are disappointed in an outcome, over time and in hindsight we see it was actually the best thing for us at that point in our lives. Like when people break up and they think that is the worst thing that has happened to them. But soon after they meet their soulmate and realize that the breakup was the best thing that had ever happened to them. Does that make sense?"

"I guess so. But what now? Nothing changes because we still have to live our lives in fear and hiding as long as Ian and Helen—if they're alive—and their people are on the loose."

"We just have to remain faithful that things will eventually work out in the best-possible outcome."

Adam was quiet as he considered this. He still didn't completely understand how faith and RTP worked, but maybe no one did. Overcome with the events of the day, he drifted off to sleep.

When he awoke, the sun was shining brightly through the windows. Maddie wasn't in bed. He rolled over to check the time on his phone—ten-thirty. He slowly rolled out of bed and took a quick shower. He was anxious to get back to his life in New York.

He found Maddie, Sancha, Mel, and Mannie gathered around the large island in the kitchen having pastries, coffee, and hot cocoa for Mannie. He kissed Maddie and Sancha on their cheeks and gave Mel a man-hug. Mannie gave him a tight hug around the waist. Adam hugged him, patted his head, and said, "You were very brave yesterday, big guy."

Mannie beamed at the praise and said, "Did you see how we commanded those lightning bolts? That was killer!"

"You've got that right. I've never seen anything like it. I'm very proud of you, but I wish you didn't have to see the...bad stuff."

Sancha said, "I agree. We told you to stay home, *mijo*."

Mannie whined, "*Mamá*, I can handle it."

Then he looked directly in Adam's eyes and said with a wisdom beyond his age, "You did the right thing, Mr. Adam."

Adam patted him on the shoulder and said, "Thanks, my man."

He wondered just exactly how old Mannie really was.

"Have some brunch," said Sancha.

"Thank you."

He grabbed a pastry and poured himself a cup of coffee. His

muscles were sore and his body was bruised, but overall he was no worse for wear, considering he had literally been struck by lightning. He wondered exactly what Jeremy had done to save him. Could he heal people like Maddie? He never got the chance to ask him or thank him for saving his life. Maybe he would do just that when he saw him again. And he knew without a doubt that he would see him again.

Mel said, "We've got guards stationed at Maddie's house in Santa Fe. If Ian or Helen show up there, they're in for a rude awakening, although we're not expecting them to be that stupid. But we're prepared just in case."

Maddie said quietly, "It's not my house anymore."

Sancha said, "Don't worry, *querido corazón*. We'll make sure your art collections are relocated. We'll help you find an even more beautiful place."

Maddie nodded her thanks and said, "I'm fine with my place in New York. I'm just thankful we're all okay."

Adam was relieved to hear Maddie mention New York. Up until then he wasn't even sure if they would be able to return to New York. He was fairly certain the KTP did not know their whereabouts in New York, but he didn't know if Maddie would want to chance going back to the same place. He didn't know if he would have to disappear from his life as he knew it.

"Speaking of New York," said Mel, "we've arranged a private jet for you. We want to avoid public transportation for now."

It worried Adam that Mel was worried enough to take these precautions, but he chose not to say anything. A ride on a private jet would be sweet. He'd never even traveled in first class. Now he was going to be traveling like the rich and famous. He still couldn't believe how much his life had changed in the span of a week.

"Any idea on the whereabouts of the KTP deserters?" said Adam.

Mel shook his head and said, "We've got our best reconnaissance teams on it. We'll let you know as soon as we find anything."

"How do you think they vanished like that so quickly?"

Sancha, Mel, and Maddie exchanged glances.

"Okay, what's up?" asked Adam suspiciously.

"We have our theories," said Mel, "but we're not sure."

Adam cocked his head, waiting for further explanation.

"Possibly subatomic teleportation," said Luis matter-of-factly as he entered the room.

All eyes turned to look at him as he grabbed a pastry and took a large bite. Adam furrowed his brow and looked at Maddie. She nodded slightly.

Luis wiped the frosting from his mouth and said, "It's like the cold war race for arms, or the race for space, but now it's the race for time travel with our minds. Whoever masters it first will have supremacy."

"You mean like in science fiction?" said Adam. "Like 'Beam me up, Scottie' in 'Star Trek'?"

"Sort of like that," said Luis, his eyes dreamy with the possibilities. "Except at this point in quantum physics, no one knows for sure who or what will come out on the other side."

"People really think this is a possibility?" said Adam skeptically.

"Absolutely. Scientists have already been successful at teleporting photons into space, faster than the speed of light. So theoretically, every particle in your body could be converted to information, down to the subatomic level. The data then could be transmitted to a receiver located wherever you intend to go."

"Many practitioners of RTP are very interested in achieving this possibility," said Sancha. "But, to our knowledge, no one has achieved it."

"But some are very close," protested Luis.

"What did you mean about not knowing who or what will come out on the other side?" said Adam.

"Well," continued Luis, "for teleportation to work, your body would have to be disrupted, particle by particle, and completely destroyed in the process. This brings up the Mind-Body Problem of philosophy. Will you still be you when you emerge on the other side? Will you have the same personality? Will you have the same mind? Will you have the same soul?"

They all sat quietly pondering the implications of what Luis had just said.

"Sounds kind of Frankenstein-ish to me," said Adam. "And you really think Ian and his gang used RTP to teleport?"

Mel said, "We think it's a possibility. Our intelligence community has reported cases of KTP members seemingly disappearing, never to be seen again. At first we thought they were being murdered and the bodies destroyed. But then some of the ones who went missing were in high standing among the KTP, and it didn't make sense. Also, around that same time, some of the peacekeepers who had been dabbling in teleportation were also reported missing. We're wondering if they had a breakthrough and teleported somewhere and can't get back."

"Or if they never made it all the way out," said Luis.

"I can't even wrap my mind around that," said Adam. "We can only hope that what Luis just said happened to Ian and the gang."

"Adam!" said Maddie as she smacked him on the arm.

"What? It's the truth."

Mannie snickered.

She shook her head in mock disappointment. "Adam, what am I going to do with you?"

"Love me forever?"

He put his arms around her waist and kissed her on the cheek several times as she playfully struggled to get away.

"Gross," said Mannie.

Everyone laughed.

Adam made a mental note to read up on this quantum physics stuff sometime.

Chapter 51

WHEN IT WAS FINALLY TIME to board the plane to return to New York City, Adam had mixed emotions. He could tell Maddie did, too. He had really grown fond of Maddie's friends and New Mexico in general. He was going to miss them tremendously. But he couldn't wait to get home to see his own friends and get back to a normal life—or what he hoped would be a normal life.

Maddie wiped the tears from her eyes as she hugged and kissed Mel, Luis, Mannie, and Sancha.

"We hate to see you go, *mi encantadora am*iga. Please promise that you'll come back soon," sniffled Sancha.

"I promise," Maddie said softly as she wiped her nose.

Adam hugged them all as well. When he saw Mannie bravely holding back tears, his own eyes welled up. He really loved this family.

"Stay brave, big guy," he said as he tousled Mannie's hair. "Come visit me in New York City sometime."

Mannie beamed. "I'd love to! Can we, *Mamá*? Can we, *Papá*? Pleeeaaase?"

"Of course we will," said Mel. "It's about time you got to see the Big Apple."

Adam gave him a high five.

"Luis, you've got to tell me more about this teleportation business," said Adam. "We're going to teleport to wherever Ian is and kick his sorry ass."

Luis laughed. "Deal!"

Maddie rolled her eyes and shook her head in mock exasperation.

Adam wished there truly was a way to teleport to home and back. That way, they could see each other as often as they wanted.

They made their way up the stairs of the private Cessna and stopped at the top for the final good-bye waves. Maddie blew them kisses through her tears before turning to enter the main cabin. Adam gave one last wave and followed her.

Once inside, the staff and pilot gave them the Namaste greeting. Maddie hugged them all and gave quick introductions. Adam thought he recognized a few of them from the KTP meeting.

The pilot said, "That was a great thing you did in arranging the meeting with the KTP. We're making strides toward our freedom, and it is an honor to transport you home safely."

Unaccustomed to this kind of admiration, Adam said, "I just started the wheels turning. It took all of us coming together to make it happen."

One of the crewmembers said, "I'm Mason. It's my pleasure to serve you today. Would you like a tour?"

Adam shook his hand. "Great to meet you, Mason. I'd love a tour."

"Right this way." Mason motioned for them to follow.

He let them into the main cabin. There was a two-seater, leather couch at the front of the aircraft, opposite the electric door they had just entered. They passed through the galley that contained a microwave and convection oven combination, a small refrigerator, an espresso machine, and a minibar. Beyond that were four spacious seats facing one another, two on one side of the aisle and two on the other, all with small laptops available for use. In the next section were two additional seats, facing each other on one side of the aisle, with a table between them set with a white tablecloth, formal place settings, a floral centerpiece, and a bottle of chilled wine. Across the aisle was a spacious couch. At the back of the airplane was a lavatory, sink, and changing area with a hard sliding door for privacy. Adam had never seen anything like it. He felt like he was in a dream.

They took a seat at the table and Mason presented them with steaming hot washcloths. Following Maddie's lead, Adam took one, wiped his hands with it, and put it back on the tray. Mason opened the wine and poured them both a glass.

"Your meal will be out soon. Please let us know if you need anything at all."

"Thank you, Mason," said Maddie.

She looked at Adam, smiled, and raised her glass.

"To a safe flight home and great times ahead."

They clinked their glasses. Adam took her free hand, leaned across the table, and kissed her gently on the lips.

"To great times ahead indeed."

The meal was one of the best Adam had ever eaten. Being a self-proclaimed chef, he was impressed by the quality of the food that had been prepared in the small confines of the airplane.

The wine flowed freely as they enjoyed the meal and each other's company in a relaxed and romantic environment for the first time in days. Adam's head was spinning a little, perhaps a combination of the altitude and the wine. Maddie must have felt it too. She grinned at him mischievously and said, "I'm not a member of the 'Mile-high Club,' but I think I might want to be."

He stopped mid-drink and put his glass down. In the next instant, they both ran to the changing area and closed the door. They kissed passionately, exploring each other's bodies with their hands as they frantically removed their clothing. He kissed her mouth and neck while caressing her breasts and between her legs.

She stroked his erect manhood. When they couldn't refrain any longer, he spun her around, bent her over the sink, and entered her from behind. They both moaned in ecstasy as the pleasure built with their rhythmic movements until they both cried out in climax.

The captain's voice came over the intercom. "Flight attendants, prepare for landing."

They hastily cleaned up, got dressed, and took their seats side by side on the couch. Maddie leaned her head on his should and said, "We're almost home."

He smiled, kissed the top of her head, and said, "I love you, Maddie."

She turned to face him, kissed him softly on the lips, and whispered against his lips, "I love you too, Adam."

Chapter 52

THREE MONTHS LATER, THE CRAZY world of the KTP and peacekeepers, Refined Transcendent Power, and the events of New Mexico seemed a million lifetimes away to Adam as he belted out his favorite number in Night Fury's first set at the Venus de Milo on Saturday night. The crowd was giving off a great vibe. Everyone was on their feet, crowding as close to the stage as they could. People were clapping, raising their hands, banging their heads, cheering, and singing along. Maddie and the regulars had staked their spots on the front row and were pressed up against the barrier, cheering them along.

The band members had given him and Maddie a bit of the cold shoulder when they had first returned, especially Zach, but they soon got over it, and rehearsals resumed as normal.

Adam was strutting back and forth on the stage, slapping people's outstretched hands as he passed them. He winked and squeezed Maddie's hand as he went by. She blew him a kiss. Strobe and laser lights bounced off the smoke in the air from the pyrotechnics. Adam was in his element.

As he was making his way back to center stage, he glanced at Maddie, as was his custom throughout his performances, and stopped in his tracks. Directly behind her, he saw two men who hadn't been there before, one on each side of her. Maddie, who was getting into the performance, seemed unware of them. He blinked. He could have sworn that the man on the left looked like Ian, and the man on the right looked like...no, it couldn't be... Paul? Then their images flickered, like his old TV screen had often done when the HDMI cable was loose. He rubbed his eyes. They must have been playing tricks on him. Maybe someone slipped something into his drink? Was he hallucinating?

Maddie looked at him questioningly, wondering why he had quit singing. It wasn't like him to forget lyrics during performances. The band played on, covering for him. In the next instant, the song ended and the house lights dimmed to darkness. He lost sight of Maddie for a brief moment. When the house lights came back on, Adam's eyes widened and his heart froze in terror. Maddie and the two men were gone.

THE END.

Acknowledgments

Thank you to my dedicated beta readers:

Dalton	Alec Greg
Jill	Zeus
Cristy W.	Rachael
Sandy	Cristy F.
Holly	Gail

Thank you, Alyssa, for using your artistic abilities to create the logo for P. A. Crenshaw Books.

About the Author

Thank you for taking the time to read my debut novel, AFTER THOUGHT, book one in the AFTER THOUGHT series. I hope you have enjoyed reading this story as much as I enjoyed writing it. If you liked this book, please take the time to leave a review and help other readers discover this book.

If you want to know when my next book will launch, please visit my website at www.pacrenshaw.com, where you can sign up for email updates and pre-launch news.

You can also find me via the web:

Facebook:
www.facebook.com/P-A-Crenshaw-104495121552669

Twitter:
twitter.com/pacrenshaw1

Instagram:
www.instagram.com/pacrenshawauthor/

P. A. Crenshaw was born and raised in a small town in New Mexico and now resides in South Carolina. An engineering manager by day, fiction writer by night, she is the proud mother of two amazing young adults and two mischievous kitties who enjoy walking on the keyboard while she is writing (the kitties, not the kids). When not writing, she can be found spending time with family and friends, reading, hiking, traveling, doing yoga, meditating, thinking positive thoughts, and expressing gratitude for life's blessings. She is currently working on her next novel, AFTER DEATH, the irresistible sequel to AFTER THOUGHT.